Vices, Villains
and the Viscount

VICES, VILLAINS AND THE VISCOUNT

The Lost Lords Series

Karla Kratovil

TULE

PROLOGUE

July 13, 1828

*I*S CRIME IN *the city rising along with the temperature this summer? Another murdered woman was found in the alley not far from where she worked. Lucy Stone was murdered Saturday in the early morning hours after leaving her job at the Queen's Head on Bow Street. According to a source, bruises around her throat indicated she was strangled to death. This reporter would like to know why this alarming pattern of attacks on young women has grown in the past months. Is it the heat that is increasing tempers or is there a killer on the loose?*

He smoothed his finger over the words on the page of the *Piccadilly Press* as he read through the short article again. His escapades were making the papers. Gaining notoriety. He smiled. Lucy, what a fine name for such a pretty girl. Her cornflower blue eyes had bulged in her pale face as he squeezed the air from her delicate windpipe. She had barely struggled at all. Frozen with fear at his first blow to her cheek. He sighed. He liked it better when they fought back. He set the paper aside and picked up the *Morning Post*. Taking a bite from his toast, he perused the headlines, looking for a mention of his kill.

Perhaps tonight after dinner at his club, he would go over to the Termage and play cards there. He was so tired of the same old places and the same boring people. It had been almost a year since he had played at the Termage, and next door to it was the Birdcage, a brothel where one could play rough for a price. He would just need to keep his beast in check. Yes, some dinner, cards, and a good fuck were just what he needed to break through his doldrums. He took a sip of tea and flipped the page of newsprint. Now, let's see if anyone else was crowing about his exploits.

CHAPTER ONE

WARM SUMMER RAIN poured outside his bedroom window. Matthew tied his dark blue cravat with practiced and efficient movements as he stared out at the wet street below. Not ideal weather for guests arriving in costume to the Blue Angel this evening. Thank God he'd listened to Val, and they had put up a large awning leading from the street to the front door. The former sailor turned club security chief had near-perfect intuition when it came to rain.

Matthew turned from the rain-splattered view to cross to his dressing table and fetch his cuff links. Didn't matter, guests would come. No one missed his bacchanal. The masquerade, in its third year, was already the summer's most sought-after event.

A knock at the door interrupted his thoughts. "Come in," he called out.

"Evening, boss." Ben crossed into the room. He carried a small tray that held a tumbler with two fingers of whiskey. "Gotcha your evening drink here."

"Thank you, Ben." Matthew took a sip, letting the pleasant burn of the fine Scottish whiskey slide down his throat.

This would be his only drink of the night. A tradition to allow himself a small pleasure before work. "How are the girls? Everything ready for the show?"

Ben rolled his eyes. "Fanny was bitchin' about her spot as usual, but generally, everything looks good. Rob says everything on the floor is ready. Val's got two additional youngins helping behind the bar tonight."

Ben, or Big Ben, as everyone in the club called him, had a unique position at the Blue Angel. He was part butler, part mother hen. Matthew was thankful that Ben handled all the behind-the-scenes drama. He supervised the kitchen staff, the maids who came in each morning to clean, and watched over the dancing girls in the show. He was one of four staff managers that Matthew relied on to keep the Blue Angel running in top shape.

"Tell Fanny she can leave the show anytime if she is so disappointed to be on the line." Matthew's lips twitched at Ben's loud snort of laughter. "I'll find another girl like her in a snap of the fingers."

"She knows this is the best job in town. She's just a complainer, that one. Maybe you can go down and give the girls one of yer famous smiles. Cheer 'em up." Ben pulled a folded newspaper from the pocket of his jacket. "Today's *Piccadilly Press* mentioned the Angel. Yer not going to like it, though."

Matthew snatched up the outstretched paper. This damn rag had been writing a series of articles they called *Vice and Crime in the City*. At first, he had been impressed at the knowledge the writer had of some of the inner workings of gangs in London. Then, the man had turned his focus on high-end brothels with a clear rub for those most frequented by toffs, and Matthew had laughed at the writer's naivety. The bias had been an obvious pander to the Press's audience. Matthew looked down at today's headline, *Lives Ruined Every Night at the Gaming Tables*. Bloody hell. He skimmed the article, looking for any mention of the Blue Angel, finding it several paragraphs deep.

One of the many gaming hells on the east side, the Blue Angel seems to cater to the working man, enticing their patrons to lose their wages at the tables. The promise of these types of places is that within their walls lay the path to easy money when, in fact, the path more often leads to ruin. Preying on the hardworking man to turn a profit is not illegal, but perhaps should be deemed a crime.

What sentimental tripe was this shit? He didn't force anyone to gamble away their money. Men were sentient creatures that did whatever they wanted. If they didn't gamble away their money at his place, it would be at one of his competitors. He threw the paper down on the side table and took a long draught from his whiskey. What this reporter didn't seem to understand was that people were inherently bad, sinful creatures. There would always be places to market to the vices that fed the masses.

"It's fine." Matthew waved a hand, dismissing the article. "Annoying, but the reporter clearly has no clue the truth of human nature. As far as the girls, I will put in an appearance when I do my rounds. I want to check on Stella anyway." He trusted Ben to know what was needed. And if he needed to be charming and give the girls a talk, then he would. The show must be flawless tonight.

It was the biggest party of the year and his favorite because many of the aristocrats were out of London at their country houses, leaving his place free of their snooty demands and endless whining when they lost to the house. Money was money, Seaton always said. Personally, Matthew preferred the "working man" to a bloody toff any day. But, as a businessman, he knew attracting a higher-class clientele could be beneficial, because Lord knew the toffs loved to waste their money. Luckily, Matthew's floor manager, Rob Morrow, was smooth as honey, never getting his temper ruffled by petulant young lordlings.

"And the awning is holding up under this downpour?" he asked.

"Yes, boss." Ben picked up the cufflinks from the table and, taking Matthew's left arm, began to fasten his sleeve. Matthew swallowed the last of his whiskey, set down the glass, and held out his other hand for Ben to fuss with the cufflink. He knew from experience that shooing Ben away would only hurt the man's feelings. Ben took care of his people and that was that.

Ben's tall stature and broad, muscled frame had won him his nickname. He had been a boxer for a decade, and that's how Matthew met and became friends with the man. The gentle giant had been desperate to get out of the fighting ring. When Matthew opened the club five years ago, he had offered Ben a job and won the man's loyalty for life. Not that he minded the mother hen thing...too much. Matthew valued loyalty in his friends over everything else. A man was nobody without the loyalty of his friends.

They headed down the back stairs, stopping at the large arched window that overlooked the main gaming room. Matthew assessed the floor. Along one wall, the long carved wooden bar gleamed with fresh polish. He and his business partner, Rhys Seaton, had built it themselves, their first project when setting up the gaming club. A massive hazard table sat at the center of the room. Above it hung a crystal chandelier, dust-free and sparkling in the candlelight. A sea of dice and cribbage tables dotted the rest of the space, ready for tonight's crowd of revelers. Matthew nodded his approval and continued down to the ground level.

He and Ben made their way to the main room and walked through the club to check that everything was perfect. Beyond the main gaming area, along the back of the house, were smaller rooms for different types of play—piquet, cribbage, loo, faro, whist, and passe-dix. Some of the rooms were for deeper play, with minimum bids to join in. Some rooms could be rented for the evening to play with a private party. He was pleased to see everything clean and ready.

At last, they backtracked to the front of the house and up the curved staircase to the theater. Tucked at the rear of the club, he'd converted the manse's old main drawing room into an intimate theater space. Long tables faced an elevated stage draped with lush, blue velvet curtains. The dancing girls were on stage in costume, practicing steps or just chatting amongst themselves. Mrs. Langley, his theater manager, was on her knees, sewing the hem of one girl's costume. The smoke of the kerosine lights that rimmed the edge of the stage and the equally potent smell of greasepaint the performers used to paint their faces pale white with bright rouge spots on their cheeks and lips all settled into his chest and made him smile with its familiarity.

"Ladies, you all look lovely as ever," he called out as he climbed the four steps to the stage. "Are you excited for tonight's show?"

"Oh yes."

"We have been practicing all week."

"The new costumes are beautiful."

The dancers replied enthusiastically. Mrs. Langley stood, giving one last look of approval at the skirt she had been mending. She turned to face him. "Everything is ready. Tonight, Jenny, Rose, Fanny, and Mary Beth will accompany Stella to the front for the opener."

Matthew nodded. Each evening, the best of the dancers performed an opening number in the grand foyer to entice customers from the tables to come to see the nightly show. "Where is my blue angel?"

"In her dressing room, getting dressed still. Late as usual." Mrs. Langley rolled her eyes, but her lips twitched in a smile. Everyone loved Stella despite her flightiness. She had the voice of an operatic diva and the kindness of an old soul, all wrapped in the lithe body of a seventeen-year-old girl.

Matthew glanced around at the dancers, putting forth his most charming smile. "Tonight, the atmosphere will be different than most nights. For those of you that are new, the masquerade is very popular. There will be large crowds, so sing and dance your hearts out. You never know who will be in the audience." He sobered his expression. "Because everyone will be costumed and wearing masks, there will be more bad behavior than normal. I want you all to be safe. If you get into any trouble, Ben will be here, watching and waiting to intervene."

Some girls nodded, but a few looked delighted at the prospect of trouble. He sighed. It was always the way of it. He couldn't make good decisions for them. These were all grown women. All except one. "Break a leg, ladies." Matthew walked across to the backstage area, heading for Stella's dressing room.

Halfway across, he was waylaid by a hand gripping his arm. "Mr. Reeves, I'm just so excited to be in the opener tonight. Thanks so much."

He glanced down into the wide blue eyes of Fanny Cooper. "All the decisions are made by Mrs. Langley."

She batted her long eyelashes. "You're the boss. Surely you influence everything here at the club."

"Not in this case. I have more than enough to worry about. I don't second-guess my managers. Keep up the good work, and I am sure you will stay in the opening number." He tried to walk away, but her fingers tightened on his sleeve.

"Mr. Reeves, if you ever get tired of your favorite, just know that I am always available for the company of such a man as yourself." Her smile was coy, but her eyes were cold and calculating.

Matthew pried her fingers off his arm. "You're new, Fanny, but that's not how I run things. I never sleep with my employees. I suggest you look elsewhere for a benefactor." He left her behind and made his way through the backstage door into the hallway that housed the dressing rooms. He knocked on Stella's door.

"Come in."

Mathew entered the room and shut the door. Stella was dressed in her costume, one foot propped up on a chair as she rolled a stocking up her leg. "Sorry I am running late. I found this poor little kitten shivering in the rain on the way back from the market. I just had to bring it home."

She finished tying the ribbons on her stocking and swept over to the dressing table with its small looking glass to pick up a pot of rouge and apply some to her lips. It didn't stop her from talking, though; nothing could stop her chatter. "Big Ben gave me some milk in a saucer, and I rubbed the poor thing down with a towel. I left it up in my room, curled up on the hearth. I think I shall name it Raindrop...or perhaps Pitter-Patter. What do you think?"

Matthew straddled the chair and rested his arms on the back. "I think you should be out front already practicing with the other girls."

"Yes, yes, I know. I'm hurrying, I promise." She turned

to face him, her wide brown eyes fringed with dark black lashes, the same color as her raven hair, glowing with excitement over her new pet. "There, I'm ready. Did I forget anything?"

He looked her over. Then pointed at her feet. "Shoes."

"Oh yes." She glanced around the small room.

Matthew sighed. "I already gave my warning to the rest of the girls. Tonight's bacchanal will be rowdier than most of the parties we host. When guests are masked, many become beasts, with no manners whatsoever. After the show, you are to go straight back upstairs to your rooms. No mingling, no hanging out behind the bar. Do you hear me?"

Stella's head popped up from under the dressing table, where she had found her shoes. "Yes, big brother." She straightened and gave him a mocking salute.

"I mean it, Stella."

"Yes, sir. I want to go see my kitten anyway. I won't get into trouble, I promise."

Famous last words. Stella never meant to get into trouble, but her newfound freedom this past year had made her reckless. And he was still getting the hang of the role of older brother. When their father died last summer, Stella had shown up on his doorstep. How she had known where to look for him, he still didn't know. But he hadn't hesitated to take her in. He understood exactly why she was too frightened to stay in the home they grew up in. Ten years younger than him, she had just been an infant when he was sent away. Matthew sighed. He would have Ben keep a close eye on her tonight.

"You know, brother, it wouldn't hurt you to get into a little trouble tonight." Stella smirked at him. "There are plenty of ladies who would love to let you seduce them in a dark corner."

"I have a club to run. No time for trouble." He got up and bent to kiss her cheek. "And you shouldn't be thinking about seduction in dark corners."

She huffed and rolled her eyes. He chuckled. A gaming hell wasn't exactly the place for a young girl to be sheltered from the city's vices. Far from it. But it was the best he could do. This was his life. At least he could offer her safety along with a sense of family, and that was something anyway. "Don't forget your mask, my blue angel."

CHAPTER TWO

B Y ELEVEN, THE party was in full swing. Matthew stood at the banister, looking down the stairs into the foyer. A steady stream of guests had come through the front door over the last two hours. Music drifted out from the main room to his right, and a cacophony of voices came from the gaming room to his left.

His floor manager, Rob Morrow, stood next to him. "More than last year, I think."

"I agree. Gonna make a killing tonight." Matthew slapped Rob on the back. "Who's in the back rooms?"

"Mr. Janson has a foursome in the green room. Lord Hoover has his mistress and another couple playing whist in the pink room. The four tables in the portrait room are full. And the burgundy room is booked, but Mr. Clay and his guest have not arrived yet."

"Give them another half hour to claim his reservation and then open it to other players. I can't afford to have the room be empty with so many people here tonight." Matthew pulled out his watch. "The show starts in an hour."

Rob nodded.

Once the show started, the gaming rooms would clear,

and the staff could take the hour to count money and IOUs. Only the most inveterate gamblers would miss the show to keep playing. These were exactly the players Matthew would personally offer loans from the house bank. His sharp gaze roamed the crowd once again.

Oh, hell no.

He spotted the one person he truly hated in this world. The one person he would never allow to step foot inside his world. "Do you see that man?" He pointed. "Tall, lean, greased-back black hair and dressed as Caesar. Get him out of my club."

"Yes, sir." Rob descended the steps and went over to Val to lean in and tell him what the boss had ordered.

Val walked over to the man and then looked up to where Matthew stood for confirmation.

He nodded. Then he watched as Val grasped the man's arm and spoke close to his ear. The man jerked back with a look of affront. But Val was not one to be messed with, and his grip tightened as he pulled the man back to the front door. Matthew folded his arms across his chest and took no small pleasure as his worst enemy was removed from the club.

Rob returned to his side. "Never seen him here before. Who was that, boss?"

"Just someone from my past. He is never to step foot into this club again. Fucking toffs," he muttered.

"Done."

Why had Jonas been here? This wasn't the typical exclusive club that he normally frequented. Had the bacchanal gotten so popular that even the snootiest of toffs deigned to come see what it was about? Matthew straightened the blue mask he had donned in deference to the masquerade theme. It covered the top half of his face and had slashing black eyebrows over the eyeholes and two molded horns rising from his temples. Tonight was a night for revelry and vices. Like the devil himself, he was happy to profit from the imprudence of others.

He continued to watch the door, on edge now at who might walk in. Why did Jonas still have this effect on him? He was no longer ten years old, soft and trusting. Life had hardened him into a man most others feared and respected. Had Jonas been looking for her? Panic solidified in his chest like ice. No, Jonas probably didn't have any idea whose club he had walked into. It didn't matter; Matthew would always protect her. Restless with his thoughts, he firmly put Jonas out of his mind and started down the stairs.

The front door opened again, and a woman in a ruby-red dress stepped inside. Her mahogany hair, long and loose, blew around her shoulders. Matthew paused in his descent, his attention stolen by her curvaceous form in the low-cut gown. She wore a mask covering the top half of her face in the same deep red as her dress. Nestled in all that thick shiny hair was a pair of devil horns, painted red with black tips. She glanced around curiously before a man stepped up beside her. He was thin as a reed; he reached up and straightened a simple white eye mask with trembling fingers. The lady smiled up at him and tucked her hand through the crook of his arm, giving it a little pat.

Matthew smiled. It was a rarity to see a woman dressed as a devil. Usually, the man was the devil and the lady on his arm, an angel. The unusual pair turned left to walk into the gaming room, and Matthew flat-out chuckled as he spotted a pair of small, white angel wings pinned to the back of the man's jacket. The two wandered off, their heads together as the lady spoke in his ear.

He continued down the stairs and followed the pair, not because he was intrigued by the lady in red. He couldn't be distracted by beautiful women, despite what his sister encouraged. No, it was time to make the rounds and see what kind of money was here tonight.

"NIGEL, STOP WORRYING. We are not here to gamble. We are here to investigate, remember?" Elizabeth said softly.

"Yes, boss. But my mother would kill me if she knew I was in a *den of iniquity*." He whispered.

Elizabeth bit back a sigh. Nigel was an excellent employee, the best writer she had, but he was more mouse than man. In a place such as this, a woman dare not arrive unattended. She had needed a male escort, and…well, Nigel was one of the few men of her acquaintance she could trust.

"Listen, let's go get a drink. Remember our main purpose. We are looking for Mary Beth. She has ginger hair, freckles, and is tall and lithe. We are here to help her if needed. Keep your eyes open for her, but don't worry. I will do all the interacting."

Elizabeth's longtime neighbor had come by earlier in the week, distraught because her daughter had run off and hadn't contacted her for several weeks. She had asked Elizabeth to use her connections to help find the girl.

"Mary Beth is so stubborn-headed, like her father. She wants to sing on the stage." Mrs. Kelley had wrung her hands. "We fought, and her da kicked her out. I know he regrets his harsh words. I just want her to come home. Where it's safe."

Earlier tonight she had tried to reassure Mrs. Kelley. "Don't worry. The tip I got that she is working at the Blue Angel came from one of my most reliable sources. Tonight, there is a large annual masquerade there. It will be the perfect time to go in unnoticed and fetch her out. I promise, if she wants to come home, I will make sure she can leave. You have my word."

Mrs. Kelley nodded, but the worry in her eyes reflected what Elizabeth was thinking. She tried to reassure the woman. "It may be that she just found a job cleaning or serving at the club." But she knew she and Mrs. Kelley shared the worry that Mary Beth was earning money on her back.

Elizabeth had squeezed the older lady's hand. Mrs. Kelley had been a good neighbor for twenty years. She owed it to her to find out what had happened to her daughter. Elizabeth understood better than most what it was like to make mistakes when one was young. She had plenty of sympathy for Mrs. Kelley's worry and would do her best to bring Mary Beth home.

"You are an angel for helping us."

Elizabeth's lips twisted into a wry smile. No, tonight she would be a devil. She would fit in far better at the infamous gaming hell, where vice and debauchery were no doubt celebrated.

She adjusted her red-beaded mask as she observed the crowd. The big room was full of people standing around talking and drinking wine. Laughter rang out from her left. Elizabeth turned to see a small group of men, all dressed as pirates. One man punched another in the arm, and all three laughed loudly again.

Behind the pirates, a large oval table took up the center of the room. There were men crowded all around it, yelling out as the dice rolled. The faces around the table were all tight with emotion—some with anticipation, some with worry. Cigar and pipe smoke filled the air and swirled around above the men's heads.

Elizabeth tugged Nigel over to the long bar. Almost immediately, two glasses of wine were placed in front of them by a barrel-chested bald man with a very crooked nose. His size and rough features should have made him scary-looking, but instead, his wide smile and cheeky wink charmed her. She couldn't refrain from smiling back at him.

For a den of iniquity, it was very clean and nicely appointed. Not at all what she had been expecting. In keeping with its name, the walls were painted a lovely sky blue and the curtains framing the windows were dark blue velvet. Across the room, there were two doors that constantly opened and closed as guests wandered through to what looked like a back hallway. What was back there? Nigel sipped his wine next to her. His gaze darted around nervously. Perhaps it had been a bad idea to bring him. He certainly didn't blend in with the brash, raucous crowd.

"Nigel, stay here and use your observational skills. I'll be back soon."

"Wait, should you be wandering around by yourself?"

"I'll be fine. Look around…there are plenty of ladies here. That's why we came tonight: the event allows for plenty of mixed company. I am almost ninety-nine percent sure that is Lord and Lady Holloway over there, dressed as Titania and Oberon."

She patted his arm and then picked up her wineglass and slowly wound her way across the room. It appeared that all the employees were dressed in solid black and wearing identical black masks over their eyes. But she didn't see any women servers, let alone any with ginger hair. She did spot a man at the end of the room, sitting in a chair that was lifted maybe six feet off the ground. His impassive expression hinted at boredom, if one didn't notice the way his eyes continually scanned the crowd around the gaming table at the center. Was he there looking for cheaters? Interesting.

A high-pitched peal of laughter rang out. Elizabeth swiveled around. A group of revelers to her right appeared to be entranced by a woman telling a story of some sort. The woman's hair was piled high on her head and powdered, her lips painted bright red. She looked like a shabbily dressed Marie Antoinette. She even had a gruesome slash of red across her neck to signify the late queen of France's demise. Elizabeth's lips twitched in amusement. But then the woman draped herself over the arm of her male companion, and he, in turn, leaned down and nibbled down her throat, making her laugh again. Definitely a prostitute. No lady would allow such affection in public.

Elizabeth continued across the room, making sure to smile and walk with confidence. She noticed a few heads turning her way with appreciative glances and barely refrained from tugging up the bodice of her dress. Perhaps this color was too loud. She wanted to fit in, but she didn't want men thinking she was a lady of the night. Nobody approached her, though. Most of the players appeared focused on the gaming.

At one of the doors to the corridor beyond, she glanced around to see if anyone would stop her to tell her she wasn't allowed. The only person who seemed to notice her was a gentleman standing nearby, wearing a blue devil mask. His gaze met hers, and his lips turned up in a smile before his attention slid back to a heavyset gentleman with whom he was conversing.

Elizabeth's heart unexpectedly sped up. What a handsome devil. His raven hair fell unruly onto his brow, and his broad shoulders filled out his black jacket nicely. She watched him and took a small sip of wine. She could feel that his attention lingered on her, even as he appeared to give it to the man in front of him. A pleasant sizzle of awareness raced beneath her skin. Perhaps it was the red dress. The dress and mask had been loaned to her by her friend Lorelei, borrowed from the dress shop she owned. The bold color and low cut of the bodice made Elizabeth feel womanly in a way she hadn't felt in years.

She moved to open the door next to her but couldn't help looking back over her shoulder. The blue devil's gaze flicked up and met hers again. She brazenly winked at him, then slipped out of the room. Her breath caught as she leaned back against the wall of the corridor. *Why had she done that?* Taking a deep breath, she rolled her eyes. So, she'd winked at a stranger…it wasn't a crime. Straightening, she smoothed her hands down her skirts. It was definitely the red dress making her feel so brazen. Besides, she wasn't likely to bump into him again, given the number of people in the club tonight.

The occasional sconce dimly lit the long hallway. Several people stumbled down the corridor to her right. One of the men grasped a woman's hand and pulled her laughing into a room. The second man smiled and followed them inside. Curious, Elizabeth turned and strolled in the same direction, hoping she looked like she knew exactly where she was going. Most of the doors were open. The rooms appeared to be for more gaming. She glanced quickly into each one as she passed slowly by.

In one room, there were several tables with four players who played whist. Another larger table of eight were playing a card game she didn't recognize. She passed by a room where the door was closed, but she could hear a mixture of male and female voices laughing. A girlish squeal of delight rang out. Frowning, she hoped that Mary Beth was not the owner of that squeal.

At the end of the corridor, it intersected with another hallway. She shrugged and turned right. As she rounded the corner, she came up short with a gasp. The man dressed as the blue devil leaned with one shoulder against the wall.

"Would you like to play?" His smile was particularly dev-ilish under a dark mustache with ends that curled up wickedly. A tightly cropped beard covered his strong jaw, adding to the edge of mystery. His deep brown eyes stared at her from behind his mask and ran over the length of her person. A flush warmed her cheeks and spread across her chest. She wished her dress covered more of her decolletage.

"Pardon?" she said.

He gestured down the hallway. "Would you like to play? I noticed you peering into the rooms."

"Oh, no. I am just curious, I suppose. I don't really know how to play anything but whist. And even then, I am not very good."

He straightened. "Well, that won't do." He stepped clos-er, and she tipped her head back to look up at him. "A devil must have vices. If not gambling, what is your vice?"

Vice? She did not have many vices, except maybe her pride or stubbornness. But she didn't think those were the sort of vice this devil meant. She glanced down at her wine and then raised it to her lips and drained the glass. "I guess perhaps mine is wine," she lied.

"Well, allow me." He pulled a bottle from behind his back and refilled her glass.

Where had that come from? "Thank you." She lifted her glass and took a more measured sip this time. She rarely drank, so she really ought to keep her consumption to just the one glass. "This is my first time at the Blue Angel. I was just wandering around, looking for a good time, but it's a bit of a maze, isn't it?" She batted her eyelashes, hoping to appear flirtatious and a bit sloshed.

"Let me show you around." He gestured down the hallway. "Each of these rooms is dedicated to a certain type of play. Faro, piquet, loo, and the sort." His hand pressed briefly on the small of her back as they turned the corner.

She could again hear laughter spilling from a room on the right. Seemed as though everybody was having fun tonight. A tiny bit jealous, she peered into the open doorway. A lady dressed as a shepherdess balanced on one foot atop a chair in the center of the room. Then the lady twirled on her toes and executed an arabesque, wobbled, and then fell into the arms of a man standing next to her.

"I told you I could do it! I used to be a ballerina!"

The man chuckled and set her on her feet. "What's next?"

"What are they doing?" Elizabeth whispered.

The blue devil leaned down to speak next to her ear. "They call this the challenge room. Everyone makes up ridiculous challenges and bets on whether they can execute them. It's loads of fun, but not for the serious-minded."

Elizabeth shook her head. That was the daftest thing she had ever heard. "Are people so desperate to waste their money?"

"Yes, they are." He leaned his forearm against the wall next to her head, crowding her with his big body. "Much of it is just for laughs, though."

She stared up at his full lips and watched as they quirked into a half smile. His proximity was as potent as the wine, making her head swim. He smelled so good, dark and spicy. "I can't remember the last time I indulged in anything just for laughs. Always far too much work to be done."

"And what about tonight?" He ran one finger across her jaw and gently tapped her bottom lip.

Her breath escaped in a soft rush. Perhaps she truly had had too much wine because wicked thoughts of kissing the mysterious man in front of her formed as she stared at his lips. She'd never kissed someone with facial hair before. Would it tickle, or would it feel like the bristles of her hairbrush, stiff and rough?

"Fair warning, if you don't stop staring at my mouth, I am going to kiss you." His voice rumbled low.

Elizabeth blinked several times before turning her head to take a long gulp of her wine. What was she doing? Allowing herself to be distracted by this devil of a man. "Actually, I am here trying to track down an old friend." Elizabeth took another sip. She was getting distracted by all the frivolity. She needed to be looking for Mary Beth. "Which way back to the main rooms?"

"This way." He led her over to another door. When he opened it, they emerged into the back of the entrance hall.

She looked back through the door, trying to parse out how the series of turns they'd taken had led them to the front. "I can't fathom how we ended up back here."

"Yes, well, the place is set up to keep people inside and playing," he replied.

Interesting. "You really know your way around. Do you frequent the club often?"

Again, the quirk of his lips was wry. "You could say I am a regular. Are you hungry? I know where we could sit and have some food. You could describe your friend. Perhaps I know who they are."

She glanced down at her wine. Oh dear, how had most of it disappeared? Food might be a good idea. She looked across into the main gaming room. How was Nigel faring? Maybe he would like some food?

The blue devil followed her gaze. "Earlier, I saw your angel chatting with an older couple at the bar."

"Oh, he's not my angel; I mean, we came together. Wait, how did you know he was with me?"

"I saw the two of you arrive, and your costume choice amused me. Precious little does at these things. More?" He tipped the wine bottle toward her glass.

She shook her head. "Well, Nigel is as pure as the driven snow, so it seemed appropriate."

"He is not your husband?"

The laugh that slipped out of her seemed cruel. Nigel was a perfectly respectable young man. And she was quite fond of his sharp mind and the dry wit with which he penned the gossip pages of her paper. She shook her head. "No, he is just a friend."

"Good."

He tucked her hand into the crook of his arm. They walked across the foyer and through another large room filled with gaming tables. Hushed conversation rumbled low through the room, broken suddenly by a loud expletive that startled Elizabeth. Smaller light fixtures hung above each card table, candlelight melting into shadows that swathed the edges of the space. Long, tufted couches ran the length of the walls. She could see the outlines of shadowed guests inter-twined with each other in the darker corners.

Before her curiosity was slaked, her companion opened another door, and they exited into a corridor identical to the one on the other side of the house. Three doors down, they entered a study of sorts. The room was dominated by a large billiards table with dark blue baize. Tucked in one corner was a small round table that could perhaps fit four. A chandelier bathed the room in a soft, warm glow.

She wandered over to the billiards table, running her fin-gertips along the polished wood edge. "Do people bet on billiards as well?"

"I am sure they do, but not here. This is a private room."
He took off his mask and set it on a side table, then crossed
to pull a cord by the door. Mere moments later, the door
opened, and a servant arrived.

"What can I get for you, sir?"

"Two of the lamb roast."

"Right away, Mr. Reeves."

Elizabeth leaned back against the table and smiled. "Finally, a name to go with the beard."

Mr. Reeves chuckled and ran a hand through his raven
hair. It was shorn on the sides, but the top was a mess of
dark curls that refused to stay put when he tried to brush
them off his brow. "Matthew Reeves, at your service."

Smiling, she turned and rolled a green ball down the table. Mr. Reeves caught her elbow and gently swiveled her
back to face him. "Don't I get to know your name?"

"I'm not sure. You see, this flirtation is quite fun, and I
don't want to ruin it by being myself."

"I certainly don't want to ruin your fun. What about just
your given name?"

She chewed on her bottom lip. What harm could it do to
tell him her name? She would never see him again after this
evening. She would have some supper and flirt, and perhaps
he could help her find Mary Beth. She untied her mask and
set it on the billiards table next to her. "Well, my father
always called me Lizzie."

"Hmmm, Lizzie. I like that." He slowly pulled her towards him. "Lizzie, what shall we do while we wait for supper?"

Then his lips were on hers, hot and seductive as hell itself. His soft, silky mustache brushed across her upper lip. Throwing her usual caution to the wind, Elizabeth gripped his shoulders and sank into the kiss. Lord, it had been so long since she had been kissed. So long since the thrum of desire had pulsed low in her belly.

One of his hands cupped her cheek as he explored her lips, his fingers sweeping over her pulse. She parted her lips and let him inside to tease with his tongue, so hot and slick. He tasted like sin. His spicy scent seemed to pour from his skin. She melted against him, clutching tight to broad shoulders as he plundered her mouth, sucking on her tongue, nibbling at her bottom lip. Every nerve ending came alive where their bodies pressed together. Then his hand seared a path from her waist to cup one of her breasts, and she moaned against his mouth at the tantalizing brush of his fingers.

A thunderous knock rang out. Matthew tore his lips from hers but didn't step back. He leaned his forehead against hers. "I'm not hungry anymore…for dinner. You?"

He was so irreverent, with his sly smile and his eyes swirling with desire for her—practical, cynical Elizabeth Harper. The craving to lean forward and dive back into his kiss was strong. But before she could say anything, more knocking came, followed by a deep voice.

"Boss, it's an emergency. We need you."

Mr. Reeves immediately straightened. His thumb brushed over her bottom lip. "This better be good," he muttered.

Boss? Elizabeth blinked a couple of times as her lust-addled brain cleared. Had she been kissing the boss of the gaming hell? A regular, he'd said. *Good Lord.* Reality came crashing over her like a bucket of cold water had been thrown in her face. What was she doing? How could she be so reckless? She ran her hands down over her skirts, smoothing out the wrinkles from being crushed against him.

Mr. Reeves crossed and opened the door. "What?" he bit out.

The man on the other side of the door was the giant bartender who had served her wine earlier. His broad face was wreathed in anguish. "Boss, one of boys went out back to have a quiet smoke and found her." He ran a hand down over his face. "She was laying in the alley, dead."

"Who?"

"One of the dancing girls. Mary Beth."

"No!" Elizabeth exclaimed. She shook her head as both men turned to her. "No, it can't be."

"Do you know Mary Beth?" Reeves assessed her with hard eyes.

"Yes, she is the friend I came to find tonight." Elizabeth slumped back against the billiard table, with a shaky hand searching behind her for stability. Mary Beth couldn't be dead.

Mr. Reeves came over and grabbed her arm. "Come with

us." Despite his gruff order, he pulled her along gently. "Where is she, Ben?"

"We brought her body into the kitchen. Boss, it looks like her neck's been slit."

Elizabeth followed the two men, her mind reeling. They all hurried down the corridor to the very end. Through an oak door, they emerged into a large kitchen. Across the room, several people were gathered around a body of a woman lying on the table in the center of the room. Elizabeth halted as they approached. Oh, dear Lord, it really was Mary Beth.

Mr. Reeves strode over to the table. "Who found her?"

A man stepped forward. "Was me, sir."

"Tell me everything that happened."

"I went outside to the alley to have my smoke in peace. Val said I could take a short break from the door. I rounded the corner, and she was there, lying on the ground."

"Did you see anyone else? Anyone running from the scene?"

"No, sir. She was still warm when I picked her up. Couldn't have been out there too long."

Elizabeth took a deep breath in and moved closer to the table. What had happened? How could anyone want to hurt this sweet girl who'd had such big dreams?

The man with the crooked nose nodded. "The show is about to start. She shouldn't have been outside at all."

Elizabeth stared down at Mary Beth. Her pale skin was a stark contrast to her bright-red hair. She wore a sparkly costume in light blue tulle, splattered with brown mud. "Show?"

"Yes, there is a nightly show in our theater. Dancing and singing a medley of numbers," Mr. Reeves replied. "Mary Beth was in the chorus line. She has worked here not too long…right, Ben?"

The large man who had come to fetch them nodded. "Just a few weeks."

She gently pushed back a lank of wet hair from Mary Beth's face. "Her mother was worried because she hadn't heard from her. She asked me to find her and make sure she was all right." A sob rose in her throat, and she couldn't stop the strangled sound from escaping. "Lord, how am I going to tell her?"

"I will tell her family. She was my responsibility," Mr. Reeves said. "Where does she live?"

"No, it's mine. I told Mrs. Kelley I would find her."

He gripped her elbow. "Lizzie, everyone who works at the Blue Angel is my responsibility. This is my world, and this happened outside my club. I will go tell her mother. You should go home. How did you get here? Do you have a carriage?"

Elizabeth stood frozen with guilt and grief, looking down at the dead woman. That's strange. There was a long thin cut across her throat. It didn't look as though it had bled like a knife wound would have. She frowned. "What would have caused this cut?"

"A blade?" Ben said.

"No, there would have been much more blood. And look here…it's beginning to bruise."

"She was strangled," Mr. Reeves said, his voice grim. "With a garrote."

Elizabeth looked up at him. "How do you know?"

"Because I have seen it before." He sighed. "Come, let's get your angel friend and get you home. No arguing." He turned to his employee. "Send for Seaton's boys. I want someone on every door, every corner around the club. And after the show, all the girls get escorted home. No one leaves alone, at least for tonight anyway. I'll take her to her parents." He looked expectantly down at Elizabeth.

She hadn't even thought about getting her body back to her parents. Elizabeth sighed. "57 Southampton King. Three doors down from me. But shouldn't we call the magistrate? Report the murder?"

Mr. Reeves's lip curled in a sneer. "No one cares about girls being murdered on the east side. And I am certainly not bringing the magistrate to my hell. We take care of our own around here."

Elizabeth glanced down again at poor Mary Beth Kelley. She knew Mr. Reeves was right. No one cared about the fate of dancing girls, or factory girls, or prostitutes. Crimes against these women never made the papers, never caused much public outrage. She fisted her hands at her sides. Well, she was outraged.

A strong hand gripped her elbow. She looked up at Mr. Reeves; his dark hair and even darker expression made him look like the king of the underworld, even without his devil's mask on. In contrast, his voice was soft, the deep timbre soothing. "Come with me. I'll have someone get you a hack to get home."

CHAPTER THREE

SITTING AT THE writing desk in her bedroom, Elizabeth rubbed at her tired eyes and glanced down at the headline of the article she had crafted in the wee hours of that morning. Unable to sleep last night, she had risen from her rumpled sheets and sat down to work out her emotions on paper. Those emotions now screamed up at her in a single word. MURDER!

Running a fingertip across the bold, shocking word, she smiled grimly. She would choose a font at least three inches tall. She would tell all of London about the killing of an innocent woman. Mary Beth's murder last night had been only one in a recent string of ghastly deaths.

Last night, as Elizabeth had looked through her notes from the past two months, she finally saw the connection. All the women killed had been attacked on the east side of town, all near their places of work. These killings had to be connected. More than that, these women deserved to have their deaths lamented. The public should be shocked and disheartened. Maybe the article would capture the attention of the magistrate finally.

She folded the penned article neatly and tucked it into a

leather folio. Before she headed to meet her printer, she should say good morning to Robert. As she left her room, she stopped in front of her tall mirror. She tucked a rogue piece of hair back into her bun and straightened the watch fob pinned to her waist. Her practical navy dress was a far cry from the beautiful red silk gown, but she looked more like herself this morning, puffy, tired eyes and all.

She walked up the narrow stairs to the third floor and paused to lean against the doorjamb to watch her son play. He sat in the middle of the large round rug, surrounded by toy soldiers, cavalry, and cannons.

"Get set. Fire," he bellowed. One small hand swept out a platoon of soldiers. "Ahhhh!"

She chuckled, and Robert's head swung around. "Mama!" His dark hair fell over his forehead and into his eyes. She needed to make time to give him a haircut.

"Hello, my love." She stepped into the room. "Who is winning?"

"The Greeks. Uncle Alex told me about how they are fighting the Turks for independence. And how we are helping with our navy. Because the British navy is the best in all the world. Uncle Alex knows lots of things about the military because he sits in the House of Lords." Robert's eyes shone with admiration.

Elizabeth ran a hand over Robert's hair, pushing it off his face. She sighed a little. Uncle Alex had become such a hero to her son. It had been a year since the Duke of Hartwick had discovered her and Robert's existence. She had kept her son's parentage a secret to protect them. But Hartwick had been searching for answers to his brother's untimely demise and found out about the two of them quite by accident. She didn't know who had been more surprised that day when Robert had opened the front door to find the duke at their doorstep. Now, they all were the most unlikely kin.

She wasn't always happy about how much the Duke of Hartwick wished to insert himself into their lives. But she did understand that Robert was starved for male role models. And, well, she supposed Hartwick was also starved for family. Why else would he allow that criminal half-brother of his to also be part of their ragtag family?

This past year hadn't been all that bad. Hartwick's wife made sure to pull him back from becoming too domineering and Lady Hartwick had become a good friend. Elizabeth usually avoided the aristocracy, preferring to write from afar about the fickle favors and betrayals of the ton in her weekly gossip page. But Hartwick and his lady were exceptions. Perhaps it was because they shared her basic mistrust of those in the ton. And, well, they were family, and the only people who had known and loved her son's father as much as she had.

"Mama, do you want to play?" Robert tipped his head up to flash her a smile that reminded her so much of his father.

Those gray eyes, clear and bright with enthusiasm, made her heart ache with the thought that Robert would never know his namesake. Never get to listen to him chatter and watch him grow. She rubbed a small circle on her chest.

Grief had a funny way of sneaking up on you, even after almost seven years.

She swallowed her emotions. "Not now, love. Bessie is acting up, and I must go after breakfast to see if I can fix her before the ladies are ready to set the type."

"Can I come?"

"Of course." She held out a hand as he scrambled up off the floor and carefully stepped around his battalions. "Let's go see what Mrs. Todd has made for breakfast."

"THANK GOD YOU'RE here," Mr. Norton's gruff voice called out.

Elizabeth pulled the pin from her straw bonnet and hung it on the hook next to the front door. "It can't be all that bad, George."

Her print chief huffed and crossed his beefy arms across his chest. "You know I can't make heads or tails of this newfangled thing. Bessie is real temperamental."

George Norton, God bless his crusty old heart, had been her father's best friend and business partner, and he had stuck by Elizabeth when she took over the *Piccadilly Press* after her father died. But the man was mired in the old ways. He still mourned the manual Stanhope Press they used to use.

Last year, she'd purchased a new steam-powered double-cylinder press. It cost her a pretty penny and took three months to come from Germany. She would be paying off the loan for the next five years, but it was worth it. Bessie could print eleven hundred double-sided sheets per hour compared to the two hundred the manual press could print. George was no spring chicken, and you'd think he would be grateful for the new, more automated machine. But no, he grumbled every day.

She took off her jacket, hung it on a hook, as well, grabbed an apron, and rolled up her shirt sleeves.

Robert took off his hat and handed it to her. "Hullo, Mr. Norton. I've come to help."

George's expression softened as he looked down at Robert. "Well now, that's a good boy. It's a fine thing you learning from your mama. She is the best print master in town." Then George winked at her.

Elizabeth stepped up to him and bussed his weathered cheek. "Flattery will get you everywhere," she said.

They walked back through the small front foyer area and into the airy print room. The back wall of the large room was all windows. Most were open to help the flow of air and mitigate how hot the room got with the steam-powered print machine.

"Good morning, ladies," Elizabeth said as she passed by where her typesetters sat on stools at a long table, getting today's edition of the paper set.

"Good morning, Miss Harper."

"Morning, little man."

Robert smiled broadly at the ladies, always the charmer.

"I came to help."

Elizabeth turned to the middle of the room, where the machine held the place of honor. "What's seems to be the trouble, George?"

"I was running the test page and the paper jammed in the second roller. I can't see why. I oiled the mechanism, but the paper keeps jamming in the second roller."

She peered between the roller and the center of the mechanism, where the ink pads would press against the paper. There was a dark blob of some sort there. "Hmm, maybe too much ink and it has congealed?" *Or...*she peered at the dark spot again. Then opened the drawer to the right, where the case of type was placed. Just as she thought, a letter was missing from the third line of text. Making sure the lever to start the machine was in the OFF position, with the latch engaged, she called out. "Robert, come here. Do you see that little dark spot there?"

Robert peered up where she pointed. "Yes, mama."

"I think it is a type tile. Can you fish it out for me?"

Robert bit down on his bottom lip and stuck his small hand between the roller and the type case drawer. After a few seconds, he pulled his hand out, the tile pinched between his forefinger and thumb.

"Good job, darling!"

George shook his head. "I didn't spot that."

She smiled at him. "We needed small fingers. Now that we know that can happen, we need to be careful not to jostle the case when inserting the type into the drawer." She crouched down in front of Robert. "What letter is that?"

Robert turned the tile to face him and concentrated. "It is a *Q*. The one with the tail."

"Correct." She gave him a kiss on the cheek. "Let's put it back in place, shall we?"

Robert nodded. And she lifted him up so he could place the tile back into place in the sentence. Then they carefully slide the case back into the drawer. "Alright, let's run another test copy."

After everything came out right with the test copy, Elizabeth turned to the ladies that set the type. "I have a new article for the front page today." She pulled it from her folio and set it on the table. A collective gasp rang out at the headline. The ladies all gathered around to read the article.

Jessica shook her head. "Poor Mary Beth. I was wondering where she got off to after her da kicked her out. I told her she should come here and work for you. But she was too good fer it." Jessica sniffed. "Some dream of hers to be a singer on the stage. Not very respectable, my ma says."

"And look what happened to her," Katie chimed in.

Well, that explained more about her row with her father. Elizabeth had to agree with Jessica's mother. Being on the stage was hardly respectable. She dearly hoped that the Blue Angel hadn't lured Mary Beth in with false promises of helping her get on the stage. Elizabeth's mood darkened. These dens of vice played on people's weaknesses and ruined lives.

"To be fair, it's not the hell's fault she is dead. There is a pattern here. Someone is on a killing spree. I want all of you to be careful when going out at night. Stick together, coming and going from work."

The four women all nodded solemnly.

"All right, let's get this article set. We've an edition to get out."

CHAPTER FOUR

MATTHEW SLUMPED INTO his desk chair and closed his eyes. What a fucking night it had been. He reached blindly for his coffee and took a deep gulp. Bright afternoon sunlight burned against his eyelids.

"Rough night?" The deep gravel of Seaton's voice came from the doorway.

"That's an understatement." Matthew took another sip of coffee.

His best friend sauntered into his office and sat across from him, stretched his long legs out, and crossed them at the ankles. "I heard about the girl. Zeke said she was strangled?"

Matthew ran a hand down over his face. "Yeah. A garrote, I think. She had a thin cut from the wire, but hardly any blood. Fucking hell, she was killed right at my back door."

"Thinking it was a message?"

"Rutledge, that bastard, he wouldn't blink about doing something like this. He's so fucking jealous over our success."

"That's cause he's still hooking crates and dodging excise

men while you're living in luxury and charming ladies and gents every night." Seaton cracked his knuckles. "I should have killed him a long time ago."

Matthew couldn't help but smile briefly. "The hell is the sweetest way to relieve people of their money. Lot better than working the odds at the fights, that's for sure."

Seaton nodded his agreement. "What do you want to do about Rutledge?"

"Nothing for now. Don't know for sure it was him. I'm going to look into it. I don't even know why she was out in the alley with only fifteen minutes till the show started"

"Could be one of Rutledge's boys was romancing her. Had her meet him out back."

Matthew nodded. It was the best theory so far. He was strict about the girls in the show. They needed to be professional, on time, and keep their beaus out of the club. He stared down into his mug. "Her mother tore into me last night. Her grief just spewed out in the form of righteous anger. How dare I lure her daughter into a life of dissolution? I tried to explain that she was in the show. Dancing. Not whoring. But she wouldn't listen. Just kept yelling."

Seaton shrugged. "Why do you care what she thinks?"

"Because I run a legitimate show. I watch out for those girls, dammit. A lot of them have gone on to work at the Globe and the Highgate. It's true some of them are looking to find themselves rich benefactors. But there is nothing wrong with that."

"No, there's not. Everyone's got to eat; take care of

themselves. Listen, you can't protect them all. You don't make their decisions for them. Like last night, you didn't send her outside to her death."

"I suppose." Everyone at the Blue Angel was like his family. Most had worked for him for the last five years since he'd opened the place. Anger mixed with the acid of the coffee in his stomach, leaving him feeling sick. He'd find out who killed her and punish them.

"Boss."

Matthew glanced up. Ben stood in the open doorway. Poor Ben had been maybe the most devastated last night. He took his unofficial job of mother hen seriously, and he blamed himself. "Come in."

Ben shuffled in. He nodded to Seaton. "Thanks fer lending your boys last night."

"Anytime. What's mine is yours."

Ben turned to Matthew. "Boss, you're gonna want to see this." He handed over a newspaper.

It was folded in half, and across the top, in big, bold letters, the headline read MURDER! He skimmed the article below it. *Last night, as revelers gambled away their money, drank away their problems, and fornicated in dark corners at the notorious gaming hell, The Blue Angel, an innocent young woman, Mary Beth Kelley, was brutally murdered in the alley behind the club. Strangled by an unknown assailant, her life snuffed out in the dangerous streets of London. She is just the latest in a string of women who have been killed on the east side.*

A barmaid at Red's Tavern, Anne Johnson, was killed out-

side of the tavern two months ago. Lucy Stone was killed walking home from her job at the Queen's Head on Bow Street a fortnight ago. And last Saturday evening, Sarah Felding was killed after leaving her job at the Birdcage in the early morning hours. All of these women were strangled to death. Does London's east side have a killer stalking working-class women? Is he lying in wait, planning to use his garrote to snuff out yet another life?

"Fuck!" Matthew slapped the paper down on the desk.

Seaton reached forward and grabbed it up. His lips twitched with amusement. "She certainly knows how to write an arresting story. I'll give her that."

"The last thing I need is to have the name of the club in the paper linked with a murder. And 'fornicating in dark corners'? It makes us sound like a fucking brothel." A gaming establishment might not be the most respectable of businesses, but hell, his girls weren't prostitutes. "You should've seen the crowd last night. The biggest night ever."

"Best crowd ever," Ben agreed.

Matthew slammed his fist down on the table. "Do you think they'll come back if they think someone's been murdered here?"

Seaton shrugged one shoulder.

Used to his friend's non-verbal answers, Matthew blew out a long breath. But then he sat up straighter. "Did you say 'she'?"

"Yes. The *Piccadilly Press* is run by Elizabeth Harper."

Elizabeth? Lizzie? Could it be the same woman from last

night? The lady in red? He clenched his fists. Had she been here looking to write an article about his club? She said she had been looking for her friend. He frowned, remembering the sorrow in her eyes as she stood by Mary Beth's body in the kitchen and some of his anger drained. But hell, if she hadn't painted his club in the worst possible light. They'd worked hard to attract more moneyed clientele. This kind of publicity would certainly scare off the toffs.

He narrowed his eyes at Seaton. "How do you know her?"

"She is the mother of my nephew."

What? "You don't have a brother."

"Actually, I do. Half-brothers. Had two. One was killed, and he had a son with Miss Harper. The other one is the current Duke of Hartwick."

Matthew held up a hand. "You're the half-brother of a goddamn duke?" A laugh erupted from his chest. What a load of shite. He glanced over at Ben, who laughed as well. They'd known Seaton since he was fifteen and running around with the Newgate gang. There was no way he was related to a duke.

"You assholes don't have to believe me," Seaton said with a chuckle. "But it's true. My mother was the mistress to the Duke of Hartwick for a time, and I am his son."

Matthew stared at his friend. "Goddamn, you're serious."

"That's how I inherited the street. This house used to be the old Hartwick manor house back when this area was a sheep and shit. He never acknowledged me, but he left me something in the end, so I hold no bad blood for him."

"Wait, really?" Matthew asked.

Seaton smirked. The long, thin scar that ran from his ear, down across his cheek to his top lip, pulling at the corner, always made him look like he was snarling, even when he was actually laughing at them, like right now.

Matthew reeled at the bombshell. He thought he knew everything about Rhys Seaton. The illegitimate son of a duke. And the lady in red was a fucking newspaper editor. "So, you're saying Elizabeth Harper, the editor of the paper, is the widow of a duke's son?"

"No, he died before they married."

"But not before he got her with child?"

Seaton nodded. "My father and him—he was the heir— were murdered. She kept the child a secret to protect herself and the baby. I found out about them last summer, along with the current duke, who I was hired to protect." He waved a hand around airily, like this was all old news.

"I know you are a private person, and I respect that, but what the hell, Rhys? You have a whole fucking family that you never bothered to tell us about?" He glanced over at Ben, who looked as shocked as him.

"I knew about them, but I never thought I would ever have any sort of relationship with them."

Matthew leaned forward. "But you do, don't you?" Why did that hurt so much?

Seaton was an enigma. Hell, Matthew didn't even know where the man kept a residence. He came and went like a fucking ghost. But as much as Seaton allowed anyone to know him, Matthew liked to think he knew him best. He'd joined Rhys's gang at fifteen, and they ran dodges in the streets of London for years. Matthew had been there with him when Rhys's mother died, and Rhys had ridden north with him when his own mother had died. Their bond of brotherhood was something Matthew cherished. Especially since his actual brother was such a bloody bastard.

"I see him sometimes." Rhys just shrugged. "Ms. Harper doesn't approve of me, so I have only met my nephew twice."

Another black mark against Elizabeth Harper. The woman was clearly a judgmental busybody. It was a damn shame. She had been so lush and responsive in his arms. He hadn't been so seduced by a woman in a long time. Matthew ran a hand down over his jaw as he tried to sift through all the information he'd just learned.

Seaton stood. "Well, let me know when you want to take care of Rutledge. I've a job that's going to take me out of town for a fortnight, at least. But let Zeke know if you need any extra eyes on the club. See ya fellas."

Matthew turned to Ben. "Send Barnes in with the books. And find out what day the burial will be for Mary Beth Kelley. I'm sure the other girls will want to go pay their respects."

"Yes, boss." Ben stepped forward. "The lady you was with left this behind." He set down the red mask on the corner of the desk and left.

Matthew took a deep gulp of his now lukewarm coffee. He stared at the mask. It was covered in red silk and embroidered with black thread. Bold, but delicate. Who was the real woman underneath the mask? Certainly not just some pretty partygoer. And not some merry widow. How long had she been raising her child all alone? How long had she been running the paper?

He reached out for the mask and ran a finger along the edge, remembering the feel of her silky skin, the sharp green of her eyes, her full soft lips, and even softer curves. He groaned at his runaway libido. Damn it, she had fucking maligned his club and splashed that poor girl's death all over the front page of her newspaper. Was nothing sacred to these people? He picked up the mask and shoved it into the drawer of his desk. Time to get back to work.

CHAPTER FIVE

T HE RAIN HAD not stopped for the past two days, and the churchyard was muddy, with the trees dripping water on the people arriving to pay their respects to Mary Beth Kelley. Matthew, Ben, Mrs. Langley, and a half dozen other dancers from the Blue Angel quietly entered the church and shuffled into a pew near the back. Across the aisle and down in front, Elizabeth Harper stood next to the skinny man with whom she had arrived at the club. In their pew were four other young women. He watched Miss Harper lean forward and lay a hand on Mrs. Kelley's shoulder. The older woman sniffed and patted her hand.

Matthew's temper rose. She'd plastered the woman's pain across the pages of the newspaper, and yet she still remained in Mrs. Kelley's good graces. He shifted restlessly in his seat. He hadn't been in a church since he was a boy. Even when he snuck into his own mother's funeral ten years ago, he had stayed in the churchyard. Spoken to her grave after the family had all left. A sinner like him didn't belong inside a church.

He glanced left at the Kelleys. The family took up the entire front pew. If the mother needed to blame him, fine by him. He knew from speaking with Mrs. Langley that Mary Beth's family had thrown her out of the house when she told them she wanted to pursue a career in the theater. Their guilt was probably eating them alive.

Dammit, so was his. Fuck, what the hell had Mary Beth been doing out in the back alley right before the show? Logically, he knew it wasn't his fault. But if one of his enemies had used that poor girl as a message to him...well, he would find out who it was. No one came to his house and harmed his people without suffering consequences.

Thankfully, the clergyman was brief, and the service was over quickly. Outside, the rain had receded to a light drizzle. He waited with the others politely for the family to exit the church. Mr. and Mrs. Kelley paused in front of him.

"Mr. Reeves, thank you for the fine coffin. We appreciate your gift," Mr. Kelley said.

Matthew nodded.

Mrs. Kelley spat on the ground at his feet. "She's dead because of you. If she had been at home or gone to work for Miss Harper, like I told her, she would still be alive." Her wave of grief hit him square in the chest.

Nothing she said was untrue, so he simply nodded again.

Mr. Kelley tugged on his wife's arm. "That's not fair, dear. She would have been home if I hadn't been so harsh with her."

A sob erupted from Mrs. Kelley's throat, and she pushed past her husband. Mr. Kelley followed her more slowly over to the freshly dug hole at the edge of the graveyard.

Matthew spied Elizabeth Harper across the grass, staring over at him from under her umbrella. He turned to the others. "I'll just be a minute." Then, following his temper, he strode across the churchyard to Miss Harper.

"Mr. Reeves. I heard you paid for the coffin. That was very generous."

But he didn't need her acknowledgment of his gift. He leaned into her space. "I don't appreciate having my club linked to a murder in the paper. How could you sensationalize that poor girl's death?"

Instead of stepping back, Miss Harper took a step forward, her umbrella tipping back as her gaze turned sharp. "Sensational sells."

"You made my place sound like a goddamn brothel. Are you trying to ruin my business?"

"This has nothing to do with your business. Nobody cares about the deaths of these working women. You said so yourself. I want to show that their lives matter. They are worth writing about, their lives worth mourning." She waved her hand toward where the Kelley family stood, watching their daughter's coffin being lowered into the muddy ground. "Your club was incidental. Besides, you peddle in vice; why are you worried about your reputation?"

"I run a gaming hell and a theater. I do not peddle in flesh." And he never would. He had seen firsthand how it could hollow out a woman, body and soul.

She scoffed. "A theater?"

"Yes. A theater. Every night at midnight, there is a show

in the theater. Mary Beth was in the chorus line of dancers. Come see it some night. My blue angel has a voice to rival any operatic diva."

"So, Mary Beth was dancing and singing in a real theater production?"

Her incredulity stung. He should be used to everyone assuming the worst of him by now. It's not like he hadn't chosen this life. He'd purposefully left behind his respectable name and his old life when his uncle died. Seaton's voice echoed in his head. *Why do you care what people think?* He usually didn't. But hell, if this woman didn't make him want to preen like a damn peacock.

She looked just as lovely today with her hair pulled back into a neat bun at her nape as she had looked with it loose and falling around her bare shoulders at the masquerade. There was a sprinkle of freckles across the bridge of her nose that he hadn't noticed that night in the candlelight. Her sharp cheekbones and small, pointed chin gave her a delicate look that belied her obvious strength of character. She stood toe to toe with him, her shoulders squared, her brow furrowed as she decided whether to believe him. Then her gaze swept down, and dark lashes fluttered as she looked away.

"I don't peddle in flesh." It was worth repeating. "Some of my dancers may take lovers if they choose. But that's none of my business."

Her mouth gaped with a small gasp. He took great pleasure in pushing her lower jaw back up with one finger. He couldn't help but needle her a little just to see that fire flash in her eyes again. "You didn't strike me as so prudish when you were kissing me in my private room the other night." He ran his thumb over her lower lip. "If you ever want another taste, come see me."

She shoved away his hand. "You, sir, are a rogue."

"I've been told that a time or two." He tipped his hat. "Good day, Miss Harper."

THAT MAN WAS a rogue, Elizabeth repeated to herself with a huff as she unlocked her front door. A menace. Strangely, she believed him when he said that Mary Beth had just been dancing in his show. And the sense of relief that Mary Beth had, in fact, been following her dream paired with sorrow that her life had been cut short before she could see that dream to fruition. Elizabeth sighed.

She unpinned her damp hat and set it on the console table by the door. Life was unfair. She had learned seven years ago just how cruelly dreams could be shattered. She set her wet umbrella into the brass stand to keep it from dripping on the floors. Because so many of her employees had been friends with Mary Beth or her parents, Elizabeth decided to not put out an edition today, instead giving everyone a day off.

The weather was miserable still. Damp and far too cool for summer. All she wanted to do was curl up in front of the fire in her reception room and cuddle with her son. Where was Robert? Usually, he heard the front door open and came running. Perhaps he was in the kitchen, pestering Mrs. Todd. She made her way to the back of the house and down the stairs to the kitchen. Sure enough, Robert sat at the large oak table, drinking milk and chattering away.

He glanced over when she came into the room. "Mama!"

"Hello, my love." She bent and kissed his head. "What are you telling Mrs. Todd about?"

"I saw a pair of frogs in the garden today. They were lying around in the muddy corner next to the back gate, where it always makes puddles when it rains. They were so loud! Mrs. Todd says frogs like wet weather. Is that true?"

"Yes, I believe so. I have only ever seen frogs by ponds. They must like to swim."

Robert giggled. "I think if they are going to live in our back garden, I should name them. Don't you? Then they can be part of the family."

Robert had been asking for a pet for months. She'd told him very firmly that she had no time to take care of an animal, and that Mrs. Todd did not need anything more to take care of either. At just under six years old, Robert was far too young to be responsible for a pet. "Well, I suppose you may name them if you see them again, but"—she held up a finger in warning—"they are not allowed in the house."

"Please, mama?"

"Absolutely not. Frogs are meant to live out of doors. Right, Mrs. Todd?"

The housekeeper nodded. "I would not like mud tracked

through my clean floors."

Robert's bottom lip jutted out a bit, but he nodded. Elizabeth held out a hand. "Why don't you come sit with me by the fire? I could use a cuddle after being out in the rain all morning."

"Yes! I'm a good cuddler." He smiled and took her hand.

"That is precisely why I asked."

"Ms. Harper, several notes arrived for you. I left the pile on your desk blotter," Mrs. Todd said.

"Thank you."

They headed down the hall and into the cozy front room. She picked up the pile of notes and then settled next to Robert on the sofa. "So, what else did you do today?" she asked.

He snuggled his small body up against her side, sliding an arm across her stomach. "We went for a walk to the park, and I got to splash in puddles. My socks got wet even inside my boots. We came back through the back garden, and when Mrs. Todd went inside to put down the vegetables she bought at the market, that's when I saw the frogs. I climbed the tree and made it all the way to the third branch before Mrs. Todd came and pulled me down."

Oh dear. The tree climbing had become quite the skill. The tree branches on the willow in their garden were quite low, but still, she wished he didn't have such an adventurous spirit when it came to climbing. The other day she had come to his room and found him sitting on top of his wardrobe, all the drawers open serving as steps. She brushed his hair back from his head. "I want you to be careful with climbing the tree. Only when there is a grown-up around. All right?"

"All right, mama." His voice sleepy, he lay his head on her breast. She wrapped an arm around him and they sat quietly watching the fire. When she was home, he always had something to tell her. She knew that she was gone far too much, but she had a business to run and household bills to pay. She glanced down as his eyes fluttered closed. His rainy-day adventures must have tired him out.

Picking up one of the notes, she broke the seal. It was from one of her best informants, the lady's maid to the Marchioness of Rollinsford. She raised an eyebrow at the tidbit Mary had written to her about. Very interesting, indeed. The next two notes also contained tips suitable for Friday's scandal page. She laid them together to give to Nigel tomorrow.

Picking up the next in the pile, she studied the very neat penmanship. It was unusual to see such nice handwriting. Most of her contacts were servants, barmen, coachmen, many who barely knew their letters. The writing was often rife with spelling errors and looked more like chicken scratch. She unfolded the missive.

Mr. Harper,

I enjoyed your article about the recent murders you featured in your newspaper. I have some pertinent information on who might be the culprit. This speculation is a delicate matter and certainly worth a pretty

*penny. Meet me at the Green Door Tavern in Cheap-
side at nine o'clock this evening. Leave your name with
the bartender, and I will find you.*

Hmm. She normally did not meet strangers out at night, but his dangle that he had information on the recent murders was enticing. She knew the owner of the Green Door. James Folger had been a long-time informant for her, always full of good gossip, seeing as his tavern was across the street from one of the city's most rowdy gaming clubs. The ask for money was typical and led her to think that the man perhaps actually did have some information to pass on. Haggling over the price of a good tip was one of her favorite things, especially with someone new.

Her tidbits of gossip came from people of all walks of life. Certainly, servants trying to earn extra quid, but also from bored wallflowers that no one noticed, but who noticed everything around them. Bartenders, coaching inn owners, and, of course, other reporters. As the saying goes, there was no honor among thieves, and she had cultivated friends across the city. This wasn't just a piece of gossip; this could be a clue to exposing a murderer. It would be worth the risk.

She smoothed a hand over Robert's dark hair. He would be fast asleep by the time she had to leave. Happy to have a quiet afternoon ahead of her to spend with her son, she hummed a happy tune and reached for the next piece of correspondence.

CHAPTER SIX

"WHY WERE YOU yelling at that woman in the churchyard?" Stella asked him as Matthew handed her down from their carriage in front of the Blue Angel.

"I was not yelling at her. We were having a simple conversation." He tucked her hand into the crook of his arm and led her inside the front door of the club.

"It was more than a conversation. Perhaps you mistake with whom you are speaking." She pointed at herself. "I am a human barometer for emotions. And that was at minimum a heated discussion."

"Afternoon, boss, Miss Stella." Chris greeted from his stool by the door.

"Chris." Matthew nodded. He and Stella headed directly upstairs. "Perhaps it was more of a confrontation than a conversation."

Stella raised one eyebrow.

"That was Miss Harper. She is the editor of the newspaper that wrote the article about Mary Beth's murder. I was not happy that she named the club. We don't need bad publicity."

"The editor of the paper is a woman? How interesting. She must be very clever."

"Clever, I will give her. But she had no business using Mary Beth's murder as a way to sell papers."

"I read the article. It seemed to me that she was trying to show that there has been a pattern of women dying on the east side."

"That's just what she said," he grumbled.

They entered his private wing. Stella reached up to remove her hat, throwing it down onto the low table in front of the fireplace. She plopped down into a chair with a sigh. "Today was so sad. I didn't know Mary Beth very well; she was new, but she seemed nice. She did have a wonderful voice."

Matthew hung his hat on a hook by the door and crossed to sit in the chair next to her. The fire crackled and danced in front of him, chasing away the damp chill that had seeped into his bones. He relished the few moments of quiet before he had to get back to work. The club's doors opened at five o'clock. Before then, he needed to have a staff meeting and speak with Mrs. Langley about hiring another girl to replace Mary Beth. If he'd learned anything from living with his uncle, it was that the show must go on.

Uncle Harry died five years after Matthew had been sent to live with him here in London. A giant man in stature and personality, he had been a safe haven for Matthew. Uncle Harry had run the Seven Stars Theater. Life there had been hectic and colorful and totally lacking in rules. The exact opposite of his childhood home with his parents. His uncle had spent every waking moment at his theater and Matthew had been ushered into adolescence by the dozen actors and dancers that worked for his uncle. Everyone had kept watch over him.

He glanced over at Stella. She had lived her whole life under their father's roof. Walking on eggshells and being quiet as a mouse so as not to attract attention. In the year she had lived with him here at the Blue Angel, she had certainly blossomed. He hoped that he offered her the same safe haven that Uncle Harry had given him—an opportunity to be herself without fear. Turns out, Stella was quite a chatterbox. Curious about everyone she met. And that singing voice, clear and melodic. She never stopped singing and humming as she went about her day. It brought him great joy to hear it, as he knew she hadn't always been allowed to sing so freely as a child.

"The newspaper lady was quite lovely." Stella glanced sideways at him with a smile.

He grunted.

"You two were standing very close. I saw you touch her lips."

"None of your business." He refused to encourage this conversation.

Stella just laughed. "She didn't seem scared of you at all."

That was true. Elizabeth Harper had not been intimidated by him in the least. He'd give her that. He had spent a long time remaking himself from a scared boy to a man who was nobody's victim. Luckily, he had grown into his adolescent bravado, reaching a height and breadth similar to that of his uncle. After his uncle died, instead of risk being sent back to his father, Matthew ran with the Newgate gang, earning money however he could. His experiences surviving on the streets of London had carved out the man he was today.

He'd had to be strong and calculating to stay alive. He and Rhys had agreed that gang life wasn't the life for them, and they worked hard to save money in order to open a real venture. This club was his investment in his future. The way he would make his fortune. He wouldn't let anyone jeopardize that, especially not a conniving newspaper editor with luscious, distracting curves.

A knock sounded at the door. "Come in," he called out.

The door opened, and Ben stepped into the room. "Chris says Jack Spencer is at the door. Says he wants to talk with you."

Jack Spencer? The owner of the Hillwood Theater. Matthew straightened. "You can show him up."

Ben nodded and disappeared. Matthew turned to his sister. "Why is Jack Spencer wanting to talk with me?"

Stella bit her lip, her eyes sliding away from him. "Um, well, he spoke with me after the show the week before last. He is very impressed by my voice."

"He approached you after a show?" Matthew stood, his agitation rising. "Without me?"

"Don't be so protective. Mrs. Langley was there. He just wanted to compliment my performance. He thinks I am talented."

Another knock at the door had Stella rising. She smoothed out her dark gray skirts. "I wish I had time to change," she muttered.

The somber dress she had worn to the funeral was just fine, in his opinion. He turned and went to open the door. "Afternoon, Spencer."

Jack Spencer took off his hat. "Afternoon, Reeves. Thanks for seeing me."

"Come in. I hear you have met my sister, Stella."

Spencer nodded and crossed the room to where Stella stood in front of the fireplace. "Afternoon, Miss Reeves."

"Good afternoon, Mr. Spencer." Stella settled in her chair.

Matthew sat back down next to her. "What's this about, Spencer?"

Spencer sat across from them. He smiled wide and toothy. "I have heard good things about your little show here, Reeves. But especially about your blue angel." He winked at Stella.

Matthew frowned at the cheek. But that was theater people for you, and this wasn't some Mayfair drawing room after all.

"I came to see the show a couple of weeks ago," Spencer continued. "And it's just as fun as people have said. The thing is, I am starting a new production. I am putting on a production of *The Deep, Deep Sea*. Miss Reeves would make a perfect Rosalind."

"No."

"Pardon?"

"My answer is no. Stella is not an actress for hire."

"But she performs for your show," Spencer sputtered.

"Precisely. She performs here at the Blue Angel, where I can keep her safe. She is only seventeen." Out of the corner of his eye, he could see Stella's pout.

"Reeves, you know I run a decent place. The Hillwood is renowned for its performances. I could make her a star."

That's exactly why he would never allow it. Matthew folded his arms across his chest and simply stared across at Spencer.

The man leaned back in his chair, his gaze sharpening. "I heard about the trouble last Saturday. One of your dancers, dead in the alley. Is the hell really the safest place for her? Many of my performers share lodgings at a respectable boarding house in Soho Square. They all watch out for each other. Think of opportunities this could open for her future."

"She doesn't need to work. I take care of mine." Matthew sighed. "Just as I know you do. Harry always respected your operation. But the answer is still no." He stood and held out a hand.

Spencer rose and shook it. "Just think about. If you change your mind, rehearsals begin in August. Good day, Miss Reeves."

Matthew showed him the door. Ben stood outside, ready to escort Spencer out through the club. No outsiders were allowed to roam unattended. When he turned back, Stella was slumped with a dejected expression. She stared into the fire.

"You know why you can't perform at the Hillwood."

"But with some makeup and maybe a wig, no one would recognize me."

"Stella…" He felt bad, but her anonymity was important. "I saw him. Here at the club."

She sat up and turned to him. "He was here?"

"Didn't make it past the front entrance. I had Val throw him out. And he's on the banned list." He sat down and ran a hand over his beard. "Never thought I'd see him so far from his clubs in St. James Square. Must have been buzz about the masquerade."

Stella's eyes were wide with fear. He reached out to grip one of her hands. "You see why I can't let you go perform at the Hillwood? Plenty of fancy people go to the performances there. You're safe here on the east side. You'll never run into Jonas at the market here or the coffee shop on Drury Lane. And he will never step foot in this club again. I promise you that."

"I know I am safe here. Mama said that if I ever felt scared, I should come to find you." She squeezed his hand. "I'm so glad I did. I love it here, I really do." She rose to her feet. "I am going to go find Pitter-Patter."

"Stella," he called out as she reached the door. "I'm glad you found me too."

She sent him a wide smile before disappearing through the door to go find her kitten. His heart clenched in his chest. She was such a gift. He had been alone for so long after Uncle Harry died. Just trying to survive. He and Rhys had an unbreakable bond of friendship, but the way Stella cracked open his heart had reminded him what it was to love someone fiercely. He would be forever grateful.

He rose and stretched, cracking the tension in his back, then headed to his study. Just as he suspected, he had a pile of invoices to approve sitting on top of the daily ledger that needed to be checked. He opened his watch fob; he had two hours before the staff meeting. After sorting through the invoices, he opened the ledger, but he couldn't focus. His eyes slid to the left and landed on the folded newspaper that lay on the corner of the desk.

His mind wandered to the woman who ran it. She had occupied too much of his thoughts over the last few days. He had no time for liaisons with complicated women. Life was complicated enough. But the fierce defiance in her eyes when he had challenged her today had made his blood heat and that kiss they had shared had been incendiary. He wondered if the prickly newspaper lady would take him up on his offer to have another taste.

CHAPTER SEVEN

RUTLEDGE COULD GO to hell. Matthew shoved his damp hair off his forehead and slammed his cap back on his head. Where was the bastard? Matthew had been standing outside the Montaque for two hours in the drizzle, the high collar of his coat barely keeping the damp from running down his back. He knew Archie Rutledge came to play deep here at the Montaque. He sneered up at the front of the hell. Gaudy and cheap, it catered to the hooks and sailors that worked near here on the docks. Rutledge fashioned himself as the leader of a gang of small-time criminals that ran this area below the Garden.

Matthew leaned back against the side of the building and lit another hand-rolled cigarillo, cupping his hands carefully over the end to block the drizzle. He needed to find out if Rutledge was behind Mary Beth's murder. And the best way to find out was to confront him face-to-face. If Rutledge was involved, the cocky bastard would be dying to crow about it. And Matthew was spoiling for a good fight after spending the day trying and failing to not think about the lady in red. He rolled his neck. Fighting was almost as good as sex to release frustration.

Then, as though the universe was taunting him, the door to the tavern across the street opened, and in the spill of light, stood Elizabeth Harper. Still dressed in the same black outfit she'd worn at the funeral, she pulled on a pair of gloves as the door behind her swung shut. In the light of the lanterns that flanked the entrance to the Green Door Tavern, her hair gleamed with golden hues that weaved through the warm brown locks. He straightened. What the hell was she doing here?

A terrified scream rent the air. He and Miss Harper both froze. It had come from the alley next to the tavern. She turned in that direction, looked up and down the empty street, and then changed her grip on the umbrella in her hand, brandishing it like a sword in front of her. She slowly walked to the mouth of the alley.

For fuck's sake. Matthew threw down his cigarillo and jogged across the street. He managed to grasp her arm right before she entered the alley. "What the hell do you think you're doing?" he growled in her ear.

Her umbrella came round to hit him, but he easily caught it with his hand. Miss Harper's eyes widened when she recognized him. She let out a long breath. "Someone is in trouble."

"And you're going to what? Pummel the bad guys with your umbrella?"

She huffed, but before she could respond, a loud crunch of wood splintering filled the air, followed by sounds of a struggle. Matthew dropped his grip on the umbrella and strode deeper into the dark. "Oy, what's going on? Do you need help?"

The struggle ceased, and as he moved deeper into the alley, he could make out footfalls receding away from him. Then, he stumbled into the body of a woman lying across the cobblestones. He crouched down. She was unconscious. He felt her neck, relieved when he found a pulse, thank God.

"Is she dead?" Miss Harper's voice came from above him.

He glanced up. "No, unconscious." He scooped up the woman. She was small and thin, and he easily straightened with her cradled in his arms. They headed back to the street. At the mouth of the alley, the light that spilled from the tavern windows made it easier to see the victim. Young, blond, the woman wore a threadbare cloak over a simple blouse and skirt. A local girl, no doubt.

"Here, let's bring her inside the tavern. I know the proprietor. James will help us," Miss Harper said.

They headed out of the alley, and she pulled open the door to the tavern.

When they strode in, Miss Harper led the way to the end of the bar. "James, someone's hurt."

A tall, wiry fellow hurried down the length of the bar. "Sarah?"

"Do you know her?" Miss Harper asked.

"Yes, she works for me. Just finished her shift." James lifted a section of the wood top and came from behind the bar. "What's happened?"

"She was attacked in the alley," Matthew said. "Is there

somewhere we can lay her down?" The woman had been worryingly still in his arms. She should have regained consciousness by now.

"Yes, this way. Caleb, watch the bar," he yelled to another man across the room.

They followed the proprietor to the back through a door that led to a large storage room. The man cleared a couple of boxes off a table that sat along one wall. Matthew strode forward and gently laid the woman down. She finally stirred. Her eyes fluttered open, filled with fear. She jerked, and her arms flailed out in defense. Matthew grabbed each of her wrists firmly, crossing her arms against her chest. "You're safe. You're inside the Green Door."

The panic receded, and she relaxed underneath his hold. He let go and stepped back. Poor girl. She took several deep breaths in, then winced in pain. Matthew's gaze dropped to her throat, where a deep red line marred her pale skin. He glanced over at Miss Harper. Elizabeth pursed her lips and gave him a small nod to tell him she had also seen the injury.

James stepped forward. "Sarah, what happened?" He helped her to sit up. "Where are you hurt?"

Sarah wrapped her hand around her throat. "He tried to strangle me. Came up from behind." Then she moved her hand to her head, right above her hairline on the right side. "And here…bashed me against a crate trying to get away."

James gently moved her hair, feeling along her scalp with his fingers. "Yep, you got a sizable bump there, girl. Come on. Let's get you home to your da." He turned to them.

"Elizabeth, thanks for helping. I'll get her home safe."

"Of course. But I think it was Mr. Reeves's deep voice that scared off the attacker." Her gaze slid to him. "I doubt my umbrella would have been as intimidating. I hope you feel better soon. And perhaps walk with a friend to get home from now on."

"Thank you both," Sarah croaked out.

Ms. Harper headed back out to the main area. Matthew followed her, watching the swish of her black crepe skirts as she expertly weaved through the crowded tavern.

"Reeves! What are you doing down here?"

Matthew turned toward the voice. Fitz, his beer distributor, waved from a nearby table. Matthew walked over and shook the man's hand. "Just handling some business and got distracted by some trouble outside."

"Saw you bring in that girl. She all right?"

"She will be. Attacked out in the alley."

Fitz shook his head. "Shouldn't be walking around these parts alone. Man or woman."

Matthew's gaze slid to where Miss Harper was exiting out the front door. "Nice to see you, but I got to run."

Fitz's gaze followed his to the disappearing form of Miss Harper. "Oh, sure. See you next week."

Matthew nodded and hurried across the room.

He exited the street just in time to see Miss Harper head into the mouth of the alley. Damn woman, didn't she have any sense after seeing that girl attacked? He caught up to her easily, catching her elbow. "What the hell are you doing?"

She blinked up at him as though she was surprised to find him next to her. "I am going to look for clues."

"In the dark alley where someone was just attacked?"

"I don't think the culprit is still lurking around."

"How little you know about crime in the city. If this is his territory, he'll be working this block all night."

"Do you really think this was about a robbery? You saw her neck. This was our murderer."

Matthew frowned. He agreed with her, not that he would admit it out loud. "What are you doing down in this neighborhood, anyway? A bit far from Bloomsbury Square."

She raised an eyebrow.

"You live three doors down from Mrs. Kelley. I remember."

"Oh, yes." She scanned the alley. "I came down to meet an informant who said he had information about these murders. But he never showed. Or, more likely, came but left when he realized I was a woman. It happens." She shrugged and tugged her arm free from his grip.

Then she walked deeper into the alley. He followed her like a damn puppy because the hell if he was going to let her wander straight into trouble. His gut told him the alley was empty, but he kept on high alert as they walked to where he had found the girl. A large stack of wooden crates leaned against the side of the building. One was cracked, the wood splintered, with a slat hanging loose.

"This is where she took the hit to her head." He pointed to the damaged crate.

Ms. Harper nodded. She looked around, but there was nothing unusual to be found. The packed dirt probably showed some signs of a struggle in the mud, but it was impossible to see in the dark. Her head tipped to one side as she walked further down. Poking at something with her umbrella first, she then bent and picked the object up.

"What is it?" he asked.

"A top hat, I think." She walked back toward the street, where the light from the tavern illuminated the pavement. "A very expensive top hat. Look, it is definitely silk."

He examined the hat, an evening hat, covered in black silk. He peered into the crown. "Wells & Co, a very high-end shop in Mayfair. What the hell is this hat doing down in Cheapside?"

"Perhaps it belongs to the killer?"

"What, a toff that comes across town to murder girls on the eastside?"

She shrugged, but a furrow appeared between her eyebrows as though she was considering the possibilities. Then her gaze flicked up. "Well, I must be getting home. Good evening, Mr. Reeves." She tossed the hat to the ground.

"Wait, you shouldn't walk alone."

"Mr. Reeves, I don't need an escort."

He gripped her elbow. "I disagree. This is not a safe area. There is plenty of trouble lurking in dark corners, waiting for a tasty morsel like you to come walking by."

"I have been taking care of myself for a very long time." She waggled her umbrella and actually rolled her eyes at him.

Matthew grabbed the umbrella. Tossing it aside with a clatter, he pushed her up against the brick wall behind her. His hand slipped around her throat, and he tightened his grip on her upper arm. Crowding her, he leaned his bulk against her. "Can you"—his thumb brushed along her jaw—"take care of yourself, luv?"

Her green eyes were wide and full of alarm as she stared up at him.

"What if I was a thief? What if I wanted to take more than just your coin? Could you stop me?"

Her lips parted, her warm breath teasing against his chin. He couldn't stop staring at her lush mouth. Her tongue darted out and licked along the plump pink of her bottom lip, and his whole body responded with a flash of desire that punched him hard in his gut. His gaze roamed her sharp cheekbones and the delicate point of her chin. He enjoyed the catch of her breath. The look in her eyes changed, no longer reflecting alarm; they heated with something new. Something he recognized from the night they kissed in his club. She swallowed and the motion rippled against his palm.

"What would you want?" she whispered.

"Another taste." The truth slipped from him. Damn her and those bewitching green eyes. He had no defenses against the challenge in them. He lifted her chin, then dipped down to kiss her. Just as he remembered, her lips were as soft and sharp as a fine whiskey. She brought her hands up and gripped the lapels of his jacket, teasing along the seam of his lips with her tongue. He opened with a groan and let the heat of her kiss spread through him. He slid his hand from her throat to grip the nape of her neck, changing the angle of the kiss and licking into her mouth, taking everything she offered.

Behind them, the tavern door banged open. Loud voices laughed and shouted. Miss Harper tore her mouth from his. She pushed him away, her chest heaving. He stepped back, equally out of breath, like he had been holding it for too long underwater. The shock of emerging from her kiss left him gasping for purchase.

She wiped a hand across her mouth. "I have to g-go home." Her voice shook, and he took perverse pleasure in the small indication that she was as affected as he was. Then she bent and grabbed up her umbrella before striding off down the street. He let her get halfway to the avenue before following her. His days shadowing marks before picking their pockets were long gone, but the skill of being invisible was second nature.

She strode up the street, her head held high, her umbrella clicking loudly against the cobblestones. At the avenue, she walked up to the line of hacks waiting to pick up customers and gave the driver her address in short, clipped tones. The driver opened the door. She clambered inside, ignoring the man's outstretched hand. As the carriage disappeared into the darkness, he couldn't help but admire her self-possession.

He walked back down the street and retrieved the silk hat. Ben would love to have such a fine item. Matthew crossed back to his shadowed corner by the Montaque. He still had a real villain to confront. Leaning back against the wall of the hell, he looked down at the hat in his hand, spinning it around by the brim. Perhaps Rutledge wasn't the culprit. He would certainly never be caught dead in something like this, and no thief worth his salt would leave behind such an expensive piece.

It had to belong to tonight's attacker. Increasingly, it looked like Mary Beth's death was part of a terrible pattern. Matthew glanced up at the front of the Montaque, its gaudy gold-painted sign creaking in a gust of wind. *Pattern.* How many of the murders had happened near a gaming hell? He tried to remember what her article had said. The Queen's Head on Bow Street, the Birdcage—which stood right next door to Castell's place, the Termage, and Red's Tavern, which was famous for its cock-and-dog fighting in the basement. All places to gamble away one's money. All on the east side. He looked down at the hat. Was the killer slumming it on the other side of town to do his dirty deeds? Or was he an avid gambler? Was he familiar with the hells? Picking his victims based on proximity to his haunts?

Matthew straightened, his desire to fight with Rutledge draining from him. He started for home, teasing out possible answers to the questions that he pondered. He wished he could tell her what he was thinking. Find out what she thought. As he lengthened his stride, he scrubbed a hand down his face. Good Lord, that woman was getting under his skin.

CHAPTER EIGHT

*A*NOTHER ATTACK ON *a woman on the east side occurred the night before last. This time, the culprit was scared away by a good Samaritan before he could finish his dastardly deed. The woman is alive and will recover. According to the victim, she left after her shift ended at the Green Door Tavern, where she serves ale. She exited the back entrance and cut up through the alley to get to Chellam Street. The victim said she was attacked from behind and choked by a strong assailant. She screamed before the wire around her throat cut off her breath. After struggling with the assailant, they stumbled backward into a stack of wooden crates. Her head knocked against one, and she lost consciousness. She wishes to express her gratitude to the man who interrupted her attack.*

Elizabeth lay her pen down and stared out the window at the quiet street in front of her house. She hadn't been able to stop thinking about the events of the other night. But not so much because of the attack that happened but because of him. Reeves. She nibbled on her thumbnail. He was so damn handsome with his dark hair and smoldering eyes. But also so frustrating and so domineering.

She huffed. She had no one to answer to, no husband or

father. She didn't let anyone tell her what to do, and she certainly didn't let anyone intimidate her. But when he had used his quick hands and brute force to push her against that wall, she had been thrown off-kilter. She should have been aghast, or at least angry. She should have told him to back away; she had no doubt he would have, despite his show of strength. But his hand around her throat had incited every nerve ending in her body to come alive. Instead of protesting, she'd kissed him back like she had been starving for his touch.

It had been so long since she had felt such heat and passion. She had ignored all of her womanly needs after Robert was born. Deep in grief, she hadn't been able to contemplate opening herself up to any type of romantic liaison. And after her father passed unexpectedly three years ago, there hadn't been time for anything but to simply get through the myriad of responsibilities each day. She had to admit that, though she was rarely alone, she had allowed herself to grow lonely.

The strange thing about her attraction was that Matthew Reeves was the opposite of her Robert. Robert had been lighthearted, smooth, and charming as sin. He had worn his privilege confidently but hadn't had any of the snobbery that so many aristocrats reveled in. In contrast, Mr. Reeves was all rough edges and bad language. He was charming in a dangerous way, like a wild dog that you are not sure if you should pet; would he let you scratch him behind the ears or snap your hand off? She chuckled. Good Lord, woman, pull yourself together.

She straightened the sheaf of papers on her desk. It didn't matter; she wouldn't see him again. She rose from her chair after hearing a knock on the door.

Mrs. Todd came into the room. "Lord and Lady Hartwick have arrived." She stepped aside, and Elizabeth's guests swept into the room.

"It's good to see you, Elizabeth!" Lucy grasped her hands, giving them a squeeze.

Lucy's husband came more sedately into the room. He offered her a small smile as a greeting. Not for the first time, Elizabeth wondered what he had been like before the attack in which an explosion left him scarred on one side of his face and body. Had he been as charming and flirtatious as his older brother? Time and tragedy changed everyone, she supposed.

Elizabeth squeezed back Lucy's hands. "It's good to see you both as well. Robert will be ecstatic." She glanced at Hart over his wife's shoulder. "It has been all Greeks versus the Ottomans in battle since we saw you last."

Hart's smile widened to a grin. He glanced around the reception room. "Is he upstairs?"

"Yes. Mrs. Todd, will you tell Robert he has visitors?"

"Yes, ma'am."

"Please come sit down." She gestured to the other side of the room, where a long sofa and two tufted wingback chairs made a cozy seating area. "I didn't think you would be back in town until fall."

Lucy's gaze slid to her husband, and she grimaced. "Yes,

well, we weren't planning to leave Belstoke either. Do you remember my friend, Violet Blakely? She was newly married this spring, and I have not heard a peep from her since. They honeymooned on the continent, but returned the first week in June, according to her mother. It has been almost six weeks with no response to my correspondence. I am worried. So, I convinced Hart that we should make a visit to the Marquess of Somerset."

Hart picked up her hand and kissed her fingers. "I'm sure everything is fine. She is probably just busy setting up her new household."

"No, it is not like her to not write. She is always full of news. Why hasn't she told me all about her travels?" Lucy frowned. "Something is wrong, I know it. Perhaps she is ill?"

Elizabeth was a believer in listening to one's instincts. "It's good that you go to visit her. She will certainly be happy to see you, no matter the circumstances."

"And surprised," Hart muttered under his breath.

Lucy elbowed him in the side. "I heard that."

Robert came barreling into the room. "Mrs. Todd said I have visitors. Who is it?"

Elizabeth gestured across to Hart and Lucy. Robert swiveled around with a delighted squeak. "Uncle Alex, Aunt Lucy!"

Lucy enveloped him in a warm hug. "How are you, Robert?"

Remembering his manners, he said, "Good, thank you. How are you?"

"I am well. We missed you."

Hart ruffled Robert's hair. "You looked like you grew this spring."

Robert puffed out his chest proudly. "Yes, sir. I grew two whole inches, mama said."

"I am not surprised. Your father was very tall."

"He was?" Robert asked with wide eyes.

"Taller than me by a few inches." Hart nodded.

Robert held out one of his small hands. "Would you like to go out to the garden and meet my frogs?"

Hart enveloped Robert's hand with his and rose to his feet. "Very much. Lead the way."

"Mama said I may not bring them inside, but they still make good pets, even if they HAVE to live in the garden," Robert explained as the two walked out of the room.

Elizabeth shook her head with an indulgent smile.

When she turned back to Lucy, the lady had an identical smile, and her eyes shined with tears. "They are so adorable together." Lucy laid a hand on her flat stomach.

Elizabeth tilted her head. "Are you all right?"

Lucy sucked in a breath. "Oh, fine."

"Are you expecting?" She raised one eyebrow.

"Yes." Lucy leaned forward. "How did you guess?"

"The teary-eyed look at your husband with Robert and the touch of your hand on your midsection are both classic tells. When did you find out?"

"I've missed two months of courses. So, early yet. But Hart noticed immediately." She wrinkled her nose. "He notices everything. We are cautiously happy. After a whole year of marriage, I thought perhaps it wasn't going to happen."

"It happens when it happens. I am so pleased for you both." And she meant it. There had been a time when she mourned that her son would never be the duke, as he would have been by birthright if she and his father had married as they had planned. But Robert's murderer had robbed her and their son of the future she thought was going to be theirs. Time and perspective had reminded her that titles don't matter. That they can be cages. Gilded ones, but, nevertheless, cages. Robert would grow up in a loving environment and learn to be an independent man. She hoped that he would be able to carve out whatever life he wished for himself.

Lucy leaned back with a sigh. "I admit to feeling quite emotional these days. You know I don't like to cry. But I can't seem to stop blubbering over every little thing."

"It is normal. And you have a doting spouse who will watch out for you. That is a blessing." Hart might be gruff, but he would do absolutely anything for his wife.

Elizabeth remembered in stark detail those months following Robert's death. Finding out she was pregnant had been a blessing in disguise. Knowing that she would have a piece of Robert had helped to pull her from dark thoughts, thoughts of dying and joining Robert in the afterlife. The child growing in her belly had given her purpose here, in her reality.

Her father had been kind, but distant. As always, running the paper had taken precedence. She couldn't complain; she'd had a roof over her head and the care she and her baby had needed. But, as she glanced at Lucy, she couldn't quite suppress a pinch of jealousy. What would it be like to have someone worry over you? To fuss? To have someone to share your fears and excitement with?

"He will be impossible. He has already hidden my quarterstaff. Hidden it! What does he imagine? That I am likely to fall and impale myself on it?"

Elizabeth chuckled.

Lucy sighed. "Tell me, what is happening with you? Did you receive your new printing press from Germany?"

"Yes, it came, and it is marvelous. It took some getting used to, but it can print triple the number of pages the old one could print in the same time."

"And what has your top story been this week? I haven't heard any news in ages."

While Elizabeth explained about the murders she was investigating, Mrs. Todd brought in the tea cart and poured them both steaming cups.

"And you think they are all connected?" Lucy bit into a teacake and chewed as she contemplated the case. "Or do you suppose the garrote has become a new fashionable weapon among criminals?"

Elizabeth shook her head. "No, none of these women had anything to steal. I think it is one man who is committing the crimes. Someone who is not in his right state of mind. A real killer." She had been thinking about the silk hat they'd found. "We found a top hat lying next to the latest victim in the alley by the Green Door Tavern. It was very expensive looking, silk. It made me think that if you were the killer, someone rich but demented, you would want a weapon that wouldn't get blood on your fine clothes. A weapon that could easily be stowed in a pocket. You could walk away from the scene of the crime without any notice."

Lucy snuck another teacake. "We?"

"Pardon?"

"You said 'we' found a top hat. Who is we?" Lucy took a bite of her cake.

"Oh, yes. Mr. Reeves. One of the victims worked at his club. Murdered right outside in the alley. He has been a thorn in my side. We keep bumping into each other." She frowned.

"Mr. Matthew Reeves? At the Blue Angel?" Lucy asked.

"Yes. Do you know him?"

"No, but I met him once. The Knot of Isis symbol is on the building that houses his club. I went to follow the clue and spoke with him about the building. His business partner is Mr. Seaton."

"Truly? What a strange coincidence. Why am I not surprised that Mr. Seaton owns a gaming hell?"

"Well, I believe the phrase 'silent partner' was used. It is my understanding that Hart's father left all the property along that block to Mr. Seaton in his will." She raised an eyebrow. "What were you doing at the Blue Angel?"

"My neighbor asked me to fetch her daughter home. The girl had left home after a row with her parents. And her mother was worried she was working as a prostitute at the club. But in fact, she was working there as a dancer. She was murdered that night in the alley behind the club."

"How terrible."

"Mr. Reeves has taken her death as a personal affront to his business. He seems quite protective of his employees." Elizabeth scrunched her nose. "He and I both ended up by the Green Door Tavern two nights ago. I am not sure what he was doing there. He just appeared behind me as I started into the alley to help the girl who screamed."

"Elizabeth! You did what?"

"You sound just like him."

"Well, he sounds like he has good sense. You must be careful. You can't be going down dark alleys at night. For goodness' sake, think of your son."

Thoroughly chastised, Elizabeth lowered her gaze. She hadn't appreciated Reeves's similar comments, but looking over at her friend's concerned expression, she could admit that she had been foolish to think she could have intervened without getting hurt. There could have been more than one assailant down that alley.

"Promise me you will be more careful," Lucy demanded.

"I promise." She nodded and then lifted her teacup to take a sip. What had Reeves been doing down on River Street? He seemed to be nearby every time she turned around this past week.

Lucy's lips quirked into a small smile. "Mr. Reeves is quite handsome, don't you think?"

"Mr. Reeves is far too handsome," she muttered.

"Is there such a thing?" Lucy's eyes gleamed with mischief.

"Definitely." Luckily for Elizabeth, Hart and Robert returned before Lucy could ask any more questions about Matthew Reeves. The four of them had a lovely visit, filled with cheerful chatter from Robert as he told them all about his new tutor and what stories he had read lately. She had been reading her own worn copy of *Gulliver's Travels* to him at bedtime, and Robert loved the fantastical stories. Hart and Lucy stayed for an early supper before Robert had to go up to bed.

As they prepared to leave, Lucy pulled on her gloves. "We will be in town just for a few days' respite from traveling. Then we will continue on to Kent to check on Violet." She turned to Robert. "We will see you again soon, in just a few weeks' time."

Robert nodded sleepily against Elizabeth's shoulder, where she had lifted him into her arms. "Safe travels," she said to the pair.

After the door closed behind them, she turned and climbed the stairs. Robert's eyes were already closed, and she smiled. The excitement of the visit had plumb worn him out. No stories tonight. Perhaps she would be able to get a couple of hours of work in before she, too, would be tired enough to go to bed.

CHAPTER NINE

WHAT WAS HE doing? Matthew paced past the row house with the discreet sign that said PICCADILLY PRESS. He was a fool to see her again. He didn't need the aggravation of dealing with the prickly but alluring Miss Harper. He paused at the corner of her street. Staring up at the Kelleys' house, he was reminded that Mary Beth's murder was his responsibility to solve. She had been part of the Blue Angel family.

His conclusion that the murders were connected to gaming establishments continued to niggle at his brain for the past couple of days. And the silk hat, in conjunction with the garrote, also bothered him, but he didn't want to jump to conclusions based on his own unfortunate past. He needed to talk it over with her. Miss Harper was smart as a whip and the only other person who was as invested as he in the murder of Mary Beth Kelley.

Striding back to the *Piccadilly Press*, he noticed a metal box with a slot at the top attached to the fence in front of her house. *What was that for?* He continued to the black-painted front door, which was identical to all the others down the row of terrace houses. At his knock, the door was answered by a servant, an attractive woman, perhaps about forty. She wore an austere black dress, but her apron was embroidered with a row of colorful ducks waddling across its border.

The woman smiled. "May I help you?"

"Good afternoon, I am Matthew Reeves. I am here to see Miss Harper. She is not expecting me, but I hoped to have a few moments of her time."

"Let's see what she says, shall we? Wait here." She gestured to a bench against the wall in the narrow front hall. Then she knocked on the first door to the right, then opened it. "Miss Harper, you have a visitor, Mr. Matthew Reeves."

Through the open door, he could see Miss Harper's head pop up from where she had been leaning over, deep in discussion with another woman seated at a desk. Her frown spoke volumes, but he wanted to speak with her, and he wouldn't be brushed off. He quickly strode across the worn wood floorboards of the hall and straight past the startled servant.

"Ms. Harper, I wish to speak with you about the clues we found the other night. I have an idea that I want your opinion about."

Besides the woman who Miss Harper stood next to, there were two other people working at desks in the room—another woman and the wiry man who had been dressed as her angel at the masquerade. Sweeping off his hat, he gave the room at large a bright smile.

Ms. Harper turned to fully face him; her eyes narrowed. "Mr. Reeves, I am busy with preparations for the next edition."

"Not a problem. I can wait." He would wait all day. Well, until four o'clock anyway, when his staff meeting took place. But it was only half eleven. He had plenty of time.

"You are not going to leave, are you?" Miss Harper huffed.

He widened his smile and shook his head. She could huff all she wanted. He could wait until she had a free moment. Curious, he glanced around. There were several desks set one in front of each other down the narrow room. Through the open front window, sunlight flooded the room and allowed in a breeze of warm summer air.

"You can wait over there." She gestured to an empty desk in front of the window and then turned her back to him, focusing her attention back to her previous conversation. "Lydia, I think if you add more description about the state of the bridge, it will let the reader understand the dire need for the bill to be passed. Start by discussing the poor conditions, then move to what is being proposed to remediate the problem, and lastly, outline the arguments for and against it. This way, the reader is invested in the politics because they already empathize with the problem."

Lydia nodded. "I see. I will work on it."

Matthew made his way to the desk and chose to sit in the chair that faced the room so he could observe her in her element. He knew the bare minimum about Miss Elizabeth Harper. Only that she ran the paper and that she was the mother of Seaton's nephew. When he'd first met her at his club, she caught his attention because of her effortless sensuality. Someone with her beauty could easily have any man she wanted. Hell, she had once seduced a ducal heir. Why did she not have a husband or a benefactor? Instead, she ran a business and raised her son on her own. Not that he didn't admire her efforts. She clearly knew what she was doing.

"All right." Miss Harper turned to her other employees. "New story ideas, tell me what you have for Thursday's edition."

The young man raised his hand. "I am working on a story about the new modiste du jour. She calls herself Madam Aubert, but I knew I recognized her from somewhere." He raised his eyebrows. "She is indeed French. Her real name is Aurelie Garnier. She was the mistress to the Royal Duke Fredrick until last spring. My guess is that his parting gift was very generous, and she has used the money wisely. She seems to know everyone in the ton. The shop has been busy."

Elizabeth nodded her head. "Good, interesting enough."

She turned to an older woman who wore her hair piled high in a rather messy bun on the top of her head. "Anne, what about you?"

"Quiet in Westminster till the fall session begins. I will have another installment breaking down the pieces of Peele's Acts. This week, I will focus on the repeal of the Petty Treason Act, and how they are replacing it with the more specific murder charge. I thought it might go nicely with your articles about the murders on the east side."

"Clever. I look forward to reading it. Lydia, keep working on the piece we just discussed. Nigel, I will hand over the tips that I think will work for this week's gossip page. Sam and Harry have articles due and are out on interviews this morning. All right, back to work."

Ms. Harper walked toward Matthew, her expression morphing to annoyance as she approached. Her face was so expressive. With her dark brows lowered and her lips pinched tight in a thin line, she made no pretense of hiding her emotions. Watching her run her staff meeting had given him a glimpse of just how capable she was, and it was damn attractive.

He understood better why she did not have a husband. He got the sense that this was a woman who didn't need a man to take care of her. If she invited a man into her life, it would be because she wanted him, not because she needed him. He leaned back in the chair and smiled. What would it be like to be the man she invited into her life?

She crossed her arms across her chest. "You are in my chair."

"Ah, makes sense. Got a good view of the room." He slowly stood but moved just far enough to prop one hip on the desk. He wouldn't be so easily dismissed by her frown.

She glared for a moment. "There is a chair right over there."

He glanced where she nodded at a chair on the other side of the desk. "I'm fine here. I need to speak with you."

She slid into her chair with a sigh, then opened a drawer

on the right side. Pulling out a stack of notes, she turned to the young man, Nigel, who stood a few feet away, waiting. "Here you are, Nigel. There is some good gossip in there. Verify and add the tidbits you think are worth printing. And I have one more for you. The Duke and Duchess of Hartwick are traveling to visit the newly married Marquess and Marchioness of Somerset at their country home in Kent. The Marquess and his wife are back from their honeymoon on the continent, and their friends are anxious to hear all about their travels."

Nigel nodded. "Have you received any more tips about the murders?"

"No, I haven't. I guess he was scared off." She shrugged.

Nigel's gaze slid over to Matthew. "I really enjoyed your masquerade, Mr. Reeves. Your club is actually quite nice." The young man blushed. "Not that I thought it would not be nice…I just meant it was very well appointed for a den of iniquity." His face flushed an even deeper red.

Matthew chuckled low. "Thank you. Nigel, is it? Come by anytime, and I will show you around."

"Oh, I couldn't. My mother would never allow it."

"Nigel, why don't you go get working on those tips," Elizabeth said firmly.

The young man sent him an apologetic look and turned back to walk to his desk. Matthew caught the smallest curve of a smile on Miss Harper's lips before she scooted her chair back, putting some space between them. "Mr. Reeves, what is it that you need to share so desperately?"

Besides his need to kiss those full lips again? Most likely, she wouldn't be open to filling that need, at least not at her place of work. He stretched his legs out and crossed them at the ankles. "I have been thinking about the other night. That hat is an anomaly. If the killer is a gentleman, what is he doing so far from Mayfair? Except then I realized that all the murders have taken place in the vicinity of gaming clubs."

Ms. Harper's eyes widened.

"The Termage is right next door to the Birdcage." He held up a finger for each establishment. "Queen's Head, the Blue Angel. And the Montague is across from the Green Door Tavern."

"What about Red's Tavern?"

"Red's is famous for the cock- and dogfighting they have in the basement. Plenty of betting happens there."

"I didn't know that." Her brow furrowed. "All gambling places. Interesting. Does he choose victims based on proximity? Whoever is nearby when he is done gaming for the evening?"

"Perhaps he is slumming it outside his fancy club. The fact that he would move around from place to place tells me he is done up. Perhaps even banned from certain places for having reached his limit of what he owes the house."

"So, he is a man with a title. Someone who would normally be afforded credit."

Matthew nodded. "Or he can play fresh again when his allowance comes in. And that damn hat. No thief would leave such a valuable hat in the street. It's worth at least five quid at a pawnshop."

"I shouldn't have left it behind," she murmured.

"I didn't. Gave it to Big Ben. It looks good on his bald head. He loves the hat. Wore it to church on Sunday."

Ms. Harper's lips turned up into a real smile. "I'm glad." She laced her fingers across her stomach. "I also have been thinking that the killer could be a gentleman. The garrote is a weapon that can kill without the mess of, say, a knife. There is no blood to splatter on expensive clothes. The garrote can easily be coiled and slipped into a pocket as you walk away from the crime. It is an elegant weapon."

Matthew lowered his brow, thinking of his own terrible experience with a garrote. Elegant was hardly the word he would use. Brutal, personal. His hand rose to scrape down his throat, the rasp of his beard covering the old wound. "It is easily concealed, but there is nothing elegant about killing someone. To strangle a person, even someone smaller than you, takes strength. And the garrote can slice the skin depending on how you use it."

"I hope your observations don't come from personal experience, Mr. Reeves." Miss Harper stared at him with those piercing, jade-colored eyes.

"It does, but not in the way you think. I have never strangled someone, if that's what you feared."

She leaned forward and opened the second drawer this time. "This tip was left in my box out front." She handed him a folded piece of parchment. "It's why I was at the Green Door the other night. The thing that caught my attention is the neat handwriting and correct speech. You see, most of the tips that I receive are from working-class folks. Often, the writing is barely legible, the sentences simple, straightforward."

"I wondered what that box outside was for." He read through the note. "Do they always ask for money?"

She nodded. "Generally. That's my favorite part. The haggling over payment." She shrugged at his incredulous look. "I am a lady who likes to bargain."

Matthew chuckled. "So, are you surmising that this clearly well-educated fellow is a friend of our killer?"

"Perhaps, or an enemy that wishes to get him in trouble, or simply a nervous observer of his behavior. There are all types of reasons people sell me information."

"But he didn't show up for your meeting?"

"No. I spoke with James Folger for a short time and then sat at the end of the bar to wait. The staff would have pointed me out to anyone who came to meet 'Mr. Harper.' It often happens that men are dismissive when they find out I am a woman."

Matthew frowned. It bothered him that anyone would dismiss her. "It must be hard to be a woman at the helm of a business."

"Why? Because a woman couldn't possibly handle the minutiae of running a newspaper?" She straightened; her shoulders snapped back.

"No, Lizzie." He liked how her name rolled off his tongue. "I have no doubt about your capability to run your business. I simply meant it must be hard to endure the snubs of those who don't think you should be doing it."

"Oh." Her shoulders relaxed. "Plenty of women run small businesses all over the city, such as dressmakers, haberdashers, candle chandlers, and milliners. We exist."

He nodded. "Speaking of milliners, I think we should go visit the shop where the hat came from. It had a number sewn on the tag. Perhaps we can track down the owner."

"I agree. I can go this afternoon. What's the number?" She pulled out a piece of foolscap and slid her ink pot closer.

"I cannot go this afternoon. I have a staff meeting at four."

"I think I should go alone. Not to put too fine a point on it, but you do not look like the sort of man who shops in Mayfair."

"I think I am insulted. What? My clothes are not fine enough?" He spent a pretty penny on his wardrobe. He had the money to shop wherever he chose. There were plenty of good reasons he choose not to shop in Mayfair. He straightened his cuffs, letting the gold cufflinks wink in the sunlight.

"It's more of an aura about you. You lack the smooth polish of a toff. And that mouth of yours. Do you ever censor your language?"

"I never censor anything about myself." He winked. "I thought you liked my mouth," he said softly, just for her ears.

Those ears went red, as did her cheeks. And there was that spark in her eyes that he remembered so clearly. That flash of heat. But then her eyes slid to the left and she cleared her throat. "Well, I think I can be more persuasive. I'll see what I can find out."

He straightened and picked up his hat. "The number inside the hat was two twenty-three. I don't know if the proprietor will give over the information on his clients easily. If you can't get the name, we can do it my way."

"Your way?"

"We'll go in at night and take a look at the books."

"You'd break in?"

"Slip in. We won't steal anything but a bit of information. Let me know how it goes today." He held out his hand. "Partner."

Ms. Harper pressed her lips together, not exactly a frown, more like a thin line of disapproval. But then she shook his hand with a firm grip. He briefly ran his thumb across the soft skin of her hand before letting go. Damn if everything about this woman wasn't a contradiction. And damn if that didn't make him all the more curious to learn everything about her.

He tipped the brim of his bowler. "Good day to you, Miss Harper."

CHAPTER TEN

A DISCREET TINKLE of a bell rang out as Elizabeth opened the door to the Wells & Co. milliner shop. The shop was quite full of customers browsing the goods on display. She glanced around. Near the front window, a row of stands, each with many arms, held an assortment of women's bonnets and men's top hats. The main part of the room was filled with long tables full of fabrics. And along the back wall, rows of colorful ribbons and other embellishments hung on hooks.

She made her way slowly through the large open room, running her fingertips over silky fabrics and fine wools. A shop like this one would certainly be far out of her price range. Her good friend Lorelei ran a dress shop, and she made all of Elizabeth's wardrobe. Elizabeth was happy to support another woman-owned business and spend her hard-earned money in the neighborhood where she grew up. Shops like this were overpriced and catered to the aristocrats who would foolishly spend any amount if someone told them the item was the height of fashion.

In what now seemed like a lifetime ago, her grandmother, the Marchioness of Rollinsford, had offered to give

Elizabeth a season in society. An olive branch extended after Elizabeth's mother died. The offer most likely came out of guilt for having cut her daughter out of her life after she married beneath her to a lowly newspaperman. At nineteen, Elizabeth had been so excited. Her grandmother had brought her to places like this one to outfit her with a whole new wardrobe. It had been Elizabeth's first time shopping with an unlimited budget, and she'd enjoyed every moment of the time she spent getting to know her grandmother.

So young and foolish. Wanting to believe the best in people. After she met and fell in love with Robert, it seemed as though her fairy tale was coming true. But when he was murdered alongside his father, all her dreams of the future had died with him. She and Robert hadn't been married yet. Her fairy grandmother had then promptly dumped her out of her life when she learned Elizabeth was pregnant out of wedlock. Elizabeth flicked back the tail end of a shiny blue ribbon as she pretended to peruse the selection.

"May I help you?"

She turned to find a young woman in a simple dark blue dress smiling at her. "Yes, thank you. I would like to purchase a new top hat for my husband. I saw a beaver worn by a gentleman that I found to be quite fine. It is exactly the hat I want to get for my Henry." She leaned in to speak softly to the shopgirl. "When the gentleman set it down, I peeked and saw your label stitched inside."

The girl winked conspiratorially. "We do make the very best hats in London. Can you describe the style of the hat you admired?"

"Well, it was black silk, and perhaps this tall." She motioned vaguely with her hands. "I think it had a brim that tipped down a bit in the front." Elizabeth screwed up her nose. "I cannot remember exactly. And perhaps it had a ribbon around the crown. Fiddlesticks, I cannot remember, but I do know it was very handsome." She gave the shopgirl a wide-eyed look of dismay. "Is there any way to look up the exact hat? Do you keep records of the hats you sell?"

"Yes, we do keep records of the custom-made hats. Each hat has a number assigned to it."

"Aha, the number two twenty-three was stitched on the label! Can we look it up and have the same hat made for my Henry?"

"Let me see what I can find out. Follow me."

Elizabeth followed the young woman through the shop to a large counter at the back end of the shop. She waited as the woman went around behind and watched carefully as she pulled a large leather volume from underneath the counter.

"Now, let's see." The shopgirl flipped through various pages. "If it was bought this year, it will be in this one. But if it is older, then it would take some searching to find the number."

An older man walked up beside the shopgirl. "Anna, what are you doing?" His voice was sharp, and his brows drawn together.

"This lady saw one of our hats out and about and wanted to order the same style for her husband. I was just looking up the number so that we could see the order."

Elizabeth sent the man a friendly smile, leaning forward slightly to see if she could glance down at the ledger. "I do so adore the work you do here."

The scrawled text on the pages was far too small to decipher upside down. Drat. The man was not returning her smile. Instead, he turned to his coworker. "Information about customer orders is not to be shared, Miss Wellesley." He lowered his voice to a furious whisper as he pulled the book from the counter. "These account books contain payment and accounts payable information that should not be seen by customers."

Elizabeth averted her eyes quickly as he glanced back over his shoulder at her suspiciously.

"I'm sorry, sir. I didn't think."

"No, you didn't. Now go straighten the ribbons."

The man turned back to Elizabeth with a disapproving frown. "Ma'am. If you would like to place a custom order for a hat, we would be happy to help you." His glance scanned her appearance from top to bottom, and he gave her a small sniff. "Do you have an account with us?"

Elizabeth straightened her shoulders. This man was not going to be helpful. He had the look of an upper-crust butler. His expression filled with judgment about her clothes and her slightly worn gloves. Typical. But she had survived a season in society. She was no virgin to snide looks, and she certainly wasn't going to take such attitude from some fancy shop clerk.

"I do not. I was curious about a silk top hat that I saw at a fete this past week. I was told it came from this shop." She gave a sniff herself. "But perhaps I should spend my money where the staff are more friendly. I will make sure to tell my grandmother, the Marchioness of Rollinsford, how terribly unhelpful this establishment is." When the man's jaw dropped open, she turned on her heel and strode out of the store.

Outside, Elizabeth let out a sigh as she straightened her spencer jacket. She shouldn't have lost her temper. But it had been amusing to see the man's expression of horror when she mentioned her grandmother's name. Not that her grand-mother gave two whits about her. She hated to admit it, but Mr. Reeves had been right.

"Miz Harper." A gruff voice called out from the street.

Spinning around, she found Mr. Reeves's hulking serv-ant, Ben—What was Ben's surname? "Hello, Ben. What are you doing here?"

"I'm here to offer you a ride home." He gestured to a fine-looking barouche next to him. "Boss's orders."

Startled, she glanced between him and the open-top car-riage. "Mr. Reeves sent you to give me a ride home? How did he know I was here?"

Ben shrugged. "He said I should come to this here fancy shop and wait for you."

"I am perfectly capable of walking home. I walked here just fine."

"He said you'd say that. Said I would need to insist.

Please, Miz Harper, I've already come all this way. Give those feet of yours a break and let me take you home. Bloomsbury is a fair walk from here."

The smile across his broad face was sweet and made a strange contrast to his crooked nose and torn ears. She glanced at the curricle, eyeing the sumptuous velvet seats. It would be nice to not have to walk home. It would save her time, especially since she had wasted her afternoon coming across town to this shop, only to find out absolutely nothing about the hat. "All right, thank you, Ben. Ben, what is your surname?"

He held out a hand to help her into the carriage. "Smith. 'Tis the name they gave me at the orphanage anyway. Everyone just calls me Ben, though. Or Big Ben."

She smiled over at him as they settled in the carriage. Ben held the ribbons with practiced ease and guided the horses into the busy street traffic. "So, Ben, how long have you known Mr. Reeves?"

"Long time. Since he and Seaton were young whelps working the odds for the boxing at the Horse and Dolphin. I was a fighter for many years." He glanced over at her with a rueful expression. "On account of my size, I was usually a good bet. When Mr. Reeves opened his own club, he asked me to come over and work for him."

"And what do you do for him at the club?"

"Whatever he needs."

What did that mean? She furrowed her brow.

Ben chuckled. "It's not what you're probably thinking. I

take care of the house, organize the food, drive him about when he calls for it. Help with security in a pinch. But he knows I don't like to fight no more."

Elizabeth relaxed her expression. Ben was Mr. Reeves's butler, although she wasn't sure he would appreciate being called one, so she kept the thought to herself. The day had turned out to be warm, and she felt a bead of sweat roll down the back of her neck. Summer in London meant the air constantly smelled like coal soot and rotting refuse. But the sun had made an appearance after all the rain of the past week, and she enjoyed looking up at the green leaves of the trees that dotted the streets of Mayfair.

"It certainly is nicer to ride through town. Thank you, Ben."

"Anytime, Miz Harper. Did you get the information you was looking for?"

She shook her head. "No, they wouldn't help me. Gave me the look. You know, like I wasn't good enough to be in the shop. I fear I lost my temper and gave up too easily. Perhaps if I had simpered a bit, I could have gotten better results."

"Places like that are only helpful to their own kind," Ben said.

"Yes, that is true. I probably needed to pretend a little better that I fit in." She picked at a loose thread on her best pair of white gloves. Maybe she needed to invest in a new pair. These were at least five years old. There were just too many things that needed to be paid for first before her wardrobe could be updated.

Hartwick had been generous with paying for Robert's tutor, and he'd wanted to give her more to pay for the rent and other expenses, but she just couldn't swallow taking any more of his charity. She had been doing just fine taking care of herself with the money her father left her and the income from the paper. She didn't want to rely on the whims of the duke. What if he changed his mind at some point? Decided he didn't want to be associated with his late brother's by-blow? Especially now that Lucy may be carrying his heir.

"Could you tell Mr. Reeves that I guess we will have to do it his way?" She sighed.

Ben nodded.

"This is certainly a nice curricle."

"He also has a town coach. Hardly ever uses either. Like you, he likes to walk everywhere."

She slid a glance sideways at the big man next to her. Ben was so friendly. He was probably a fountain of information about the enigmatic Matthew Reeves. "Where does Mr. Reeves reside?"

"At the Blue Angel. Him and his sister. A few of us do as well. Mrs. Langley, the theater manager. Also, some of the girls, Val, and Allan the bean counter. Mr. Reeves wanted it to be a safe place for those who needed one." He shrugged. "It varies who's with us. Keeps me on my toes. But I like taking care of people."

A safe place. Interesting. "Mr. Reeves said the girls are in a dancing show? But they also have rooms at the hell?"

Ben's back straightened as he snapped the ribbons. "Yes, the show is a musical featuring Miss Reeves. It's a proper show." His voice sharp. "I heard about what you wrote about the Blue Angel. It's not a brothel."

Taken aback by his vehemence and his glower, Elizabeth felt bad about her assumptions. But what would one expect her to surmise? There definitely had been ladies of the night at the masquerade. Her assumptions were not that far off from the norm. "I'm sorry about that. It was based on my first impressions at the masquerade." When there was no response from Ben, she twisted in her seat to look up at his profile. "I'm glad to hear it is a real theater show. Mary Beth was a nice girl. I used to watch her when she was young. Her dream was to be an actress on the stage."

Ben's ramrod-straight posture deflated. "She had a good voice. She was new, but Mrs. Langley thought she had potential. I'm just sorry I couldn't keep her safe."

"Ben, there wasn't anything that you did wrong. You didn't know she stepped outside. It still bothers me. What was she doing in the back alley minutes before the show was supposed to start?"

"Haven't been able to figure that out. No one saw her leave the backstage area."

She mulled over that. How did the killer lure Mary Beth outside? It had to be someone she knew; otherwise, why would she leave the safety of the club? Or perhaps the threat was already inside, and she fled outside to get away from it? These unanswered questions had been keeping her up at night. She would love a chance to speak with the other girls that danced at the club. Somehow, she doubted that Mr. Reeves would let her, based on his ire after her initial article came out.

"Ben, the name of the club, what does it mean? Is it named for someone?"

"Don't rightly know. Never thought much about it. Gonna have to ask the boss yourself."

Yes, she would. She had plenty of questions left for Matthew Reeves. He was a puzzle, to be sure. A man who grew up on the streets but spoke like a well-educated man. A man who essentially fleeced people of their money for a living. But also made his club a safe haven for those who worked for him. God only knows, with a man like Rhys Seaton as his business partner, what other unsavory dealings he was involved in. But she didn't fear him, even when he'd had her pressed against the brick wall in that dark alley with his hand around her throat. She shifted restlessly in her seat. Instead, she had come alive, ready to submit to whatever he demanded with those wicked lips.

They turned onto Bloomsbury Square, and Elizabeth gave Ben direction to her house. As the carriage pulled up in front, she saw the flick of white curtains in the front window of Mrs. Lindow's house next door. Her lips twitched; arriving home in such a fine conveyance would make her the object of gossip today. Ben helped her down.

"Thank you for insisting. My feet appreciated the break." She grinned up at him.

Ben tipped his cap. "Boss's orders. Good day to you, Miz Harper."

CHAPTER ELEVEN

MATTHEW PULLED THE slim pick from his pocket. Wells & Co. had a surprisingly hefty lock on their back door. Not that it would be a problem for him; there wasn't a lock that he couldn't open. An important skill that had made him valuable to the gang he ran with after his uncle died. His uncle had invested everything he had in his theater, and when he died, the theater died with him. Matthew had only been fifteen and far too green to even think of running the business.

The talent had all left for jobs with other venues, and his uncle's partner had sold the building and kindly given Matthew his share of the proceeds, as his uncle had instructed in his will. As an adult, Matthew now recognized how lucky he was that the man hadn't swindled him out of his inheritance. Charlie had watched out for him. Matthew continued to return the favor now that Charlie was too old to work on the stage any longer.

Returning home to his parents hadn't been an option. He hadn't been able to stomach the fear and resentment that had still churned in his gut at being sent away, at his father choosing his brother over him. So, Matthew had made the choice to care for himself. He'd never regretted his choices, except perhaps on the day of his mother's funeral. He had cried at the loss of the one person who had loved him and tried to keep him safe. In the end, she hadn't been safe in that house either. Stella told him their mother had swooned and fallen down the stairs, breaking her neck in the tumble. But the doubt and fear in his sister's eyes said volumes about how 'accidental' their mother's death had really been.

The scrape of a door opening down the alley made him freeze for a moment. He stepped back against the wall, blending into the shadows, and took a drag from his cigarillo. But the voices that emerged from the nearby business floated down the opposite way from where he stood. He clamped his smoke between his teeth and turned back to the lock. With his tools, he played with the mechanism until he heard the telltale click of the lock opening.

He opened the door and swiftly slipped inside. The back room was filled with shelves full of inventory. He briefly wondered where their workshop was located. Probably in a part of town with cheaper rent.

Through the shadows, he moved to the front room. The curtains had been pulled in front of the large front windows. Matthew sighed in relief. He glanced around in the dark and spotted the shape of a kerosine lamp. Taking his cigarillo, he lit the wick with the glowing end. Lifting the light, he scanned the shop's interior. Fancy, indeed. Ben had relayed Miss Harper's experience here earlier today. His lips twitched in amusement, thinking about how put out she must have been that he had been right.

He stood behind the back counter of the establishment. Crouching down, he ran the light across the shelves. Neat and orderly, there were more rolls of ribbon and various supplies. Ink pots, pens, foolscap, and then, in the last section, a row of cloth-bound books. He slid one out and laid it on the counter. The inside showed that it was an account book from 1827. He reached down for the next one, which was marked with the current year.

Flipping through, he figured out that the book was organized by item. He turned pages until he found men's hats. By scanning the order numbers, it was easy to find number two twenty-three. His finger traced across the page, and his breath caught. *Fuck.* The gut feeling haunting him for the past two weeks since he'd seen the mark across Mary Beth's throat had been spot on. No matter how much he'd argued with himself that he was allowing his own childhood trauma to interfere with logical thinking, here it was, neatly penned across the page.

His brother's name—Jonas Perrin, the Viscount Griffen.

The hat in the alley belonged to Jonas. Jonas had appeared at the Blue Angel the night of Mary Beth's murder. Had he killed her outside in retribution for being thrown out of the club? Matthew scraped a hand down over his face, his fingers instinctively finding and tracing the old scar hidden under his beard that ran across his neck, under his chin. Who knew why Jonas did anything? His brother's mind was not right, never had been. God dammit, did Jonas know the

Blue Angel belonged to him? Had he figured out where Stella had escaped to? Or was it a strange twist of fate that had brought him to gamble at the Blue Angel that night?

Jesus, if there was even a chance that Jonas knew Stella was at the Blue Angel, she was in danger. Their brother had kept his sister's disappearance quiet, but Matthew knew Jonas had had a private investigator looking for her. Matthew had looked into the investigator and found that the man had been quietly asking friends in Norfolk and Stella's acquaintances from finishing school about her whereabouts. No one guessed she would ever come all the way to London and certainly not to the east side.

But the whispers that another one of Viscount Griffen's children had gone missing was too juicy a piece of gossip to not be passed along. Their father was probably rolling over in his grave that Stella had also escaped. Matthew's constant worry in the past year had been that someone who knew Stella in Norfolk would spot her and inform Jonas. Not that Matthew had any intention of letting her go without a fight. Jonas might hold the title and clout that came with it, but Matthew had plenty of money to send his sister safely abroad if needed.

He traced his finger over the name on the page. Jonas was a danger to more than just Stella if he had been strangling women all over the east side. A chill ran down his spine as he thought about the note that had led Elizabeth to the Green Door Tavern. Could it have been Jonas? Did he lure her there to harm her? Or had he wanted her to be a witness?

If Lizzie was in his sights, she was certainly in danger. He slammed the accounts book shut and slid it back into its place. He must go tomorrow and talk with her. Tell her everything he knew. She certainly needed to be a damn sight more careful than gallivanting about town at night with only an umbrella as a weapon. He turned out the lamp and let himself out as silently as he had entered. He walked down the back alley and emerged onto the street. Fishing out a coin for the lad who watched his horse, he said, "Thanks, Tim. Good hunting tonight."

"Anytime, Mr. Reeves." The boy tipped his worn cap and scurried away, back to picking pockets outside the theaters down in the Garden.

Matthew mounted his horse. He needed to get back to the club. Friday evenings were always busy. But as he rode down the street, his thoughts drifted back to his brother, and instead, he guided his horse west to Berkeley Square.

———— ∾∾ ————

THE LARGE SQUARE was lined with the grand homes of some of London's wealthiest peers, the address only second to St. James Square. Jonas had let the house last year. What a bachelor wanted with such a large mansion was beyond Matthew's comprehension. The lights blazed in the front windows. Matthew stroked down his horse's nose when Bax nudged his shoulder with a soft whinny. "Hang in there, boy. We won't stay long. Just wondered what he is up to tonight."

Would he go gaming? To his fancy club to dine and drink? Matthew popped open his watch and tilted the face to catch the moonlight. Quarter past ten. Perhaps Jonas was already out for the evening. Then, a clatter of horses' hooves sounded from down the street. A town coach pulled up in front of the house. Matthew immediately recognized their family crest gleaming in gold paint on the door. A couple of minutes later, his brother descended the front steps. He was dressed in formal evening attire, his dark hair slicked back and his face clean-shaven.

"Let's see where he's going," Matthew murmured to his horse. He mounted and set off a short distance behind Jonas's coach as it exited the square. Turned out his brother wasn't going far. Two streets over, the town coach pulled up in front of a stately home in Grosvenor Square. Matthew snorted derisively. Fucking toffs. Can't walk two blocks? He passed the grand house and found a spot down the block where he let Bax nibble on the grass of the great lawn that filled the center of the square. His brother descended from the carriage and disappeared into the house. Matthew tied his horse's reins to a low branch of a tree. "I'll be right back, I promise."

Then he skirted around the house. In two swift moves, he was over the fence. He straightened the sleeves of his jacket as he strolled to the back garden. Expansive and perfectly planned in the French style, shadowed marble statues stood among neat squares of blooming flowers. He stayed away from the long terrace, where light from the ballroom spilled out. Keeping to the shadows, he puffed at his cigarillo.

A bright, sparkling scene played out through the tall French doors that lined the back of the house. Glittering headpieces and colorful gowns interspersed with black formal wear danced across his view. And that's when he saw Lizzie. Standing next to an ajar door, her lace fan fluttered back and forth. She stood alone, apart from the rest of the guests. She wore a gown of subdued navy-blue silk. It had white lace trim along the low neckline and at her wrists.

Even from here, he could see that her throat was unadorned by jewelry. Such a shame. That long, lovely neck should be dripping in jewels—emeralds perhaps, to match her eyes. He swallowed hard as he thought about kissing down the creamy skin of her throat until he reached the delicate swells of her breasts. Dammit, this woman was so damn distracting.

What the hell was she doing here? His breath froze in his chest as he realized that she was in the same room as Jonas. God dammit! He took two steps forward before pausing. He certainly couldn't go in there. He wasn't dressed properly and would stick out like a sore thumb. And he couldn't risk Jonas seeing him. Even though it was unlikely his brother would recognize the adult version of him, he would not take the risk of exposing himself. He had Stella to protect. Stepping back, he took another drag of his cigarillo. He would simply have to watch and make sure Lizzie got home safely.

CHAPTER TWELVE

T HE WOMAN ACROSS from him was beautiful. Her dark blue gown highlighted her creamy skin and the long lines of her neck. Her brown hair was piled simply in a crown of curls. Her delicate facial features were highlighted by sharp cheekbones and perfectly arched eyebrows. She wore no adornments, which was unusual, but she did not need anything to distract from her serene beauty. Simply staring at her as she softly fanned herself calmed his beast. What would she smell like? Certainly not heavily scented perfume, like so many of the other ladies here tonight. No, this lady probably smelled like fresh soap or perhaps a delicate lavender.

She moved away from the open window and strolled along the edge of the ballroom. He followed. He had to know her scent. She even walked gracefully, winding past other guests with purpose. Although she spoke with no one. She was no fresh debutant. Was she visiting someone this summer? He tapped his fingers against his leg. He stopped when she paused. Her rosy lips curled up in amusement as she watched Beltram make a fool of himself. In his cups, as usual.

What would those lips taste like? His eyes drifted back down to her throat as he imagined it marred by bruises. They would show up so well against the pale skin there. He would be able to pull her close and take in her scent as he strangled the breath from that long, elegant neck. She wasn't like the others. No, she was far lovelier. He would have to seduce her first, his beast demanded. He had to know what she tasted like. He would know her scent, drown in it. Then afterward, he could take pleasure in watching her slip away with his hands around her throat. This one would be different.

Lost in thoughts of all the beautiful bruises he could put on her alabaster skin, he frowned when another man stepped next to her. He couldn't hear what they said, so he moved to pass slowly behind them. He was rewarded when he heard the man address her as "Miss Harper." The name didn't ring a bell; she must be visiting someone, like he'd first thought. He would ask Lady Cheltenham who Miss Harper was staying with. He strode away to find their hostess.

CHAPTER THIRTEEN

*I*T'S SO HOT *in here.* Elizabeth fanned herself. She'd moved next to an open French door that led to the balcony outside, but the night air felt just as warm as the air in the ballroom. At least the outside air was fresh in comparison to the heavily perfumed air inside. After taking in one more breath of fresh air, she forced herself to move along the edges of the room, making a slow circle while she noted who danced with who. A loud shout of laughter drew her gaze across the room. Lord Cheltenham roared as he watched Lord Beltram mop up spilled wine from Lady Beltram's heaving bosom. The lady was red-faced and smacking her husband's shoulder as he drunkenly apologized.

Elizabeth's lips twitched. Funny as it was, the incident was hardly newsworthy. Nights like this could be interesting or plain boring. Lady Cheltenham had invited her to make sure her party was described in detail in the paper. But so far, all Elizabeth had were a few notes about the tropical theme that the hostess had obviously spent a great deal of money to achieve. She continued her stroll around the edges of the room, pausing again to stare blankly at the crowd of dancing guests.

"Dead boring tonight, isn't it?" a male voice commented from next to her.

Elizabeth glanced over and frowned. Harry Kimmel from the *Morning Post* stood a couple of feet away. His stupid, lopsided grin accompanied a roll of his eyes. She made a noncommittal noise and turned her gaze back to the crowd.

"Come now, Miss Harper, surely you're not still mad about last month?" He chuckled.

"I certainly am. Sending false tips to throw my man off the scent was low, even for you, Kimmel."

"It's hardly my fault if your puppy is so gullible."

Elizabeth winced. Nigel was quite green. Which is why she was here tonight instead of him. He was a brilliant writer, sharp and witty, but he needed to work on his investigative skills. He didn't have a cynical bone in his body, and he was far too trusting. But he was only twenty; there was time yet for him to grow and learn.

Her silence didn't seem to bother Kimmel, who kept talking. "I hate summertime. No one of interest is in town. Just a bunch of social climbing nobodies who don't have their own estates to escape to."

"Careful, Harry. Your snobbery is showing." She glanced over at him. "There are some peers of note here. Plenty don't care to be away from the entertainments of town."

He grunted. "You always were kinder than most toward the toffs, being from the same lofty breeding ground and all."

"That's simply not true. I have as much cynicism as the

next person. I simply have more manners than you. Good evening, Mr. Kimmel." Elizabeth walked away from the other reporter.

It was no secret who her grandmother was, and weasels like Kimmel would always throw it in her face. No matter. He was just a peon in the machine that was the *Morning Post*. Harry was just jealous that the *Piccadilly Press* was hers and she could write about anything she saw fit to print. She stepped out of the ballroom to the less crowded portrait gallery. Staring up at a painting of a sixteenth-century ancestor of Lord Cheltenham, Elizabeth listened to nearby conversation. To her left, two matrons, their fans fluttering madly, spoke about the one woman's daughter's marital prospects. On her right, a group of young men strolled by, laughing at a crude jest one made that had Elizabeth wrinkling her nose in distaste.

She moved away, down the room. It was so damn hot, and her fan was doing little good. Then, like a miracle from above, a tendril of cool air drifted over the back of her neck. She turned to find a door stood ajar. She walked over and peered out. It led out to the garden. Another breeze raced across her overheated skin, tempting her to step outside. Slipping through the door, she drew in a deep breath of humid air. Still, it was better than the air inside the house. She hadn't made it more than five feet from the door when male voices stopped her in her tracks. Her instincts had her stepping back into the shadows next to the house. The moon peeked out from behind clouds, throwing its light across the grass beyond the veranda.

"It's been in the papers. Four women so far," one man said.

"And you actually think it's him?"

"I fear it is him. The paper said the women were strangled. Same thing that happened to his mother."

"Peter knew that boy wasn't right in the head. But he kept him in line. We need to watch out for him, now that his father can't."

"But if he is the one killing those girls, we need to stop him, not cover for him."

"Stop him how? Having him committed? Can you imagine the scandal? We owe it to Peter to protect the family name. His son is the last of the line. Besides, who cares about a few dead prostitutes?"

Elizabeth raised her hand to smother her gasp.

They weren't prostitutes, you bastard.

She squinted, but could only see the backs of two evening jackets. One man was taller than the other, but they stood in shadow, and she couldn't decipher any details about the two men. The shorter of the two men tipped his head back and drained the contents of his glass.

"Listen, I will talk to him. Scare some sense into him. He just needs a firm hand." The taller man clapped the other on his shoulder.

"That would be good. He will listen to you. Tonight, I saw the editor from the *Piccadilly Press* inside. She has run several articles about the deaths. My wife was telling me about it over breakfast this morning. Harriet loves that scandal rag. What if she is digging around? Why would Lady Cheltenham invite those newspaper people to her party?"

"They are here to report on the decorations and who is dancing with who. Don't worry so much, George. I will take care of things. Come, let's get another brandy before your wife comes looking for you."

Elizabeth glanced left and right for a route of escape but, thankfully, the two men walked away from where she stood and climbed the stone steps that led up to the veranda. She let out a sigh of relief. Tipping her head back, she stared at the moon peeking from behind clouds. The killer was definitely an aristocrat. One of them.

She moved out to walk through the garden beds. The roses perfumed the air, and more clouds blew across the sky, gathering to hide the stars. The fact that the killer was a peer of some sort complicated how to catch him. Especially if he had others that were willing to protect him. No magistrate was going to take action against a peer, solely based on her conjuncture.

"Should you be out wandering dark gardens at night, Miss Harper?" the rasp of a familiar voice interrupted her thoughts.

Mr. Reeves stepped onto the pea gravel path in front of her, his sharp features briefly lit by the end of the cigarillo he puffed on. Elizabeth took a step closer to him. "You mean with rogues like you hiding in the shadows?"

"Precisely." A wolfish grin spread across his face.

"What are you doing here?" she asked.

"I could ask you the same question."

"I am working. The hostess invites representatives from the papers to make sure her event is featured in this week's columns." She quirked an eyebrow in question at him.

"I have news for you. About the hat."

That wasn't an answer to her question, but she was too curious to bother with his evasiveness. "Did you go to the shop?"

"Yes, I've just come from there. I found out the owner of the hat is Lord Griffen."

Griffen. Good Lord. Her heart stuttered into an uneasy rhythm. She needed to sit down.

"You look very pale all of a sudden." Mr. Reeves grasped her elbow. "Do you know him?"

She walked over to a stone bench nearby and plopped down. The breeze picked up, blowing around the loose tendrils of hair that framed her face. She nodded. "His father ruined my life."

CHAPTER FOURTEEN

A ND JUST LIKE that, the heavens opened up, and it began
to pour. Matthew tipped his head up to the sky. Her
words rang inside his head. *His father ruined my life.* How
could his father have damaged this strong, beautiful woman?
How would they have ever even interacted? He glanced
across at Elizabeth. She jumped up with her hands in the air,
catching raindrops, her expression incredulous as water
dripped off the end of her nose. Then her gaze met his, and
they both burst out laughing.

When she let loose, her chest heaving with laughter, her
eyes crinkled at the corners, she looked so damn beautiful.
Matthew cupped her cheek, wiping away rain with his
thumb. Then, against good judgment, he kissed her. He
couldn't help himself. Fuck, his attraction to her was messy
and about to become so damn complicated, but as his lips
slid against hers, it was worth every ounce of risk. Her hands
came up to frame his face and she kissed him back with
warm lips and slick tongue. With a groan, he tugged her
tight against him.

Rain poured down on them, but he didn't care. Her
body pressed against his set him aflame. He'd never felt this

kind of hunger for a woman before. Pleasure between partners was always fine, taken and given easily. But he couldn't explain this bone-deep need for her. He pulled his lips away fractionally. "We should get out of the rain." She nodded but kissed him again. Smiling against her lips, he said, "Come, Lizzie, did you bring a carriage?"

She nodded. "Yes, I hired one for the evening. I certainly can't go back inside like this. I guess it's time to go home."

"Can I escort you home?" He brushed back sodden curls from her forehead.

She stared up at him for a long moment, and he thought maybe she was going to tell him to go to hell. That she could get herself home just fine. But then she nodded. He exhaled in relief. Grabbing her hand, they ran through the rain, heading across the lawn and down to the mews. The lamplight glowing from the open doors of the stable was a beacon as they exited the gardens and stepped onto the dark lane behind the house.

Once inside, Elizabeth went to find her driver. Matthew gave one of the stable hands two quid to get his horse and take him home to the Blue Angel. He felt guilty for leaving poor Bax tied up for so long. He climbed into the carriage after Elizabeth and settled next to her on the bench. She snickered behind her hand. He slid an arm around her shoulders. "What's so funny?"

"The horrified expressions of the stable hands and my driver. I must look a fright. A real drowned rat."

"Certainly not a rat." He leaned over and kissed her

temple. "Perhaps something adorable, like a drowned rabbit or a drowned hedgehog."

She wrinkled her nose. "You look like a drowned panther. Sleek black hair and dangerous smile."

"Hmm, I like that." He indulged himself and nuzzled her neck, kissing a spot behind her ear when she tipped her head to one side to give him better access. Her small sigh of pleasure had him wanting to ravish her right here in the carriage. But he leaned back instead. She deserved more than a quick swive in a hired hack, that was for sure.

Matthew took her hand in his, weaving their fingers together. She had good hands. Long, strong fingers with short, neatly trimmed fingernails. Calluses marred the tips of her fingers. He ran his finger over a callus on her middle finger. "What are these from?"

"Setting type. It is a tedious process. Now, I have ladies who come in and do the job for each edition, but for years, I set type for my father. He had me learn each part of the business by doing. He was a big believer in learning as you go."

"You hire a lot of women?" he asked.

"Typesetting takes delicacy; the tiles are small. You need small hands, so women are naturally better at the detailed work."

He weaved his fingers back through hers. "Will you tell me about what happened? You said Lord Griffen's father ruined your life."

She sighed.

"Please?" He kissed her fingers.

"I will, but let's get back to the house first. It is a long story and I want to change into something dry."

He nodded. Elizabeth leaned her head back against the squabs and was quiet the rest of the way to Bloomsbury. When they arrived, Matthew paid the coachman and sent him off. He could walk home from here. He followed Elizabeth into the dark house. She moved easily through to the front room and lit a taper, then crossed to light another pair on the mantle.

"I will just go upstairs and change. Please make yourself at home." She crossed to open a window, and a damp breeze raced through the room. When she turned back to him, she frowned. "You are just as wet as me. I can bring you down a towel."

"I'll be fine." He pulled off his jacket. "I will dry."

"I will be just a few minutes." She swept out of the room.

Matthew hung his sodden jacket on the back of a wooden ladder-back chair. His shirt was only slightly damp, but his cravat was a limp wet rag, so he removed it as well. He set his hat on the seat of the chair. Moving across to pick up one of the tapers, he wandered around the room. At one end was a large desk covered in papers, inkpots, and pens. He smiled at the mess. Nice to know that *Miss I can handle everything* wasn't perfect. He spotted a candelabra and lit the candles, bringing it back over to the low table in the center of the seating area.

The extra light afforded him a better look around. He

spotted a small army of tin soldiers on the floor in front of the cold hearth. Squatting down, he reached for one; the little soldier was battle-worn, its paint scratched and the hat dented. A squeak of door hinges had him twisting around. Was she back already? But the door didn't open fully. When he held up his taper, he could see the outline of a small head poking through the slightly ajar door.

"Is someone there?" Matthew stood.

The door opened further, and a small boy came across the threshold. "Hullo."

"Hello," he replied. "Are you Robert?"

"Yes." The boy let go of the door handle. "Who are you?"

"Matthew Reeves. Shouldn't you be abed, Robert?"

"I heard my mum come home and voices downstairs. I just wanted to see who was here."

"I see. Well, your mum will be right back, so you might want to scurry on back to bed."

"I won't be in trouble. I want to make sure she is all right." Robert's small shoulders straightened. "It's my job as the man of the house."

"I promise you I won't cause her any harm. Your mother and I are friends." Matthew shoved his hands in pockets and tried to look non-threatening. The boy had gumption for only six years old. Or was he seven? He nodded to the army on the hearth. "Is this your regiment?"

"Yes, sir." Robert came closer. Still eyeing him warily.

Matthew crouched down again. "Who are they fighting?"

Apparently, that was the right question because Robert hurried over. "They are fighting the Ottomans. We are helping the Greeks to win independence. The British army is the best army in the whole world. We have been sending big ships to Greece to help as well. But I don't have any Navy boats. Just army regiments. But look at all the cannons I have." He pointed to a neat line of artillery lined up behind the soldiers. "If you want, you can be the cavalry. I like to be the cannons."

They worked together to fight the imaginary Ottoman empire. Matthew had no idea what he was doing, but Robert gave orders, and he sent his cavalrymen where the boy instructed. It turned out that he didn't need to worry about playing the right way; the battle was pure chaos. Matthew flung one of the cavalrymen backward with a loud "Ahhhhh" of agony, and Robert hooted with laughter. He swept his hand through one of the regiments, scattering soldiers and yelling "Ahhhhh" as well.

"Robert Edward Harper, what are you doing out of bed?"

Both he and Robert swiveled their heads to where Elizabeth stood in the doorway with her hands on her hips. Robert scrambled up first. "Sorry, mama."

Matthew rose to his feet. "We were just fighting the Turks."

Elizabeth pursed her lips together. "I am aware. It is always the Turks." She raised her eyebrows and gave her son a stern look. "Robert, why are you out of bed? It's very late."

"I wanted to see who was down here." He walked over to his mother and grasped her hand in his small one. "I just wanted to make sure you were safe, mama."

The kid had charm, and his wide-eyed look of concern seemed to melt Elizabeth's annoyance. Her expression softened. "Off to bed with you." She bent to kiss the top of his head.

"'Night, Mr. Reeves." Robert gave a little wave and scampered off.

Elizabeth went to the doorway and listened for a moment and then stepped back, shutting the door. "Sorry about that. He is far too curious for his own good."

"Curiosity is a sign of intelligence. He is very well-versed in current events of the British empire."

"Yes, that's from his Uncle Alex. The current Duke of Hartwick." She still stood by the door. She had changed into a light blue dress and taken her hair down. The damp locks had been brushed out and fell past her shoulders in long, loose waves.

He pushed down his desire to pull her into his arms and continue where they had left off in the rain. There was too much to say. Too much that tied them in ways that he never expected. Matthew held out a hand. "Will you come sit?"

Elizabeth nodded. Crossing to him, she held out a towel.

"Thanks." He accepted it and rubbed it vigorously over his head to get some of the damp out.

Then she went and sat on the long sofa. Her posture was ramrod straight; hands clasped together in her lap.

Matthew dropped down next to her. "You don't have to tell me what happened if it is too painful."

"No, it's all like a dull ache now." She didn't look at him but stared across at the tin army regiments. "My mother was the daughter of the Marquess of Rollinsford. She was disowned when she married for love to a lowly newspaperman. She was happy in the life that she chose; we were happy. Then when I was eighteen, she died."

He squeezed her hand. "That's tough. My mother died when I was at a similar age."

She did look over at him then. "My grandmother came to the funeral and met me for the first time. She offered to sponsor a season in society for me, and my father reluctantly agreed. I was so excited. She bought me a whole new wardrobe. I took lessons on manners from a private tutor. Not that my mother hadn't taught me good manners." She shook her head. "But I digress. This isn't about her. At a ball, I rounded a corner and ran into the love of my life, Robert Barclay. We had a whirlwind courtship, and he asked me to marry him. But when he went to his father, he was told that a verbal agreement had been made many years prior to marry him to the Viscount Griffen's daughter. But the daughter was still too young, only ten years old at the time."

"Who was Robert's father?" he asked.

"The Duke of Hartwick."

Matthew whistled long and low.

Elizabeth sent him a wry half smile. "Yes, well, the Duke decided to support Robert and canceled the informal betrothal. But Lord Griffen was not happy and demanded satisfaction."

She shifted in her seat to face him, pulling her hand from his. "Robert went to the duel as his father's second. Both he and his father ended up dead." Her hand rose to rub at the spot over her heart as though it still pained her to talk about it. "Later that night, Robert and his father were found in a carriage down on the Strand. Their deaths were attributed to a robbery gone bad. But I knew they had started the day at the duel. My father and I agreed that it was a cover-up. I was devastated. Two months later, I realized that I was pregnant. It helped to pull me back to life. I had a piece of Robert growing inside me; I had to persevere."

His mind reeled. Her story lined up with what Seaton had said about her. Although Seaton hadn't given the details of his father's and half-brother's deaths. What a bloody mess. Matthew didn't have many clear memories of his father. He had been a tall, dour figure. One who hadn't spared any time or attention for his younger son. Would he have been a killer, though? His father had always extolled the strict following of rules and morality.

"Why kill the second?" he murmured.

"I didn't know the answer to that for many years. The current Duke of Hartwick, Robert's younger brother, Alex, never accepted that their deaths were a random act of street violence. He had been quietly investigating for years. Two years ago, one of his father's cohorts met with him to unload his guilt about knowing what happened. The carriage they met in was hit by a homemade explosive. Lord Galey was killed, and Hartwick was badly injured with burns that left scars along his face and torso. Further investigation last summer unearthed that his father had a group of friends since school days that, through a traumatic incident, had bonded and all looked out for each other. They were all there that day of the duel.

Apparently, none of them thought that Lord Griffen would actually kill Lord Hartwick. And when it happened, Robert was wild with anger. He yelled that he would get revenge on all of them for allowing it to happen. That he knew all their secrets, kept in a journal his father had." She shook her head. "Someone then shot Robert in the heart."

Matthew watched a single tear roll down her cheek. He enveloped her hand in his again. "How do you know all this?"

"Seaton. He had been hired by Lord Fleming to protect Hartwick from further harm, and he brought Fleming to Hartwick House. Lord Fleming told us what really happened that day but would not disclose who killed Robert. He is still protecting his friends, even at the expense of people's lives." Her tone was full of well-earned bitterness.

Matthew sighed. "Seaton received the property that houses the Blue Angel and the rest of the block from his father at his death. When he told me his father was a fucking duke, I laughed in his face. I have known him since we were fifteen, and trust me, nobody would ever guess he was an aristocrat's bastard."

Her lips briefly curled up into a small smile. "Yes, well, he was a great help to Hartwick when his wife was kidnapped by Lord Griffen."

Matthew's mouth fell open in shock. His father had kidnapped a lady? A duke's wife? "Wait, why?"

"This journal of secrets the elder Hartwick kept. I do not know what it contained about Lord Griffen, but it must have been explosive enough of a secret to make him desperate. He ransomed Lady Hartwick for the book. Which the younger Hartwick didn't even possess. Seaton found out where they were keeping her, and he and Hartwick rescued her." Elizabeth stared at him curiously.

Matthew tried to wipe the shock from his expression. His "play by the rules" father had kidnapped and tried to ransom a duchess? Perhaps he shouldn't be shocked. He knew exactly what secret his father would do anything to hide. Having an heir that was mentally unstable would forever tarnish the family name. And with his spare lost to the streets of London, he would have been desperate, indeed. He ran a hand over his beard. "Good Lord, what a tale."

Elizabeth nodded. "The elder Lord Griffen died that night. An explosive detonated on his boat."

He couldn't help but wonder if his brother had been there. If he'd wanted to be free of their father's control. Would Jonas have killed their sire? Matthew stared at the dancing flames of the candelabra on the table, his mind racing to put the pieces together. His brother, let loose from his father's control, could be devolving into the killer that he had always been.

When they were young, his brother would capture small animals and torture them before snapping their necks. He would bully the smaller children in the village as well. Pushing and smacking to see how far he could hurt someone before they would quit fighting back and run off. Matthew hadn't played with Jonas, preferring to stay safely at home with his books. Jonas hated his academics, always getting into trouble on purpose so their tutor would banish him from the schoolroom as punishment. But even with all he knew about his brother's cruelty, he had never expected Jonas's attack that night long ago. Never thought his brother would try to kill his own kin.

CHAPTER FIFTEEN

"I F THE SON, Perrin, who is now the new Lord Griffen, is our killer, it makes this very hard to prove." Elizabeth frowned. "He will have powerful friends looking out for him." The conversation she overheard tonight reinforced that assertion. "We will have to have more proof than just a silk hat at the scene of the crime."

She leaned back against the tall back of the sofa. She was tired already, just thinking about the difficulty of proving a peer of the realm was a murderer. Like father, like son. Dear lord, was the whole family rotten to the core? She sighed.

"We will figure something out. No man should be above the law." Matthew's expression was harsh and forbidding. "I promised myself to mete out retribution to Mary Beth's killer, and I mean to follow through."

The power that he radiated, born from his anger, was very attractive. Still, she much preferred Matthew's mischievous smile, or when his eyes were lit with desire, over this expression clouded with anger. Tonight, she would ask him to stay. They had been edging around their powerful attraction to each other for the past two weeks. The plain truth was that she wanted him. His lips on hers, his body warming her bed.

As she had rehashed the events of the past, she realized the truth in what she'd told him earlier. The pain from that time was a dull ache, like a bruise that would always remind her of her love for Robert. Even that love, which had seemed all-consuming during their courtship, now felt fuzzy, like the edges of a lovely dream. Matthew had awakened something in her, a need that she had been ignoring for a very long time.

Matthew stood. "I guess I will head out." He grabbed his jacket off a nearby chair and shrugged into it.

"No." She scrambled up. When he turned back to her, she placed her hands on his chest. Screwing up her courage, she raised her gaze. "Stay."

He stiffened. "I don't know if that is a good idea."

"Oh." Perhaps she had read too much into his previous flirtation. "Of course. You should go." She smoothed her hands over his damp shirt. "I understand."

He gripped one of her wrists. "No, I don't think you do. It's complicated."

Embarrassment rose as a wave of heat crept up her chest and neck. "I do understand. I am complicated. With a young son and a business to run, there is no doubt that you can find less complicated bedmates." She turned to head toward the door. "Let me show you out."

Matthew's arm snaked around her waist. He twisted her, roughly pulling her flush against his hard frame. "Lizzie, I have wanted to bury myself inside you since the moment I saw you stroll into my club." He tipped his head back to look up at the ceiling. "I am trying to be a gentleman."

"Why? What I want is the devil."

"Fucking hell," he muttered. His eyes burned dark and dangerous when he dropped his gaze to her mouth.

She shivered in anticipation. It didn't have to be complicated. She was a mature woman who wanted to invite a man into her bed. She didn't need permission to take a lover. Elizabeth indulged her urge to touch him, running her hands up his muscled chest. Then she curved them around his neck, lifting onto her toes to kiss him.

His response was immediate and fierce as his lips slid against hers, hot and demanding. She melted against him as both his arms banded around her. Yes, yes, she wished to meet all of his demands. Their tongues tangled as he licked into her mouth. He tasted like tobacco and sin.

She pulled her mouth from his. "Come with me upstairs."

He froze for a moment but then nodded. Taking his hand, she led him out of the room. To the left, down the hallway, they climbed the stairs. "My bedroom is on the right. It looks out onto the garden."

Matthew glanced at the room across the hall when they paused at her door.

"Don't worry, it's empty. Both Robert and Mrs. Todd sleep on the third floor. That used to be my father's room."

His shoulders relaxed. He wrapped his arms around her from behind and nuzzled her neck as she opened her door. A sharp bite of pain startled her as his teeth scraped against her neck. "Did you just bite me?" she gasped.

"I want to eat you whole, Lizzie. I mean to nibble every inch of your delectable body." His tongue laved at the spot he'd bitten, sending a shiver of pleasure through her.

They stumbled into her room, and Matthew locked the door behind them. She crossed to the mantle to light the candelabra with the taper she'd brought from downstairs. Shy suddenly, she sucked in a fortifying breath and then turned to find Matthew roaming her room, his fingers running over the washbasin and the vanity table. He walked past the bed and pushed open the window. The lace curtains fluttered around him.

He turned back to her. "Come here, Lizzie. Will you let me undress you?"

She bit down on her bottom lip, glad for the dim lighting. What would he think of her body with its round stomach and generous hips? She had never had the svelte figure that seemed perennially popular, but having a child had filled out all her curvy bits further. *Courage, girl. You've never had any complaints before.* Robert had been a big man, and he had worshipped her body during their lovemaking. She moved across the carpet to Matthew's outstretched hand.

"What's this for?" he brushed his finger over her lip, which she still had trapped between her teeth. "Having second thoughts?"

She shook her head. "It is just that it has been a long time since I've done this. Seven years, in fact."

His eyes widened, but his thumb continued to soothe her abused lip. Then he bent and kissed her. Slow and sensuous, his kiss erased her worries. There was nothing but the feel of his lips, the soft brush of his beard, and the burn of her desire for him low in her belly. She gripped his wrist as he plunged his fingers into her hair, cupping her cheek. Lord, she could kiss him endlessly.

His lips never left hers as his hands lowered to sweep across her bare shoulder, tugging her dress to the side, exposing more skin. She reached behind her back and undid the three buttons that closed the bodice. The pink lawn fabric slid off her shoulders and exposed the top of her breasts and the lace trim of her chemise above her corset.

Matthew tore his lips from hers. With a hum of appreciation, his fingers skimmed light as a feather across the swells of her breasts. "So beautiful," he murmured.

She let the dress slide down her arms and fall to the floor. Matthew spun her around and a low groan erupted from him as his hands slid underneath her shift to cup her bare bottom. "Christ, woman, this ass is a fucking feast." He gave one cheek a squeeze before his fingers moved to make quick work of the ties to her corset. She let it fall to join her dress on the floor. The soft rasp of his beard on her shoulder was followed by hot open-mouthed kisses, leaving a wet trail up her neck. His hard erection pressed firmly against her bottom. She wiggled against it and was rewarded with another groan, which vibrated in her ear.

"Tease," he whispered.

"I am not the tease." She turned in his arms. "You, sir, are still fully clothed."

He stepped back. He held his arms wide. "Want to take care of that?"

She couldn't stop the smile that stretched. He did indeed look like a panther, beautiful and dangerous. Lean and muscled, his hair mussed by her hands, and his eyes filled with desire, he was devastatingly handsome. She stepped forward and smoothed her hands across his chest, up to those broad shoulders, and slid his jacket off. It slithered to the floor with a soft whoosh. Then she rose onto her tiptoes to run her tongue lightly over the exposed section of throat between the V of his shirt collar. Matthew tipped his head to one side to give her better access. She took advantage, stretching to kiss up to his earlobe before nipping at it. "You're too tall."

Unbuttoning his vest, she then made quick work of pushing it off to join his jacket on the floor. Impatiently, she shoved his braces off his shoulders and tugged his shirt from his trousers. Underneath, his skin was hot and smooth. Her fingers discovered a light dusting of hair across his chest. "Hands up," she instructed.

Matthew chuckled but raised them above his head. Elizabeth pulled the shirt up until she was on her toes again, but only just managed to get it over his head. "Too tall," she muttered.

With his hands still trapped above his head, Matthew grinned down at her. "Let's take care of that." He shucked off his shirt and strode across the room to pull the chair from in front of her desk. Placing it in the center of the room, he sat. "Come here, Lizzie."

She walked to him slowly, enjoying the way his gaze roamed her body with such hunger. He kept it banked, tightly coiled. How could she let it loose? What would it take? She pulled her shift up her body slowly. Pulling it over her head and exposing her naked body.

His growl echoed. Quick as a jungle cat, Matthew grabbed her hand to guide her on his lap to straddle his legs. "Better?"

She leaned in to kiss him. "Mmm, much better."

His arms banded her close, and his mouth devoured hers. The games were over. She all but felt his control snap as his hands roamed down to her bottom, squeezing roughly, kneading the flesh. She plunged her hands into his hair, giving it a sharp tug, tilting his head back to devour his lips. He moaned into her mouth. With hands at her hips, he rolled her core up his hard length. The wool fabric of his pants giving her clit extra friction that felt amazing.

"Again," she demanded, breaking away from his lips.

His smile was wicked as he rolled her hips again.

Lord, that felt so good. She grasped his shoulders and, this time, she took control, moving her core against him just right. Her head fell back as she reveled in the stimulation.

"That's it, luv. Rub that hot cunt on me."

Her head snapped up as she gasped at his dirty words.

All but black, his dark eyes burned with desire. "Use me.

Find your pleasure."

Shamelessly, she did. She rolled her hips against his hardness, chasing her orgasm. Panting, mindless with how good it felt, how good he felt. She closed her eyes and focused on the building pressure in her core.

His hand pressed against her sternum, pushing her to lean back. She should have felt off-kilter, but with his other hand splayed between her shoulder blades, he held her steady. His tongue licked a stripe across her breast and then around the tip.

She moved her hips frantically as he suckled on her breast. *Oh God.* Her clit throbbed as her orgasm exploded. She moaned low, biting hard on her bottom lip so not to make too much noise. Matthew cradled her back with his strong hands, supporting her. She couldn't help but pulse her hips a couple of times against him as she slowly came down from her bliss. He was so hard underneath her. She needed that hard length inside her, filling her. Right now.

She lifted her heavy eyelids and glanced down at Matthew, whose face was still buried in her bosom. He smiled up at her like a cat that had drunk all the cream. "You are gorgeous when you come, my girl. Simply stunning." He licked across one breast lazily, as though he could sit and sample her all night, as though the throbbing length nestled between her legs didn't matter.

She ran her hands down the sides of his beard. What would the texture feel like rubbing the inside of her thighs? But not now. Now, she needed him to be inside her. She wanted him to let his animal out. She climbed off him. "Trousers off."

"Be my guest." Again, he spread his arms wide with a wicked smile.

She flipped her hair over one shoulder, letting it fall over her breast. Then slowly leaned down. He insisted she undress him, then she would let him suffer. She ran her fingertips up the bulge in his trousers from the bottom to the top. Then, using her nails, she lightly scraped along the skin right above the waistband.

"Minx," he murmured.

Elizabeth smiled. She slid a button loose and the next one, making her way slowly across the fastenings. But she didn't touch his hard shaft...yet. "Up."

Matthew stood. He toed off his shoes. The unfastened placard of his trousers was no match for what lay underneath. His thick shaft sprang free to stand proudly from a thatch of dark hair. She licked her lips and reached out to wrap her hand around his length. She squeezed it before running her hand up the soft skin.

His head fell back, his eyes closed in bliss. "Lizzie..."

She stepped forward, giving his shaft a hard squeeze. "Matthew, look at me."

His head snapped up.

"I want to lie with you. To have this gorgeous cock fill me up. But you may not spend inside me."

His eyes widened. Then he cupped her jaw. "Yes, of course. You have my word."

This was such a risk. Having been reckless before, she fully understood the consequences. She didn't wish to let her desires overwhelm her common sense, but good Lord, she wanted this man. Staring up into his eyes, she tried to assess his sincerity.

His hand slid down to her throat, squeezing gently. "You can trust me to take care of you." Then his lips crashed into hers, stealing her breath as he seized control, his tongue teasing and tasting, leaving her no choice but to submit.

CHAPTER SIXTEEN

FUCKING HELL, THIS woman was going to ruin him. The hand she had wrapped around his cock squeezed tight as he devoured her sweet mouth. He was going to embarrass himself and come all over her hand if he didn't take control of their bed play. And play it was. He'd never been with a woman who battled for control as she did. Then she brought her other hand around and slapped his arse. He growled against her mouth.

Her lips curled up into a smile.

"Oh, you want to play, you wicked thing?" Matthew scooped her up over his shoulder. Stepping out of the puddle his trousers had made around his ankles, he then strode with her to the bed and tossed her into the middle. He crawled over her. "Hands above your head," he ordered.

Lizzie shook her head. "No, I want to touch every inch of you." She threaded her fingers into his hair and pulled him in for another scorching kiss.

Happy to sink into her delicious mouth, he kissed her slow, enjoying every taste. As he sucked on her tongue, he grabbed her wrists and dragged her arms above her head. Now, he had her how he wished, stretched beneath him, a feast of creamy pale skin and luscious curves. He had never wanted a woman as he craved her.

"Spread those pretty thighs for me, Lizzie."

She did as he asked and he sank down against her heat, giving a roll of his hips and finding her so slick and ready for him. They both groaned low. She bucked her hips and writhed desperately against his grip on her wrists. God, she was breathtaking. He bent to suck one rosy nipple into his mouth, her moan gratifying.

"Matthew, stop teasing. I need you to…"

"I know what you need." He sank into the heat of her pussy in a slow slide. Fuck, she felt so good. He closed his eyes and concentrated on banking back his orgasm. He had promised to not come inside her, and for fuck's sake, he was no green boy. Opening his eyes, his gaze locked onto hers. It felt as though she snared his soul with those witchy emerald eyes. He rolled his hips and they began to move together in a rhythm that felt as natural as breathing. He captured her lips once again; their kiss messy, mostly the two of them panting against each other's mouths. He let go of her hands to grasp her hip as he searched for the angle that would make her moan. His pace became increasingly frantic. His orgasm raced down his spine.

"Lizzie, come for me. I want to feel you strangle my cock," he begged as her nails scratched up his back.

Her head tilted back, her long neck arching. "I'm so close. Don't stop."

Oh, hell no. He wouldn't stop till she came apart beneath him. Bending, he placed open-mouth kisses along her throat, making his way down to the juncture with her shoulder. Then he bit the tender flesh, the animal inside him needing to mark her.

"Yes, yes, Matthew!" Lizzie cried out.

He allowed himself two more thrusts into her tight cunt before he pulled out. He grasped his cock and painted her stomach with his orgasm. Sitting back on his haunches, he grinned down at her spread out before him. He ran his finger through the mess he'd made on her stomach, seeing his seed marking her skin almost as satisfying as filling her up with it.

She raised her arms above her head languidly and grinned back at him.

"Satisfied, my gorgeous girl?"

"Mmm hmm…"

"Stay there. Let me clean you up." He slid off the bed and crossed to the dresser, where a washbasin and a neat stack of cloths sat on top. Dipping a cloth into the water, he closed his eyes briefly. *What was he going to do?* Now that he had her in his arms and had witnessed her in the throes of passion, he would keep her. Had to keep her.

The question was whether she would have him for more than one night. Especially once she knew about his past. He squeezed out the excess water. No, she couldn't know. No one could know. It was the only way to keep Stella safe. He had been hiding his true identity his whole life, and this was no different. He wasn't that boy any longer. Sucking in a deep breath, he turned and returned to his Lizzie.

CHAPTER SEVENTEEN

LATER, AFTER HE'D dressed, Matthew leaned down to kiss one of her bare shoulders. "I must go, Lizzie." It was two in the morning. He'd been missing for far too long. The club could run without him, but he really should get back.

Lizzie turned her head so she could peer up at him with heavy eyelids and a small frown. "No. Get back into bed."

He swept her hair from her brow and indulged them both by running his fingers through the thick locks, scratching her scalp gently. Lizzie let out a low purring sound, and his cock twitched. How he wanted to get back into the bed. He sighed. "I must go to work, luv. Will you come tomorrow night and see the show?"

She nodded. "What time?"

"Eleven. But if you come at nine, we could have a late supper together in my private room." And he could get under her skirts again. "Yes?"

"Alright. Tomorrow evening."

"I'll send my coach for you." Then he bent and took one more slow taste of her lips. With a groan, he pulled away. "I'll see myself out."

The walk back to the club helped to cool his blood somewhat, but he knew he would be thinking of her delectable body nonstop until he could have her again. Damnation, he had really let his cock lead him straight into an impossible situation. Taking his hat off, he ran a hand through his hair. If he was honest with himself, it wasn't his cock that was the problem. He had enjoyed one night with lovers in the past and walked away without thinking of them again. But this time, his heart had taken an unfortunate dive. After hearing about her past and meeting her son, he couldn't admire her more. And dammit, good things didn't just happen to people like him; he certainly planned to keep her as long as she would have him.

The club was crowded when he arrived. "How's it been tonight, Chris?" he asked his man at the door.

"Busy, boss. Val's been looking for you."

Matthew nodded and headed into the main room. A good crowd circled the hazard table and plenty more were bellied up to the bar. Ben caught his eye. Matthew crossed to where Ben stood next to a table of men playing loo. When he was next to him, Ben tilted his head fractionally toward the far side of the table where Lord Gerling played, his pile of chips large and his smile wide.

Matthew watched the play for several hands. Then he saw it—Gerling's gaze slid to the man across from him, who tapped three times with his middle finger at the edge of the table. Gerling flipped one of his mother-of-pearl chips over and under the knuckles of his left hand. But it was the flick of the lace cuff on his right sleeve that caught Matthew's attention. Gerling fumbled the chip, and suddenly, a card slid into his set. He placed down a black king, giving him the winning trick.

"Evening, lads." Matthew approached the table with a smile. Laying a firm grip on Gerling's shoulder, he squeezed hard. "You're done, my lord. I need you to come and chat with me. Now."

The man's partner shot to his feet and scurried away. Matthew tipped his head to Ben, who strode after him, easily catching him by the collar of his jacket. "Fresh deck, John," he said to the dealer. Then he grasped Lord Gerling's arm and hauled him up. "We can make a scene, if you like."

"No, no." Gerling smiled and held his hands up. "I will come." Then the man had the gall to reach for his winnings.

Matthew growled low and gave him a small shove, directing him away from the table and toward a door to the back rooms. Once they were down at the end of the corridor, he pushed Gerling up against the wall and pinned him with a forearm to his throat. "Haven't you heard the phrase, 'cheaters never prosper'?"

Gerling's eyes began to water. "I-I wasn't cheating."

"Really?" Matthew grasped the man's right arm and shoved his sleeve upward, revealing a small band around his wrist, which held two more aces. He threw them to the floor in disgust.

Ben appeared through the door with the man who'd tried to run. Holding him by his scruff with one of his giant hands, he gave the man a little shake. "Name."

"Holbrook, B-Bob Holbrook," the man stuttered.

Matthew slammed Gerling's hand against the wall next to his head. "Now, normally, I take a finger off for cheating."

A sob came from Holbrook, and Gerling tried to speak but couldn't draw a breath.

"But tonight, I am in a good mood, and I don't feel like getting blood on my clothes. So, instead, you two are going to get gone. And you are banned for life. Don't even think of showing your faces in my part of town again."

He let off the pressure on Gerling's throat. The man slumped forward as he gulped in air. They pulled both men to the exit door and pushed them out into the alley. Back inside, Ben turned to him and chuckled. "Have you ever taken off someone's finger?"

"No, but they don't know that." Matthew straightened his sleeves.

"Been missing this evening. Is the newspaper lady the reason for your good mood?"

"Yes, well, the night has had its ups and downs. Do me a favor and tell Val to put those two on the banned list. I am going to go upstairs and have a drink. Come get me if you need anything down here."

"Sure, boss."

Matthew climbed the back stairs to his wing. At the doors, he nodded to Frank, who leaned against the wall. "Stella go to bed?"

Frank nodded. "She came through here about an hour ago. Seaton is in your study."

Seaton was back? "Thanks, Frank."

He made his way down the hall to the study. Inside, Seaton sat across the table from Stella, playing cards. They both looked up when he came through the door.

"Matthew, where have you been?" Stella asked.

"Out." He walked over and kissed the top of her head. "What are you doing still up?"

"Keep Rhys company since you were missing. He is teaching me how to catch when someone is cheating at cards."

He turned to raise an eyebrow at his friend. "Is he?"

Seaton shrugged and petted the kitten in his lap. "It's good to know when someone is trying to fleece you."

He couldn't disagree with that. "Hmm, we could have used you down on the floor tonight. I had to kick Gerling and his friend out for hiding cards. Fucking toffs think they are so smart."

"Who caught it?" Seaton asked.

"Ben. He has a nose like a bloodhound for this type of thing. Can always sniff out a sharp."

Stella tried to hide an enormous yawn behind her hand.

"Time for bed?" he urged gently. They all kept night hours, but there was no need for Stella to stay up once the show was done. She should get some sleep.

Stella nodded. "Yes, I think I will." She rose and accepted her kitten from Seaton.

"Thanks for keeping me company, lil sis." Rhys flashed her a rare smile.

Stella came over and gave Matthew a hug. He still wasn't used to her spontaneous shows of affection. Not that he was complaining. He exchanged a look with Rhys over her shoulder as he patted her back. "Good night, Stella."

After she and her kitten had gone, Matthew crossed to his desk and poured himself a whiskey from the crystal decanter that sat on one corner. He didn't bother to offer Rhys any; his friend never drank alcohol. Then he took his sister's seat across the table from his friend.

"Glad to see you back." He didn't ask what kind of job Seaton had been doing and Rhys didn't offer.

Rhys nodded. "Just got back into town this evening. Ben said you'd been to Mayfair to break into some fancy hat shop."

"Yeah." He filled Seaton in on how he'd gone to confront Rutledge, but instead ended up in an alley saving a young woman from being murdered. How Miss Harper had found the top hat and how they had decided that the killer was probably a toff. Matthew took a sip of his drink. "It's Jonas. The ledger in the hat shop says it was his hat in that alley. He certainly fits the bill as a killer."

"Unless his valet is borrowing his accessories and killing young women," Seaton said with a wry grin. "What are you going to do about it?"

"Nothing. He is not my responsibility." He took another gulp to help swallow his lie. Damn it, he didn't want anything to do with Jonas. "He is a fucking viscount. Above the law."

"The law?" Rhys snorted.

"Getting into it with Rutledge is one thing, but killing my brother, who happens to be a peer? I'm not that foolish. I have to think about Stella now."

"Yeah, and he's a threat to her too."

Matthew just shook his head. He stared down into the amber liquid in his glass. He thought about Mary Beth and the other girls that Jonas had most likely killed. He'd vowed to find out who the culprit was, but he had never imagined it would be his brother. It wasn't a lie that it made stopping Jonas more difficult. Money and the title made for a safe cocoon around men like him.

"I almost had him in my hands last summer," Rhys said. "I underestimated how clever he was. He gave me the slip on the waterfront. I am almost certain he set up the explosion that killed your father."

Matthew raised his head with a start. "You were there? Did my father really kidnap Hartwick's duchess?"

"Yes. She was the one who saw your brother set up the powder keg below deck. Jonas told her not to worry, as it wasn't meant for her. I gave him chase through the boats that night, but he got away."

"Elizabeth told me some of it. She told me about the duel that led to her fiancé's death."

"Ah, so you were with her tonight."

Matthew ran a hand down his face and slumped back into his seat. "Yes."

"Don't you think sleeping with her is rather complicated?"

"Pardon?" Matthew straightened.

Rhys sent him an arched look. "You smell like sex."

Fuck. But he smiled despite himself. Spending the evening in bed with Lizzie had been worth it. "Fuck, yes, it is complicated. But she is worth it. Everything about her is complicated, from her past to the son she is raising on her own. She is prickly and sharp-tongued and smart as hell. She invited me to her bed. You can't seduce a woman like that. She chooses you."

"Are you going to tell her who you really are?"

"I have told her who I really am. I am Matthew Reeves. I took my uncle's name for a reason. I haven't been Matthew Perrin for almost twenty years. They didn't want me, and I don't want anything to do with them."

Rhys nodded, but his eyes slid to look past Matthew, his expression pensive. Damn, how could a man who said so little convey his worry so starkly? Rhys was pondering the possibilities and working out what things would become trouble. Matthew knew his friend too well. "Fine, I will think on what to do about Jonas. My father should have fucking had him committed years ago." He stood, too restless to sit still anymore. He would go back downstairs. Go see what Val had needed earlier.

"And Elizabeth Harper?"

"I'm going to keep her." The possessive thought slipped out unbidden. Seaton's eyebrows rose. Matthew felt a flush creep up his neck. Shit, what was wrong with him? "I mean, that's up to her. But I will surely fight like hell to stay in her bed." He jerked his head toward the door. And Rhys stood and followed him out of the room. "I've invited her to come see the show tomorrow evening. I know she'll want to talk about what to do about Jonas. She'll want him punished. Perhaps she will have an idea of how to corner him."

CHAPTER EIGHTEEN

E LIZABETH LET HERSELF through the back door of 151 Charlotte Street, her friend's dress shop. "Lorelei?" she called out. It was early, not yet eight in the morning, but she knew Lorelei would have a pot brewing as she got her shop ready to open for the day. And this morning, Elizabeth dearly needed a friend and a hot cup of tea.

"Elizabeth?" Lorelei came through the curtained doorway from the front of the shop. "What a lovely surprise!" Her friend's black hair was uncovered and wound down over one shoulder in a long braid. Lorelei was one of the most beautiful women Elizabeth knew in real life. Her petite, curvy figure was modestly shown off in a perfectly tailored dress of sumptuous green silk. Lorelei always wore her own creations. She said it was the best advertisement of her skills.

"I've brought back the red dress you lent me." Elizabeth held up a bag she had slung over her shoulder.

"Thank you. Come in, come in. Do you want a cuppa?"

"Most definitely." She set the bag down on a nearby table and followed Lorelei to a pair of stuffed chairs in the corner. She sank onto one and accepted the mug of tea her friend passed to her. The steam that rose was fragrant with notes of bergamot and lemon. "Thank you."

Lorelei sat and stared at her over the top of her mug. She straightened. "You had sex."

Elizabeth boggled her tea and almost spilled the whole thing. "What? Why would you say that?"

Her friend narrowed her eyes. "Are you denying it? You can't fool me. You know I have the sight."

"No, I'm not denying it." She took a sip. "Damn you and your intuition."

"It's not my fault I can read people so well. And it's been so long for you. Your whole aura is different today."

Elizabeth rolled her eyes. "I don't appreciate that being pointed out, but yes, it has been a long time. By choice. You know I don't need men complicating my life."

Lorelei waved her hand around dismissively. "Who is it you have allowed into your bed?"

"Matthew Reeves, the owner of the Blue Angel."

"It was the dress! I knew it would look gorgeous on you." Lorelei set her mug down and clapped her hands together. She leaned forward. "But what is this frown all about? Wasn't it enjoyable?"

"All too enjoyable. Amazing, in fact." She sighed. "What am I doing? This feels so risky. I don't like to take risks. But he is so…" What was it about Matthew? Certainly, he was darkly handsome, and his self-possession was attractive. Was it the way his eyes twinkled with mischief? Or the way he had challenged her with his teasing that made her want to kiss him just to see what he tasted like?

Lorelei raised an eyebrow, waiting for her to finish her thought.

"He is so intriguing. I have been drawn to him from the first moment I saw him."

Her friend sat back with her tea mug in hand. "I think you should take the risk and see him again. We both know that life can be unpredictable at best and heartbreaking at worst. Even more reason to hold on to good things when they present themselves."

She and Lorelei had first bonded over a shared understanding of grief. Lorelei had lost her husband in a terrible carriage accident after only two years of marriage. Then her father died from heart failure a year later. Luckily, her mother's family supported her after the tragedies and helped fund her dream of turning her father's tailoring shop into a dress shop featuring her own elegant designs.

"You are right. Last night was enjoyable, and there is nothing wrong with having a liaison. I am a grown woman." But with a son to care for, which made taking risks less appealing. She had to think about Robert first and foremost.

But last night, when she had walked in and saw Robert and Matthew playing with the soldiers on the rug, the simple scene had made her well-guarded heart yearn. Is that what she wanted? Did they need someone to complete their little family? No, she and Robert were doing just fine. And Matthew Reeves was hardly a family man. He ran a gaming hell, for goodness' sake. She met her friend's searching gaze. "I will just keep it simple. Enjoy my affair with a handsome man and try not to think too hard and make it more complicated than it needs to be."

Lorelei nodded her approval.

"He has invited me to come see the show at his club tonight. Do you, by any chance, have something in my size that I could wear?"

"I have just the thing!" Lorelei rose to her feet. "How do you feel about warm apricot?"

IT TURNED OUT that the apricot-colored dress was actually a gorgeous iridescent silk confection. Elizabeth smoothed her gloved hands down the shimmering overskirt that had a multitude of tiny orange rosettes sewn throughout. Then she took a deep breath and started up the front stairs of the Blue Angel.

The front door opened, and a man with sandy-brown hair and a neatly trimmed mustache greeted her. "Good evening, Miss Harper. You are right on time," he said with a grin of approval. "Right this way."

"Good evening, Mr. ...?" she asked.

"I am Rob Morrow, the Angel's floor manager. Mr. Reeves is expecting you and asked me to keep an eye out while he makes his rounds to speak with guests."

With guests? "You make it sound as though he is throwing a fancy garden party."

Mr. Morrow smiled. "Hardly. But he does make sure to

make nice with all the high stakes players." He leaned down to speak more softly next to her ear. "It's his least favorite part of running the place. Makes him grumpy to play nice. So, I'm glad you are here to brighten his mood."

She chuckled. "That sounds about right. My last visit here was a whirlwind and ended in tragedy. I hope tonight I can have a chance to observe everything that goes on."

"I must insist on your discretion." Mr. Morrow's expression turned serious. "Mr. Reeves assured me you were here strictly as a social call."

She gave the floor manager a reassuring smile. "I am simply a guest of Mr. Reeves. I never write about my personal adventures." Elizabeth made a small cross over her heart.

The man's shoulders relaxed. His smile returned. "Let's go find him then, shall we?"

They walked into the first room, the one with the large oval hazard table. There were plenty of people in the hell this evening, but she had no trouble finding Matthew. He stood a head taller than most. His messy curls were hard to miss in a sea of hats. As though he could sense her perusal, he turned, and their gazes collided. He said something to the man next to him and then strode across the room toward her. His eyes roamed the length of her with heat flashing in their mahogany depths. A syrupy warmth spread through her as he approached. She stepped forward as if pulled to him by an invisible cord.

Matthew came to a stop in front of her and reached for her hands. He lifted them and kissed her satin-covered fingers, first on one hand, then the other. "I'm so happy you're here. You look beautiful."

"Thank you for inviting me." She stared up at him. The noise and people around them disappeared. All she could think about was the way he'd looked last night. His bare skin burnished by candlelight and all that powerful muscle climbing over her, on top of her. She bit down on her bottom lip and Matthew gripped her hands tighter.

"Rob, we are going to have supper in my private room before the show tonight. Don't bother me unless someone is dead." He placed his hand at her waist and guided her through the room toward the back hallway.

Elizabeth scrunched her nose. "Really? Did you just say that after what happened last time?"

He shrugged. "Bad choice of words, but I mean it. Nobody will bother us this time." When they had made it through the maze of corridors, past all the private party rooms, he opened the door to his private room and ushered her inside. The snick of the lock followed, and then she was in his arms.

Elizabeth laughed as he buried his face in her neck, trailing kisses up to her jaw.

"I missed you. I was a fool to ever leave your bed." He cupped her jaw and kissed her.

Sinking against him, she kissed him back. The simple press of lips soon became messy, with open-mouthed kisses and tongues tangling as both of them succumbed to the flare of desire between them. Lord, this man was the fire. She gripped his shoulders and let herself be consumed. When she was in his arms, everything else disappeared. Within the iron clasp of his arms, she could only feel. The hot stroke of his lips, the slick caress of his tongue, the hard pressure of his cock against her belly. Her core grew damp in response, yearning for the frantic press of their bodies like last night.

Mathew picked her up off her feet and walked across the room. The solid surface of the billiards table pressed into the back of her thighs as he set her down on top. She slid her hands into his hair, gripping his head to keep his mouth on hers. His hands roamed down her back and back up, coming around to cup her breasts, his thumb trailing over the silk, causing her nipple to pebble under his touch.

She giggled at his low groan. "There was no room for a corset under this gown. It fit so nicely and was such a pretty color I decided to wear it anyway."

"Are you telling me you are not wearing anything under this gown?" The husky scratch of his voice sent heat curling down her spine.

"Just my stockings." Elizabeth leaned back onto her hands to give him better access as his tongue dipped below the silk to trace a wet path across one breast. He roughly pushed one of the puffed sleeves off her shoulder and she moaned as his tongue laved at her nipple that he was able to free. He tugged roughly at the neckline, searching for further access.

"Matthew, don't tear this dress. It's only on loan."

"I'll pay for any damage." His comment was muffled as

he pulled her nipple into his mouth.

She grasped his hair and pulled his head back so he was forced to look at her. "And what about attending the show? Shall I go with a torn dress?"

Matthew's lips tipped in a wicked smile. "You're right." He gently pushed her sleeve back up onto her shoulder. "I promise not to ruin your dress. It's beautiful." Then he slid to his knees and slipped his hands under the hem of her skirt, caressing her calves. "And so are you. All I could think about today was your soft skin, your lush curves, the soft moans you gifted me as you rubbed your pussy up and down my cock."

"I couldn't stop thinking about last night as well," she admitted. "About the hot trail of your tongue across my body, your strong hands touching and teasing, the delicious weight of you on top of me as your cock pushed inside of me."

His eyes closed with another groan. When they snapped back open, his expression was feral. He pushed her skirts up over her knees. "There was one place I didn't get to taste last night."

He kissed the inside of one thigh above the ribbon of her stocking, searing the skin with his warm lips. His tongue traced a wet path slowly up to the juncture of her legs. "Pull those skirts up higher, luv. Let me see your pussy."

She scrambled to grasp her skirts and keep herself propped up on her elbows. The soft scrape of his beard grazed the sensitive skin of her thighs, making her quiver in anticipation. Then his hot breath ghosted across her sex. His eyes flicked up to her face, and the dark pools of desire in them had her sex clenching. But if she thought he would go slow, torture her, she was so wrong. Matthew buried his nose in curls. His tongue flicked out, and she moaned at the delicious sensation of having his mouth on her. Then he proceeded to devour her, licking and sucking until she was writhing on the table.

"Matthew!" she sobbed out as her sex pulsed.

His hands spread her thighs, and he pulled back to blow air over her wetness. Her head popped; she glared at him. "What do you think you are doing?"

"Just enjoying the view of your soaking wet pussy." He had such a filthy mouth. His beard was covered with evidence of just how wet she'd made him, and his grin was wide and mischievous. He knew exactly how to drive her wild.

"You are a naughty tease." She hooked one leg around the back of his neck and pulled his head back to where she wanted it, where she needed him. "Get back here."

He let her grip his hair and guide his mouth back to her sex. The first swipe of his tongue almost had her coming at the relief of having his hot mouth on her again. And when he slid two fingers inside her, she moaned and bucked her hips.

"Yes, I know what you need, luv," he murmured against her.

His fingers twisted and thrust as he ate her with fervor, as though she were his last meal. Her orgasm crashed through her, and she threw her head back as she came apart against his talented tongue.

Elizabeth lay staring at the ceiling as she came down from her crisis. How did he know just how to unlock her? Matthew kissed the inside of her thighs. His beard tickled now that she was so thoroughly satisfied. He chuckled when she jerked her leg. "Ticklish, luv?"

"Apparently, post orgasm, every touch seems more pronounced." She leaned up and threaded her fingers through his silky hair. "Come here, please."

Matthew rose to his feet and leaned over her, caging her with his arms. She grinned up at him. "You are addictive, Matthew Reeves." She combed his hair back from his forehead. "Perhaps we could continue this liaison? One night was certainly not enough."

In response, Matthew leaned down and kissed her with a filthy, open-mouthed kiss. She could taste herself on his tongue. He smelled like sex and tobacco and his lips slid against hers, firm and demanding. Trapped beneath him, she sighed against his mouth and wrapped her arms around his back. The connection they had was as natural as breathing. How could she have lived so long without being able to kiss this man? Without knowing his touch, his scent?

He lifted his head fractionally. "Yes, one night was certainly not enough." Then he straightened and held out a hand. "Come, let's have something to eat."

Confused, she looked down at the bulge straining against his falls. She trailed her fingers over it. "What about you?"

"As you pointed out, it is no time to get disheveled. There will be time for me to get you messy later, after the show." He gave her a swift, hard kiss. "You will stay after, won't you?"

She nodded, and he helped her off the billiard table. Shaking her skirts out so they fell nicely, she followed him across to a smaller table where two silver cloches covered what she assumed was their supper. Matthew sat and then grabbed her around the waist to settle her onto his lap.

"Matthew!"

"Indulge me." He rolled his hips against her bottom. "Let me torture myself."

She giggled. She wondered how long he would last before he was flipping up her skirts again and sinking into her still wet sex. She clenched her thighs together. To distract herself, she uncovered one of the trays. Underneath was a plate laden with roasted chicken, green beans, and baby potatoes. The aroma of rosemary and thyme wafted up, and her stomach growled. She picked up a green bean and held it in front of his lips.

He opened and took a large bite. Next, she speared a potato and fed him that as well. His eyes stayed on hers as he chewed. Then he reached for a chicken leg, holding it up to her lips. She tore a piece off from it, the juicy meat melting in her mouth. And that's how they continued, feeding each other little bits of food until they were both satisfied.

Elizabeth reached for a linen napkin and wiped her mouth. "That was delicious. Compliments to your cook."

"Thank you." Matthew wiped his mouth off as well. "It should be good, for all the money I pay the man. He is French and very moody, but you can't attract quality clients without excellent food."

"Everything you do here, it's all to keep the clients here and playing. If they have good food and entertainment, they won't leave for other establishments."

He tapped the end of her nose playfully. "Smart lady."

"We are not so different in our approach. It is the same with the paper. The flashy headlines, the gossip pages, it all attracts readers to the paper. And then, hopefully, they stay and read the articles that matter. We try to highlight events and issues that affect the everyman and everywoman in the city. If more people in society would care about the problems of their neighbors, then maybe we could all work together to solve them."

"I admire your passion. Mine is simply to make money."

She shrugged. "Well, I also have to sell papers. No newspaper can survive without circulation numbers. For years, I tried to convince my father to add the gossip pages to attract more customers. But he was stubborn, stuck in his opinions about what was newsworthy. When he died, it was the first thing I implemented, and I have sold triple the number of papers. Last year, I bought a new printing press to accommodate our growth." She was proud of how she had grown the paper.

"That must have cost a pretty penny."

She grimaced. "I'll be paying off the loan for at least the

next five years."

A knock sounded at the door. She jumped off Matthew's lap. "Lord, I hope no one is dead."

The doorknob rattled. "Matthew, can I come in?" a woman's voice called out.

Matthew sighed and stood as well. He adjusted himself and buttoned his jacket, hiding the erection straining against his trousers. He sighed. "That will be my sister."

She smoothed a hand over her hair. "Am I a mess?" she whispered.

He straightened the sleeves of her dress and then walked around her, inspecting. "Don't worry. You look beautiful," he said next to her ear. Then he tugged and retied the bow of her sash.

Elizabeth sucked in a calming breath as he walked over to unlock the door to let his sister in. A young woman, the spitting image of Matthew, bounced into the room. Her dark hair was swept up into an intricate crown of ringlets. A tiny blue tiara nestled into the front of her topknot. She wore a frothy dress of blue tulle that ended mid-calf. The skirts swirled as she entered.

"Ben said you had a guest, and I just knew it had to be you." The girl bounded over with a wide smile, showing off even, pearly white teeth. "You are Miss Harper, the editor of the *Piccadilly Press*, correct?"

"Yes, it's nice to meet you," she replied automatically.

Matthew shut the door. "This is my sister, Stella Reeves."

"It's so nice to meet you," Stella said. "I admired your

article on the murders that have happened. Unlike some people"—she turned to glare at Matthew—"I understood that you were trying to shine a spotlight on their deaths when no one else cared about them."

"Exactly." Elizabeth was surprised at this young woman's understanding of the issue.

Stella walked over to the table, snagged a potato, and popped it into her mouth. It didn't stop her from talking around it. "So, what else have you two figured out about the murderer?"

"Please excuse my sister's total lack of manners. For goodness' sake, sit, Stella, if you are hungry."

Stella shook her head. "I shouldn't eat with my costume on. Mrs. Langley would kill me if she knew. I am just being nosy because Matthew doesn't tell me anything."

So, it was a costume for the show. Elizabeth smiled at his sister. Her personality was as sparkly as the glass beads sewn onto her dress. "Well, we found a silk hat laying at the scene of the latest attack. Which is a very strange place to find such a nice top hat. Matthew went to the shop where the hat came from and found out that it was purchased by Lord Griffen. Now, we must figure out how to trap such a powerful man before he attacks anyone else."

Stella's face went ashen. Her eyes widened and slid to the left to stare at her brother.

Oh dear, perhaps she'd frightened the girl.

Matthew's jaw tightened. He nodded.

Stella placed a hand to her chest.

"Don't worry, you are safe here," his deep voice reassured her.

Elizabeth looked back and forth between the two. They seemed to converse without speaking. Then Stella exhaled a long breath.

Elizabeth went over to her and grasped her hand. "I am sorry if I frightened you with talk of murder."

Stella gave a small smile, half the vivacity of her bright enthusiasm when she'd first walked in. "If you will excuse me, I have to finish getting ready for the performance."

"Of course. I am looking forward to watching tonight."

Stella crossed the room and grabbed Matthew's hand on her way. "A word, brother." She all but dragged him from the room, pulling the door mostly closed behind them.

Elizabeth tilted her head. How strange. What was the silent discourse between them all about? She crept forward to stand next to the gap that was left open.

"What are you going to do to stop him?" Stella's voice was low, but the strain in her tone was obvious.

"I don't know yet," Matthew replied.

"You aren't going to kill him, are you?"

"No, of course not. I don't care to get hanged for murder, thank you."

"What about Seaton?"

"Why do you think he would kill him?" Then Matthew sighed. "No, he offered, but I told him no."

"Good. I want him to be stopped, but he is still our brother."

Brother?! Elizabeth gasped. Both Stella and Matthew swiveled to stare at her. She shoved the door all the way open. Shock raced through her, and she started to shake. No, it didn't make sense. Matthew grew up on the streets. He owned a gaming hell, and his sister was an actress on the stage. "Viscount Griffen is your brother?"

Stella nodded. "Yes, he is our older brother."

"Stella," Matthew hissed.

"What?"

"You can't just tell anyone who you are. Especially not a newspaper reporter."

His comment felt like a slap in the face. Anger swelled up to replace her initial shock. "Bloody hell, Matthew! After all that I shared with you last night about my past, you were just going to keep to yourself the fact that you are the son of the man who ruined my life? To a man who got away with murder? I trusted you!"

Matthew ran his hand through his hair and then sighed again. "I can explain. But not out here. There are reasons I could not tell you."

"Like what? That I am a reporter?" she spit out. His lies hurt. His distrust hurt. Pain seared through her chest. She'd given herself over to a man who she didn't even know. Oh God, he was a Perrin. Part of a despicable family of entitled murderers. What had she done? Allowed herself to be pulled in by falsehoods and false charm.

"Partially," he said. He held out a hand. "Let me explain."

"No." Taking a step back, she glanced down the hallway. She needed to get out of here. Slapping away his hand, she rushed down the corridor. At the corner, she blindly turned left. Then, at the end of a long carpet runner, she pulled open a door, and to her relief, she emerged into the large gaming room. Taking a shaky breath, she pushed forward through the crowd of people, which seemed to have multiplied twofold since she arrived. Frantically, she looked around for the exit to the front hall.

A hand gripped her elbow. "This way," a gravelly voice instructed. Mr. Seaton guided her through the throng of gamblers and opened a large door to escort her out to the front hall.

"I have to leave." Her voice came out shaky, and she breathed in to steady her racing emotions. "I want to go home."

"Stay here. I will get your wrap." He was only gone a matter of minutes before returning with the silk wrap. "I will take you home."

"You don't hav—" She had arrived in Matthew's carriage. "Thank you."

As they walked to the front door, Seaton looked back over his shoulder and Elizabeth followed his gaze. Matthew stood on the balcony that overlooked the hall. His hands gripped the railing. The anguish on his face caused her to stumble. Should she have stayed and listened to his explanation? No, he was a Perrin. How could she trust anything he said? She cut her eyes away. "Take me home, please."

Seaton nodded. They walked out into the balmy night air. He guided her to the right and down to the corner. The night air was cool, compared to the heat of the crowded club, and Elizabeth gulped in long breaths as she tried to calm herself. Seaton easily kept pace with her angry strides. At the corner, he gripped her elbow when she would have blindly stepped into the street.

"This way." They went right again. In just a few moments, they stood outside the mews. "I will go in and get the barouche. Stay here."

Elizabeth blinked at his commanding tone, but she nodded, and he walked into the stable.

What was Matthew doing running a gaming hell if he was an aristocrat? Why did he use a fake name? Why was Stella not supposed to say who she really was? How could he have not told her who he really was last night? Instead, he let her take him upstairs and… Lord, the things they did. The way he made her body reawaken. She covered her face with her hands. How could she have been so stupid to be fooled by a Perrin?

The *clip-clop* of horse's hooves made her raise her head. Matthew's curricle pulled to a stop in front of her. Seaton stretched a hand down. "Come on, Elizabeth."

She automatically put her hand in his and let him help her settle into the carriage. The back hood was raised, and she was happy for the privacy it provided. Sighing, she leaned back against the squabs. Seaton flicked the reins, and they moved through the streets in silence for a while.

Then Seaton spoke. "I assume he told you about his family connection?"

"He didn't tell me," she said bitterly. "I overheard him and Stella discussing their...brother." She twisted to face him. "Do you know?"

He nodded. "Reeves and I have been friends a long time. There isn't much we don't know about each other."

She examined Mr. Seaton's profile. Physically, the two friends were opposites. In contrast to Matthew's dark messy curls, Seaton's blond hair was always neatly trimmed short. He was clean-shaven; she had never seen him otherwise, and the scar that ran down his cheek gleamed white in the moonlight. "You have been friends since you were in the same gang, right?"

He nodded. "Matthew joined the Newgate boys when he was fifteen."

That didn't make any sense. Why would he be running with a street gang if he was the son of a viscount? "And?"

"And Matthew's past is his to explain. Perhaps you should give him a chance to." Seaton's gaze slid over to her. "Unless you were only interested in a good fuck. Then don't worry about it and simply move on."

She gaped at him; her cheeks flamed hot with embarrassment at his crude words. Glad for the darkness, she pulled her wrap tighter around her and stared straight ahead. She would not be ashamed of having a liaison. The attraction between her and Matthew had burned hot from the very beginning. Maybe Seaton was right. She barely knew Matthew. Their night together had been wonderful, but perhaps she should cut and run. It was dangerous to want someone this much. Why did the prospect of not seeing him anymore make her feel so desperately sad? She had to think about her son. She needed to be careful about who she let into their lives.

CHAPTER NINETEEN

MATTHEW STARED, UNSEEINGLY, at the front door where Seaton had just escorted Lizzie out into the night. God dammit! That couldn't have gone any worse. He gripped the railing tight, his knuckles going white. The look of betrayal on her face had been like a knife to his chest. Why hadn't he just told her last night? Hell, she had been a thorn in his side about these murders for weeks. He didn't owe her anything, certainly not his secrets. He had reasons to keep his identity hidden, but if he was honest with himself, he hadn't expected how spending the night with her would shift something within him. How fucking far his heart would fall.

A hand landed on his arm, giving it a gentle squeeze. "I'm sorry, Matthew. I didn't mean to tell her about Jonas. Why was she so upset?"

"It's a long story." He turned to face his sister. "Actually, it has to do in part with you."

Stella tilted her head. "It does?"

"Yes. I will tell you about it in the morning. But now you need to get into the theater room. The show is starting soon."

She nodded. "Matthew, will you go after her? Women always want you to go after them when you fight."

His lips twitched in amusement at her advice. "I think not tonight. I will let her temper cool off. She will have questions; she can't help wanting to know all the answers." It was one of the things he loved about her—the way she must figure out all the angles. "Go on now, or Mrs. Langley will be angry that you are tardy."

Stella gripped his arm again. "Will you be all right?"

"Of course. I'm fine." He patted her hand.

"We will talk in the morning? I won't forget."

He nodded. Her part in the tragic events was blameless, but she deserved to know what their father had done. She needed to understand how important it was to keep her identity a secret. He turned back to the railing. Looking down at the full house, he should have felt pleased to see so many patrons. All his plans and hard work were paying off. But the scene blurred, the sounds of conversation fading as his thoughts drifted back to Lizzie, as she had been earlier, spread out on top of his billiards table, her skirts bunched up and her sex glistening with arousal. He ran a hand across his mouth. Fuck, she had tasted divine. And the sounds of pleasure that fell from those gorgeous lips had him addicted.

He hadn't been able to concentrate all day, numbers in the ledgers meaningless as he recalled every detail of their night of passion. Their chemistry was incendiary, but afterward, having her in his arms, her leg draped over his thigh and his nose buried in her hair, had felt so good. She was right; she was complicated. He certainly didn't need complicated. And yet, he did need her.

THE NEXT MORNING, he sat across the breakfast table from Stella and gave her the short version of the events that had led to the murder of Lizzie's fiancé.

"That's so sad." She set down her teacup. "I did know that I was betrothed. Father and Mother were endlessly telling me to behave, to watch my manners, because one day I was to be a duchess." She slumped back into her seat. "I was not happy about any of it. I hated my lessons and the way they treated me like some doll. Pretty, but empty-headed. I wanted no part of being married to some damn duke."

Matthew chuckled. Her language was definitely being influenced for the worse. "Well, you are free to marry whomever you want now. I won't let Jonas sell you off to some stuffy aristocrat."

Stella sighed. "I can't believe Father would kill his best friend like that."

"Me either. But I do know he was capable of cruelty," he said bitterly. "He simply got rid of me when I was ten. Protecting his precious heir was far more important."

Stella pursed her lips together, and her eyebrows lowered in confusion. "Is that really what you think?"

"It's what I know." He stabbed a piece of bacon with his

fork and stuffed it into his mouth.

"Matthew, did it ever occur to you that they sent you to Uncle Harry because they were trying to protect you from Jonas? Mother always told me that if anything happened to her and I was afraid for my safety, I should come find you at Uncle Harry's. That I would be safe there."

The piece of bacon he had been chewing suddenly got stuck as he tried to swallow. He reached for his coffee and took a gulp. This alternate truth tilted his world on its axis. To keep him safe? But they never visited, never interacted at all with him after he was sent to Harry. Well, his mother had written to him on his birthday and at Christmas. But increasingly, during those five years he had been with Harry, he had grown more hurt with every passing year at being discarded so easily. And each year, angrier.

But now, being faced with another possibility, perhaps he could see that they had, in their misguided way, wanted to protect him from further harm. Still, they had chosen to keep and coddle his disturbed brother. His father had always thought he could control Jonas's impulses, to fix him. He sighed and took a more measured sip of his coffee.

"How did you find me? If Mother told you to go to Uncle Harry?"

Stella reached for a scone. She shrugged. "The actors at the Seven Stars were very nice. The house manager there told me about the Blue Angel."

Frank still ran the backstage at the Seven Stars. He had been far too valuable for the new owners to replace when the theater was sold after Harry's death. Now, the Seven Stars was under new management once again. This time, it was purchased by a man who already owned two other theaters in London. Declan Howell appeared to be building an empire. Not that Matthew begrudged him the success. Declan had been Uncle Harry's star actor back when Matthew first came to London almost twenty years ago. His public persona had been brash and intimidating, but in reality, he had been kind and tolerant of a kid who had been largely at loose ends around the theater.

Matthew attempted to change the topic. "Wednesday afternoon should be fun. I'm interested to see what improvements Mr. Howell has made to the old place."

Stella wouldn't be deterred. She eyed him over the rim of her teacup as she took a sip. "And Miss Harper? When will you go and explain things to her?"

Matthew shifted in his seat. Truth was, he didn't know if he could explain things properly. She already hated his family. He had lain staring at the ceiling in the early hours of the morning, trying to figure out what to say to make her understand that he was not a Perrin. That he had only ever presented her with his true self. This man he'd molded himself into. "I will give it a few days. She has a business to run. I don't want to bother her at work."

"Sounds like an excuse for cowardice to me, brother."

He sent her a glare but couldn't deny the truth in her observation. Instead of replying, he stuffed another piece of bacon into his mouth.

CHAPTER TWENTY

H E WATCHED ELIZABETH Harper emerge from the
print shop in Bloomsbury. She had also stopped in on
Monday this week. It had been a pleasant surprise to find out
that she was the editor of the newspaper that extolled his
exploits. Almost made him believe in fate. Certainly, her
fascination with his kills was a sign that she was the woman
for him. Now, he watched her adjust her hat as the breeze
bent back the wide brim. She had a lovely face and an even
lovelier body. Soft curves a man could sink into when
swiving.

He had been following her all week. After seeing her at
the Cheltenham party, he thought she would be his next
victim, but the more he observed of her, the more he knew
that he would keep her. She may even make a good wife. He
needed to be married and have an heir. She was obviously
fertile; he had seen her walking with her son in the square on
Sunday morning. And she came from aristocratic stock.

His father's warning echoed in his head. "Never harm a
gently bred lady. They are off limits." But if she belonged to
him, he could treat her however he liked.

He ambled after his target. She always walked at a fast

clip, with long, purposeful strides. He couldn't wait to take her and have her wrap those long legs around him while he pumped his seed into her to make his heir. All that porcelain skin would show his marks beautifully. She would make the best pet. But first he needed to find a good opportunity to compromise her, to have a taste. Then he would convince her she belonged to him.

She was walking home. He could tell by their route. Her house was a neat row home in the middle of the block. The sign outside proclaimed it also her place of business. He kept across the street and puffed on his pipe. The fragrant smoke of his special blend of tobacco always soothed his racing mind. Through the front window, he could see her sitting at her desk. A man who worked for her approached the desk and stood too close. He clenched his fist. She's mine!

The man walked away, and she turned in her chair to embrace the small boy who ran up to her. He grimaced. The boy would have to go. He would be in the way of their new family. He would need her to concentrate on raising his heir. No more newspaper, nothing to steal her time away from him.

CHAPTER TWENTY-ONE

"I'M GLAD TO see the old place looking so good," Matthew said to Declan Howell. "A fresh coat of paint does wonders."

Howell grinned. "It's far more than paint. But this old girl birthed my career, and I am rather fond of her. I couldn't pass up the opportunity to buy her."

Both of them stared up at the newly painted façade of the Seven Stars. The brick exterior had been whitewashed and the trim painted black in a dramatic contrast. A new sign, with the distinctive arch of seven stars, hung over above the massive double doors of the entrance. "Those doors are new," Matthew commented.

"Yes, they were carved in Italy. I had them shipped in. Took months, but I think they make a statement." Howell shoved his hands in his pockets.

"I'd say." Matthew walked up to examine the doors more carefully. Famous scenes from Faust, Hamlet, and many other plays had been carved into panels inlaid into the twelve-foot-tall doors. Matthew ran his fingers over a carving depicting the balcony scene from Romeo and Juliet.

When he turned back around, he froze. Lizzie stood

across the street among a group of men waiting behind a roped-off area. She looked beautiful this afternoon. Her hair was pulled back into her practical knot, and a jaunty facsimile of a men's hat in blue sat pinned at an angle in her hair. She was speaking to the man next to her, but her eyes kept flicking across at where he stood. Fuck. There was no way in hell he could let her slip away. Stella was right; this was no time for cowardice.

Matthew nodded at the group. "What's that about?"

Howell glanced over. "Oh, reporters. My publicity man is supposed to talk with them, but he is not here yet. He's got a spiel about the history of the place, the new show, etc." He waved a hand around airily. "I am in charge of giving the tour to patrons such as you."

Over Howell's shoulder, Matthew saw Stella come around the corner. She barreled toward them at top speed. "I'm here! I'm here. Have you begun yet?" She was breathless, whether from rushing or from excitement, he couldn't tell. She slid to a stop with a laugh. "I'm sorry to be late. Pitter-Patter got into my wardrobe and made a huge mess of my chemises, trying to make a nest for himself. He is such a naughty boy."

Howell's eyebrows shot up.

Matthew sighed. "Declan, let me introduce my sister, Stella Reeves. Stella, you haven't missed anything. This is Declan Howell, the owner of the Seven Stars."

Stella pushed the oversized brim of her bonnet back to look up at Howell with a wide grin. "It's a pleasure to meet you. I am terribly excited to get a tour of your theater."

Howell looked a bit stunned, but he recovered quickly. "A pleasure to meet you, Miss Reeves. We will get started in a few moments. But first, I must know who is 'pitter-patter'?"

"Oh, he is my kitten," Stella replied. "I found him in the rain; hence, the moniker."

Howell nodded, as though that made perfect sense. Matthew chuckled softly. His attention slid back to Lizzie. She had a small notebook out and was jotting down notes with a pencil. The man next to her still chattered, and she glanced up at him occasionally and nodded. Was he bothering her? Then the man reached out to put his arm around her shoulders and peer down at what she was writing. Lizzie pulled away and shut her notebook. Matthew growled. Lizzie's gaze snapped up to stare at him across the street, even though she couldn't have possibly heard him.

"Howell." Matthew turned. "I have a friend who is one of the reporters over there. She is the editor of the *Piccadilly Press*. Do you think we could invite her to join us on the tour, as a favor to me?"

"Certainly." Howell nodded. A carriage rolled to a stop near them. "Go fetch her. I see my other guests have just arrived."

Matthew glanced at Stella, who gave him an encouraging smile. Then he strode across the street.

Lizzie looked startled at his approach. Then she crossed her arms across her chest. "What do you want, Mr. Reeves?"

He gave her a small smile. "I wished to invite you to join us for a tour of the theater with the new owner."

Several of the other reporters around her murmured with surprise. The man next to her spoke up. "Can I come too?"

Matthew shot him a hard look. "No."

Elizabeth stared daggers at him.

He held out a hand. "It's an exclusive opportunity to speak to Mr. Howell."

"Harper, if you don't want to, I will take your place," a man from behind her said.

She glared over her shoulder at the man and then huffed out a breath. She slid her hand into his. Matthew guided her under the rope and tucked her hand into the crook of his arm. She immediately pulled her arm from his. "Why are you here?" she whispered furiously as they walked across the street.

"You're welcome." He couldn't help but chuckle at her prickly reaction. "This theater used to belong to my uncle before he died. I am a patron and was invited to get a private tour. Consider this an olive branch. I would like to speak with you about the other night. There are things to explain."

She shook her head. "I'm not so sure there are. Your family...I can't. I need to think about my son."

Her halting words were hard to hear. But he wasn't surprised by her reluctance. He came from a family tree rotted by greed and madness. Why would she want anything to do with him? He sighed. They stepped up onto the pavement in front of the theater. "May I introduce Miss Harper, the editor of the *Piccadilly Press*. This is Mr. Howell, new owner of the Seven Stars."

"It's a pleasure to meet you," Elizabeth replied.

"And you remember my sister, Stella?"

Elizabeth nodded stiffly.

"It's lovely to see you again, Miss Harper." Stella gave her a warm smile. Bless the girl's sunny disposition.

Howell turned to a couple standing next to him. "Let me introduce Mr. and Mrs. Kensington, two of my most valued patrons. Where is Monty?"

A phaeton rolled up with a dramatic whistle coming from the man at the reins and the horses came to a perfect prancing stop. The man stood and doffed his hat with a flourish. He gave a bow. "Sorry I am late." He hopped down from the tall conveyance with the grace only a young man could pull off.

Howell raised a hand and gestured for one of his people. The employee hurried over to grasp the leads of the pair of horses.

"Glad to see you made it. Everyone, this is Hugh Montague, another patron of the Seven Stars." Howell finished introductions and then, with the dramatic flourish of a true showman, he threw open the great doors and raised his hands in the air. "Welcome to the new Seven Stars Theater!"

Stella clapped her hands enthusiastically. Matthew took her hand and guided her inside. Elizabeth followed along, walking next to the Kensingtons. Matthew couldn't stop from admiring the swing of her hips. She moved with such grace. *What was he doing?* He had all but decided to let it be. To let their love affair be only one glorious night. But the moment he saw her across the street, he had to speak to her, to touch her, to explain things he had never spoken to anyone about. She had gotten under his skin and become his addiction.

Entering inside the Seven Stars, he was struck by nostalgia. Howell really had invested in the project. The seats had all been recovered in a rich burgundy velvet. The carpeting down the center aisles was new as well.

Howell guided them to the stage. "The floor of the stage has been sanded and refurbished. The lighting uses gas. I had a line pulled in from the street."

"I see my money is being well spent. Very impressive, Howell," Mr. Kensington said.

Matthew nodded in agreement. The gas lamps that lined the front edge of the stage would illuminate the actors and sets far better than just the overhead chandeliers. "Harry would have thought it capital."

Howell smiled. "I hope the old man is haunting the place so he can see."

Elizabeth looked back and forth between him and Howell. "Who is Harry?"

"Harry Reeves was the original owner of the Seven Stars," Howell replied. "He gave me my first big break as an actor. This theater launched my career. He passed away fifteen years ago?"

"Fourteen," Matthew corrected. "If the theater has any

ghosts, it would be him. He loved this place. Worked himself to an early grave, some said, but he had a passion for putting on a great production. He was a true showman."

"Well said." Howell slapped him on the shoulder. "Let's go onto the stage and take a peek behind the curtain."

They walked to the side of the stage, and Matthew turned the small brass knob that opened a wall panel, revealing a short staircase that led backstage. Stella scampered ahead up the stairs, but Elizabeth paused next to him. "How did you know that was here? It looked like part of the wall."

"Reeves was raised in this theater. He is one of us." Howell grinned as he passed them to escort his guests to the backstage area.

Elizabeth tilted her head as she stared at him. He knew her mind was buzzing with questions. Her natural curiosity was what made her such an observant reporter. He took perverse pleasure that she wanted to know his story, despite her earlier denial that she wouldn't let him explain his past.

He gestured to the stairs. "After you."

They climbed the stairs and emerged stage left. Howell described how there would be new sets for the new show opening this evening. Matthew walked over to the rope pulley and cranked open the main curtains. Stella stood in the middle of the stage and gasped as the curtains lifted.

"Oh, Mr. Howell, it's magnificent!" She stepped forward and began to sing. It was a ballad from the show at the Blue Angel, her solo. Her voice filled the empty auditorium, the clear soprano rising and falling effortlessly with the melody.

Matthew's chest filled with pride. Stella had an amazing talent, and he was so glad that she had the freedom to enjoy it. Everyone else had gone silent as they all stared at her in wonder. When she finished the last notes, clapping erupted. Stella turned and executed a graceful curtsey. "The acoustics are lovely."

"Your voice is extraordinary, my dear." Howell turned to Matthew. "Where the hell have you been hiding her, Matthew?"

"Stella sings at the Blue Angel. Where I can keep an eye on her." He gave Howell a hard look. "She is only seventeen."

Declan Howell actually flushed red. That was a new one. He cleared his throat. "Yes, well, plenty of singers are younger than that when they get their start."

"Not my sister."

"Of course." Howell turned his winning smile back on. "Come, let me show you the back gallery. The skylights are new." He winged out an arm for Stella. "This way, everyone."

As the others walked away, Matthew grasped Elizabeth's elbow. "Can we speak for a moment?"

She glanced at the others and then back at him before nodding.

"Lizzie, I'm sorry I didn't tell you right away." He shoved a hand through his hair. "I keep my past a secret for good reasons. I am not used to sharing that part of myself with anyone."

Her stare bored into him for a long moment. "I can accept that you have reasons for not telling me."

"I told myself that I would just let you walk out of my life. That it was for the best. But seeing you today, I know that I cannot. The pull between us is undeniable." He wanted to touch her so badly his chest ached with the effort to keep his arms by his side.

"It is the same for me," she said. At that admission, he reached out and grasped her fingers. The connection was fleeting as she took a step back. "But I must be careful about who I allow into my life. I have to protect my son. He is the most important thing to me."

"Then you already understand why I have hidden my parentage. My brother is looking for Stella, and she came to me for safe haven. Keeping her identity a secret is my priority." He watched Elizabeth's brow scrunch. "Ask me your questions. I know you have a slew of them. I promise to answer truthfully."

"How is it that you grew up here, in this theater?"

"When I was ten years old, my parents sent me to live with Uncle Harry, my mother's brother. He was a businessman, and this theater was the love of his life."

"Why would they send you to live with him? It seems as though the Viscount would disapprove of theater people raising his son."

Matthew stuck his hands into his pockets and rocked back onto his heels. "I don't know their reasons. It is a complicated tale that is perhaps for another time and a more private space."

"And how did you end up with the gang? And in the gaming hell business? Why do you use your uncle's name?"

Matthew laughed out loud at her string of questions. Fucking reporters. He smiled. "You are asking for my entire life history, Lizzie."

She frowned. "You said that you would answer my questions honestly."

"Yes, I did. But all of that would take time to tell." He reached again for her hand. Would she allow him to explain? "Perhaps we could have dinner, and I could spill all my secrets to you?"

Her eyes heated, their green depths flashing.

He tugged her closer. His eyes fastened on her ripe berry lips.

But she shook her head. "I don't think that is a good idea. I don't seem to have any self-control when it comes to you."

"You should never tell your opponent your weakness," he murmured next to her ear. He licked the spot right underneath her ear and reveled in the soft sigh that escaped her lips.

"Are we opponents?"

"Hell, no. I certainly don't want to be."

Elizabeth stepped back, her expression serious. "I admit that I am curious. I would like to hear your story. Perhaps, we could take a walk after this tour? Big Ben told me you like to walk everywhere."

He nodded. "It's left over from when I couldn't afford conveyance, not even a horse. I ran the streets as an adolescent, and I suppose that it seems natural to walk where I need to go."

"I feel the same. I don't need or have the extra money to have a horse or carriage at my disposal. My feet work just fine." A grin spread across her face, and he couldn't resist pressing a brief kiss on her lips.

Before she could sputter about him taking liberties, he pulled her across the stage. "Let's finish the tour. I'm sure you have a million questions for Mr. Howell as well."

CHAPTER TWENTY-TWO

WHAT WAS SHE doing walking along through Covent Garden at night beside the one man she had firmly decided not to ever see again? Matthew slipped his hand into hers and squeezed gently. Elizabeth sighed. Why was she so weak of conviction in his presence? His strong grip felt right in hers, and she didn't pull away.

After the tour of the Seven Stars, Mr. Howell had invited all of them to dine. It had been an entertaining evening full of laughter and tall tales from the theater's history. At least, she assumed they were exaggerations. Certainly, some of the debauchery couldn't actually be true. Everyone else had stayed to watch the opening show. But she needed to get home. She wanted to be able to tuck Robert into bed. "Don't you need to be at the club?"

"Yes, but it is early yet, and I have excellent staff."

They walked east for a while before he pointed to a narrow house with peeling paint and crooked shutters.

"That is where I lived for a number of years with Seaton and a few other boys from the Newgate gang. Four of us shared a one-room flat on the top floor, but it was still better than the prospect of being sent home after Harry died."

They paused and looked up at the building. "When I was ten, I woke from a deep sleep where I dreamt that I was drowning, gasping for breath underwater. In reality, my brother was sitting on top of me with a garrote at my neck, trying to choke the life from me. Stella, barely a year old, began crying from the crib in the corner. Nanny came in and was able to intervene and pull Jonas off of me."

"Dear God," she murmured.

"Luckily for me, this was Jonas's first attempt at killing a person, and he didn't understand the force it would take. The thin wire cut me as he was pulled off of me." He lifted a finger and drew a line across his throat under his chin. "I still have a scar here."

He began to walk again, and she followed along. The street lamps flickered in the gathering darkness. She didn't feel frightened; Matthew would not let any harm come to her.

"I remember sitting next to my mother as she petted my head and soothed my sobs. My father angrily paced the length of the carpet in his study. It was my mother's suggestion to send me to Harry. I have recently begun to understand that they were trying to keep me from further harm, but all I could feel afterward was confusion about why I had been sent away. The confusion morphed into anger. Why had my father chosen to keep my brother close, but so easily discard me?"

He sighed. "I was angry for a long time. And after Harry passed, I found a new family belonging to the gang. Seaton and I became close as brothers. His mother was a prostitute, and he was often set loose in the city as a boy when she entertained clients. He and I had similar goals—to save enough quid to open our own place one day. To have enough money that we didn't have to answer to anyone. And that is the sad tale of young Matthew, who took his uncle's surname to keep from being found by his real family. Though I doubt they even cared enough to wonder what happened to me."

Elizabeth stopped and faced him. "For once, I am at a loss for words." She cupped his cheek, watching various emotions race across his expressive features—anger, sadness, resignation. She pressed a soft kiss to his lips. "What a brave boy you were."

Matthew looked off to the left and then, with his hand still in hers, began to walk. "I think the more apt word would be scared. I was terrified by that night when my brother attacked me. The only time I have ever been home since was for my mother's funeral. And even then, I stayed hidden in the trees outside the churchyard. A year ago, when my father was killed in that explosion on his yacht, Stella turned up at my door. She was frightened to be alone with Jonas, and rightly so. He has been discreetly looking for her using a private investigator."

"What do you suppose he wants with her?"

"Who knows? My guess is he sees her as his property and is angry to have lost her. He would have total control over her. Could marry her off to whomever he pleases or keep her locked in the house. I don't care to imagine what goes on in his broken mind. He doesn't know where I am or even if I am alive, so Stella is safe at the Blue Angel with me. She saved my life once, and I will protect her with mine."

It was indeed a sad tale. She understood that Matthew's mother would have wanted to send him somewhere where he would be safe. And that the Viscount would have let his son be raised by a man in the theater business, family or not, said volumes about how he had also feared for his son's safety. But it was certainly telling that Matthew's father had been so worried over how his family would be viewed if it came out that his heir was mentally unstable that he would keep a viper in the bosom of the family. A secret worth killing over; and kidnapping a duchess. Elizabeth would bet anything that Hartwick's father had all the details written in that damn book of secrets.

Elizabeth glanced sideways at Matthew as they walked up Broad Street. This turned everything she thought she knew about him on its head. He hadn't grown up a spoiled, pampered spare to a rotting aristocratic tree. Instead, he'd had to make his own way in life. She admired that. But, nevertheless, he had been a criminal, a street thug. And now he made his success in the ruin of others. Hardly the type of man she wanted around her young son. And yes, she was wildly attracted to him. But the daring, wanton woman she had been a few nights ago was not truly her. She was a businesswoman and a mother, first. She had been foolish to think that she could have a simple affair.

As they approached the square, she tugged him onto the lane that ran behind the houses. "My neighbors are nosy. I would prefer not to arrive at the front door with a strange man."

He nodded.

When they reached her house, the back gate was ajar. "That's strange. We always keep this closed." She hurried into the back garden. "Oh Lord," she gasped. The back door was also open. Matthew swept past her as she stood frozen in place, her mind racing over all the possible reasons why.

"This lock has been forced. The latch is broken."

His comment spurred her into motion. "Robert." She hiked up her skirts and raced past him into the kitchen. It was empty. In the shadows, it looked undisturbed. Her heart beat too fast in her chest as she hurried up the short staircase to the main floor. "Mrs. Todd?" she called out. "Robert?"

Matthew was right behind her. He opened the sitting room door, and they found the fire low and Mrs. Todd's knitting on the arm of one of the chairs. Next, Matthew strode across the small entryway. "The front door is unlocked as well."

She crossed to open the door to her workspace. It was dark, the moonlight spilling over empty desks. Spinning around, she headed up the stairs. "Mrs. Todd! Robert!" she called again.

Each flight of stairs felt endless as fear twisted in her chest. She had to find her son. She called out his name again and again. Matthew kept pace right behind her. When she reached her son's room, she burst inside. "Robert!"

A scrape of a key turning in the lock echoed in the empty room, and the closet door creaked open. Robert barreled out and into her waiting arms. She hugged him against her in relief. Mrs. Todd emerged more slowly from the closet. Her eyes were wide. She laid a hand on her chest. "Thank God, you're home."

"What happened?" Matthew asked.

"There was a man in the house," Robert said.

"'Tis true. I was putting young Robert here to bed. And we heard a large bang from downstairs. Then heavy footsteps walking about. When I heard the footsteps on the stairs, we decided to hide in the closet. So I blew out the candles and locked us inside."

"You absolutely did the right thing, Mrs. Todd," Matthew said. He walked over and lit the lamp with flint from his pocket. The warm glow filled the room and eased the terrible tightness in her throat. She hugged Robert tighter.

"We heard the man—I think there was just one—open and close doors as he walked around. He spent a lot of time on the first floor. But he did come up here briefly."

"We were very quiet, mama. Just like the mice from my book."

Elizabeth ran her hand over his hair. "Good job. You did exactly the right thing." She stood, pulling Robert up into her arms. "Thank you for your clear thinking, Mrs. Todd."

"Well, I don't know about clear thinking. I was scared out of my mind," she replied.

"Come, let's go downstairs, and I will make some tea for everyone," Matthew said. "I want to secure the back door as well."

He led the way downstairs, and when they entered the kitchen, he lit several candles. "You ladies sit down. Robert, come help me. Do you know where the tea is kept?"

Robert scrambled down from her lap. "Yes, sir, in that cabinet over there."

"Go fetch it while I put water in the kettle."

Elizabeth was about to say it was on too high a shelf, but Robert was already dragging a chair over to climb on. She watched him unlock the cabinet and carefully pull out the tin. He handed it to Matthew.

"Good job, Robert. Now, where are the cups?"

She laid her hand on top of Mrs. Todd's hand and gave it a squeeze. "Thank you for keeping my son safe." She swallowed hard and tried to keep the tears that burned in the back of her eyes from falling. The terrible possibilities of what could have happened to Robert and Mrs. Todd flashed in rapid-fire through her mind.

"I always will. The two of you are like family." Mrs. Todd let out a long breath. "I don't understand. Was it a robbery? Did he steal anything?"

"We looked through the rooms so quickly as we searched for you that I am not sure," she replied. "I don't have anything of value. I can't imagine why anyone would pick this house to rob." Then it came to her. "Unless it had to do with the paper. My shingle out front makes it easy to find me. Could it be retribution for something written in the paper?" Had the *Press* put her family at risk?

Matthew came over to set two mugs of tea down in front of them. "We will take a closer look around. But first, let me see if I can fix the door latch." He disappeared out the back door, and she heard the garden gate squeak shut. Then he returned and crouched to look at the latch on the back door. "It's bent, probably from someone kicking it in." He came inside and shut the door. Then he dragged the wooden cabinet that held her dry goods in front of it. "That should keep it secured until we can repair the lock."

Elizabeth turned to Mrs. Todd. "You stay here and settle your nerves. Robert, keep Mrs. Todd company. You may have a biscuit. I am going to go look around."

Matthew nodded. He picked up a lamp, and they went through the main floor. The sitting room was undisturbed. But across in the office space, the desks had been rifled through. Her desk by the window had drawers left open. Her ledgers were out of order on the shelf. Nothing appeared missing. Why would a thief want anything from this room? It was just papers. Perhaps some notes on what would be in the next edition of the paper.

Matthew turned the lock on the front door. "I think he must have left through this door. Which is so strange. What kind of thief would leave through the front door?"

They went up the stairs, and this time, when she entered her room, she actually looked around. Before she had been so frantic to find Robert, she'd entirely missed the mess. Her wardrobe had been rifled through, undergarments hanging out of drawers, and hangers pushed to one side.

"Look at this." Matthew stood over by the bed.

She gasped when she came up next to him. A deep-green silk gown lay on the bed, the sleeves smoothed out to the sides like a dress for a paper doll. Next to it, laid just as carefully, was a chemise, a corset, and a pair of white stockings with matching green ribbons.

Matthew pointed down. A pair of heeled slippers was set neatly by the bed. "He chose an entire outfit from your wardrobe. This was no thief."

"Do you think it's Griffen? How would he know who I am?"

"Fuck if I know. You have written about his exploits several times now. Perhaps he was fucking flattered." He grasped her shoulders and turned her to face him. "You can't stay here. Come stay at the Angel. I will keep you safe."

Her first instinct was to decline. To say she would be fine. Elizabeth glanced at the clothing on the bed. The man, whoever he was, had been in her bedroom. Had touched her things. She shivered. There was no way she would be able to sleep here tonight. Hartwick and Lucy were out of town, and Lorelei's flat would not be big enough to have the three of them stay. She looked up at Matthew, his dark brows lowered in concern. His grip was firm and reassuring. She nodded.

"Good. Let's check the other rooms and make sure he didn't leave any more unpleasant surprises. Then you should pack a bag for the night. We can return tomorrow to get more of your things." He rubbed his hands briskly up and down her arms. "Everything will feel better in the morning light."

Exhaustion, physical and mental, washed over her. She laid her forehead against Matthew's solid chest. He wrapped his arms around her, and she was safe in the circle of his embrace.

CHAPTER TWENTY-THREE

MORNING LIGHT SLANTED across the bed as Elizabeth cracked open her eyes. She blinked, trying to orient herself. The dark wood walls and navy-blue canopy were unfamiliar, but as she turned her head to the side, the familiar sight of her son sprawled next to her on the bed made her smile. Robert always slept on his stomach with his arms and legs akimbo. She reached out and ran her hand over his hair, so glad that he was safe. Racing through the house last night had been some of the most terrifying moments of her life.

What had Griffen been looking for? Had it even been him? What would have happened if he had found where Robert and Mrs. Todd were hiding? All her questions rolled around in her gut, increasing her anxiety. She sat up with a sigh, left the bed, crossed to the window, and pushed open the sash. Warmth skated inside on a light breeze. She pulled her long braid over her shoulder, and after removing the tie, she began to pull apart the plait. Running her fingers through her hair, she finger-combed through the loose waves. This was her favorite time of day. The world quiet, and she could breathe before her day began. The only time of day when her hair could be loose and not tightly wound into her typical chignon.

When they arrived last night, Matthew ushered them in the back door and up the back stairs. A man sat on a stool in front of the doors that led to the wing. He was sent to fetch Ben, who had then proceeded to fuss over them excessively. Ben had cooed over Robert, who had been half asleep on her shoulder, and then ushered her and Mrs. Todd into two bedrooms next door to each other. Mrs. Todd offered to help prepare the beds, but Ben was having none of that. Elizabeth chuckled. Ben had simply flummoxed her house-keeper as she watched him efficiently make the beds. Matthew made sure that Ben had things well in hand and then excused himself to check on things downstairs.

She rooted through the satchel she had quickly packed last night. Pulling out her brush, she worked to untangle her long locks. Matthew had looked so grim. He thought that the intruder had been his brother. She paused the downward stroke of her brush. His brother. She still struggled to reconcile all that he'd told her last evening. He had grown up very differently from what she had expected after learning his true identity. And now, he protected his sister from their brother. Despite her concerns about his family and his profession, she had felt so safe within the circle of his arms.

Elizabeth got dressed and wound her hair into a simple bun. Robert moved around, rubbing his eyes sleepily.

"Good morning, darling." She walked over to the bed.

He sat up, and with his habitual cheerfulness, smiled up

at her. "Good morning, mama. Are we at the Blue Angel?"

"Yes. If you get dressed, we can go find some breakfast."

Robert nodded and scrambled off to go empty his bladder in the chamber pot placed in the corner. "Will we go home today? Is our house safe? Will that man come back, do you think?"

His barrage of questions didn't surprise her. "I think we will stay here for at least a few days. I need to get the back door fixed. Then the house will be safe again. And I will have a good lock added to the back garden gate as well."

Robert came over and wrapped his arms around her leg as he gazed up at her with serious gray eyes. "I'll set up my soldiers to guard the front windows."

"That will be very helpful. Let's get you dressed. I brought a fresh shirt and trousers for you."

She held Robert's hand as they emerged from their room and made their way to the double door at the end of the corridor. The stool outside the door was empty, but there was a maid sweeping the wide main staircase. She looked startled to see them, her gaze bouncing between her and Robert.

"Pardon," Elizabeth said. "Could you direct us to the kitchen?"

"Surely. Down the stairs, then to the right through the big gaming room, at the corridor on the other side, go left, and the third door is the stairs that lead down to the kitchen. Sure you don't want me to fetch Big Ben for you?"

"No, that won't be necessary. We'll find our way." Elizabeth hoped it was true; this club was a maze.

She and Robert found the kitchen without any trouble. Perhaps the layout made more sense than she originally thought. The front of the place housed the main gambling rooms, separated by a grand foyer. Up the stairs was the theater, and to the left was Matthew's private wing. To the right, she assumed, were more bedrooms that perhaps housed the other staff members. Behind the main gaming spaces were two long corridors, one in each direction from the center of the house. These were the private gambling spaces and high-stakes rooms.

Down here in the basement, they passed a warren of storage rooms containing food stores and barrels of wine and beer. Finally, they reached a large kitchen. In direct contrast to the quiet of the main floor, it was a hive of activity.

Scullery maids stood at the sink, scrubbing pots. Two adolescent boys peeled an enormous bucket of potatoes. Big Ben stood with a notebook in hand, next to a short, rotund man with a long mustache. She spotted Mrs. Townsend sitting at a long table in the center of the room and headed over to her. "Good morning."

Ben's head popped up from where he was scribbling into his notebook. "Ms. Harper! Good morning. Can I get you a cuppa?"

"Yes, thank you. That would be lovely."

Ben snapped his notebook shut and strode toward them. "And you, lad? A cup of hot chocolate, perhaps?"

Robert craned his head back, with his mouth hanging

open, to stare up at the massive Ben. He probably only had hazy memories of him from last night.

"Oh no, that's too precious," Elizabeth interjected. "We couldn't possibly."

"Nonsense. Nothing but the best for our guests. Boss's orders." He turned to set a large kettle onto a burner of a massive stove. Matthew certainly had not skimped on the quality when outfitting his kitchen. She sat down next to Mrs. Todd and pulled out a chair for Robert, who scrambled up onto his knees with a wide smile on his face at the prospect of having hot chocolate, which was a treat they only indulged in on Christmas Day.

"He wouldn't allow me to help with anything this morning," muttered Mrs. Todd. "I've never felt so useless in my life."

Elizabeth smiled at her exasperated tone. Mrs. Todd was accustomed to being in charge of things. "Well, I must go to the house this morning before the staff arrives, so I would be grateful if you could entertain Robert." She frowned. "Perhaps for today, stay inside the Angel. I will return as soon as I can. But with tomorrow's edition to prepare for, I will also need to go to the print shop."

"Of course, dear. Robert and I will be fine. You be careful."

"I will."

After they had tea and chocolate, Ben fed them ham and coddled eggs for breakfast. He bustled around the kitchen, whistling off-key. The man he had been speaking with was

Mr. Gregory, Matthew's expensive French chef. The man had greeted them with a charming smile and then left with one of the young men who had been peeling potatoes to go fetch ingredients for the day's menu from the market. Elizabeth checked the watch fob pinned at her waist. It was nine o'clock, and she needed to get going.

"Alright, I must be off." She kissed the top of Robert's head. "You mind Mrs. Todd. I will be back later."

He nodded, his upper lip still covered in hot chocolate. She picked up a napkin and wiped his face. "There, handsome boy. Be good."

Ben followed her to the door. "Maybe you shouldn't go out alone, Miz Harper. The boss wouldn't like it."

"Nonsense. I will be fine. And please call me Elizabeth." She turned before he could argue further. She hurried back up to her room to grab her hat and satchel. Just as she emerged back into the hallway, a door diagonal to hers opened, and Matthew emerged. His hair stuck out at all angles, and he wore pajama pants and a satin banyan in midnight blue. The vee of the robe allowed her a peek at the dark chest hair that covered his smooth olive skin. She swallowed hard as a warm, syrupy desire to put her hands on him spread through her chest.

He blinked and scratched at his beard. "I thought I heard someone out here." His gaze roamed over her from head to toe. "Where are you going?"

Trying to shake off the intimacy of seeing him fresh out of his bed, Elizabeth sucked in a deep breath. "To work. I have a paper to get ready."

"It's too dangerous for you to go out alone."

"Nonsense. No one is going to attack me in broad daylight. I truly appreciate you letting us stay here for a few days. Strangely, I do feel safe here at the club. Mrs. Todd and Robert are downstairs in the kitchen with Ben." She gave in to impulse and stepped closer to him. Her nose filled with his scent, spicy with the tobacco he smoked. "But I have a job to do. I would think you would understand that. Now be a good boy and go back to sleep."

Quick as a cat, he snagged her wrist and tugged her against him. "I can sleep when I am dead." His lips slid across hers in a languid kiss that had her knees turning to jelly. She slid a hand into his hair and held on as the kiss became more desperate. His lean, hard body pressed into her soft curves, setting her on fire. She wrenched her lips from his. Damn it, how did he manage to ignite her blood with just a kiss?

"I have to go. My staff will be waiting at the front door if I don't get back to my house." She couldn't resist running her thumb across his bottom lip. A low growl rumbled in his chest, and she worried that he wasn't going to let go of her, or even if she really wanted him to. But then, he released the grip he had around her waist. She stepped back and hurried down the corridor before he could change his mind and convince her to stay.

Two hours later, Elizabeth concluded her staff meeting. "Let's finish the last pages. Anne, give the advert section a final proofread. I need to take everything over to the print shop by three."

The metallic clang of a hammer sounded from the back of the house. She twisted around with a frown.

"What was that?" Nigel asked from behind her.

Another loud clang rang out. "I don't know. But I will find out. Back to work, all of you."

She strode through the house and, following the banging, down into the kitchen. The back door was open, and the cabinet that had held it closed was shoved to one side. A man crouched in front of the lock, prying it off with a hammer and a metal wedge. Behind him in the garden, she spotted Matthew, his arms crossed over his chest as he watched.

"What is going on?" she asked stupidly.

Matthew raised one eyebrow. "I would think it obvious. We are fixing the broken latch."

"I was going to get someone to fix that." She had planned to look at her budget and see where she could find the money to pay for the repairs. She just hadn't had a chance to sit down yet.

Matthew held out a hand. "Come outside for a moment."

The workman in the doorway stood with the bent latch in his hands. "Mornin', ma'am," he said, as she stepped around him. "I'll have a new one put on in a jiff."

"Thank you." She followed Matthew over to the tree that Robert liked to climb.

"I realize you could have hired someone yourself, but I know Jacob over there, and he could get the job done immediately."

"I will pay you back if you tell me how much he charges."

Matthew waved a hand dismissively. "No need. I've handled it."

"I must insist." He was impossible. "It's my house and my responsibility."

"Truth is, Jacob owes me some quid, so he is happy to do the job for free as a way to settle the debt." He shrugged.

Elizabeth narrowed her eyes to study his nonchalant demeanor. People all over town probably owed him money. She snorted softly. Then she noticed the top of a carriage parked outside the wall in the lane.

Matthew followed her gaze. "Oh, I brought the carriage to help bring more things you might need for the next little bit while you all are staying at the Angel. Have you gone back upstairs?"

His concerned expression left no doubt he meant specifically had she gone back into her bedroom, where the disturbing scene with her clothes was laid out.

"I haven't." She grimaced. Focusing on what needed to be finished for Friday's edition had been easier than thinking about her house being invaded by a stranger. Despite the fact that she didn't need Matthew's help, it was nice to know she, Robert, and Mrs. Todd would be safe at the Blue Angel. She glanced over at the door where the workman was fitting the new latch to the doorframe. It was also nice that she wouldn't have to track down and pay for the repairs. It wasn't so much that she minded having help. It was just that it had been a long time since she'd had anyone offer.

"Would you like me to come up with you?" Matthew asked.

"It wouldn't be proper."

"Since when do I care about proper? Since when do you?" His smirk was a clear challenge.

"Oh, all right. Yes, I would like you to come with me. I have been avoiding it all morning." She turned on her heel and strode back across the small garden, but didn't miss his low chuckle.

Upstairs, in her room, she ripped the dress off the bed. The green gown was old, a relic from her one season in society. A dress that was entirely impractical in her current life and decidedly out of fashion. She grabbed a hanger from the wardrobe and hung it in the back where it belonged. Her burgeoning anger burned away the fear she had felt last night.

"How dare he come into my house and touch my things? Threaten the safety of my child?" She grabbed up the shift and folded it neatly, then rolled the stockings into a neat ball. Finally, she picked up the corset and turned to put the items in the chest of drawers only to find Matthew standing in front of it, folding her undergarments that had been rifled through. She gaped at him.

He held out a hand for the items she had. "What? Have you mistaken me for a fine gentleman all of a sudden? You don't think I know how to fold clothes?"

She passed him the chemise and corset. "You are a man, after all. I don't think my surprise is so unfounded." Then she moved to open the small cabinet door she kept her stockings in. She sent him a glance as he continued to carefully put the things in the drawers back to rights.

"When you don't have a lot, you learn to take care of what you do have."

They made quick work of putting everything away properly. Then she pulled out a few dresses and other things she would need. She paused with indecision. How long would she hide at Matthew's club? A few days? A week? She turned to him, clothing grasped in her hands. "We have to figure out a way to stop him."

Matthew nodded, his dark eyes serious. "We will. And until then, I will keep you safe. I promise."

She sent Matthew to the third-floor closet to fetch a small valise. Once her things were packed, they went upstairs to pack bags for Mrs. Todd and Robert. Matthew took a small cinch-top sack and gathered at least half of Robert's army off the floor. Again, he surprised her with his thoughtfulness. "Who are you, Matthew Reeves?" she muttered under her breath as she added Robert's favorite stuffed bear to the bag.

Matthew's strong arms wound around her waist from behind. Bending down, he pressed a kiss to her neck. "Maybe you should take a risk and find out?" His voice was sultry in her ear. "I can think of a dozen ways we could get better acquainted."

CHAPTER TWENTY-FOUR

ELIZABETH HAD CONVINCED Matthew to leave her at the print shop and take the carriage with the bags back to the Angel. Being in the shop with George and the ladies had helped settle her nerves. The hum and clang of the press and the smell of ink all worked to spread the sense of familiar purpose through her chest. She had a paper to run. Stories to tell. The *Piccadilly Press* was her father's legacy, and she was proud to be the caretaker of it. She liked to think her paper had a unique perspective.

Hmm...perhaps that was how they could lure Griffen into revealing himself.

She crossed her arms over her chest and stared at the printer as it spit out newsprint. Matthew said that perhaps his brother liked seeing his transgressions in the paper. Could they challenge him somehow in print and then trail him to catch him in the act? No, too dangerous. What if he eluded them and another woman was killed? However, if anyone could handle a dangerous situation, it would be Matthew and his partner, Rhys—bloody—Seaton. Hartwick seemed to trust Seaton, but she knew that the man was probably involved in all sorts of criminal activity. It wasn't as though he even tried to hide it.

"Ms. Harper, could you come look at this?" Ella called out from the tile table.

Elizabeth walked over to where the ladies were furiously finishing setting the tile for the last section. "What is it that I am looking at?"

"Here. Shouldn't this be an apostrophe? This is the store's sale, not that 'Harrisons' is plural, right?"

"That's a good catch, Ella. You are correct."

Ella grinned. She turned back to her work and muttered softly, "I knew it."

Elizabeth smiled. Ella was a quick learner. Though she hadn't had much schooling, the young woman was like a sponge with information. Elizabeth would have to send her home with a good book on grammar if Ella was interested. With her sharp mind, she may make a good reporter someday. When the last edition had been printed and ready to post, Elizabeth gathered her jacket and hat. She looked outside. The sun was low, but she should make it back to the Angel by suppertime. "Goodbye, George; you'll set those out in the front for the morning?"

"Yes, Lizzie. Be careful walking home now," George Norton replied.

She hadn't told him about the break-in at her house. She didn't want to worry him. Or explain about where she was staying. She pinned her hat into place and walked out into the warm summer evening. A young man, maybe twenty, if that, lounged against the outside of the building. He straightened and stepped in front of her with a tip of his cap.

"Evening, ma'am. Are you Miss Harper?"

"Yes, I am." She looked him over warily. Lanky, dressed in black trousers, a jacket, and a jaunty blue neck scarf, he appeared non-threatening. "Who are you?"

"Name's Harry. I'm here to walk you to the Angel. Boss's orders."

Boss's orders. Elizabeth rolled her eyes. She knew Matthew had given in too easily earlier when she had insisted he needn't wait for her. She looked down at her watch fob. Five o'clock. He was probably already preparing the club for guests this evening or he would have been here himself. The man was so managing. "Alright, then. I hope you don't mind a brisk pace. I don't stroll."

Back at the Blue Angel, she headed up the back stairs to Matthew's wing. She could hear the noise of voices and the click of glasses drifting up from downstairs. She put away her hat and satchel and then made her way to the sitting room in search of Robert and Mrs. Todd. When she walked in, she found Robert sitting on the floor across from Stella. Three rows of cards lay face down between them.

Mrs. Todd sat in a chair nearby with her stitching in her lap. She rose to her feet. "Glad you're back safe."

"Mr. Reeves made sure of that by sending one of his men to walk me home," she replied.

Mrs. Todd nodded with approval. "Well, now that you're back, I will just go down to the kitchen and see about getting some supper for Robert. The two of them have been playing cards for a good hour now." She set her stitching on the small side table and left to go find Big Ben.

"Hello there." Elizabeth approached the pair on the floor with a smile. "What are you playing? You're not teaching him to gamble, are you?" It was only partially a jest. Stella seemed like a sweet girl, but she didn't know much about her. What had it been like to grow up in Lord Griffen's house? What had made her come to find Matthew? She should be having her season out in society. Wasn't that what all young girls of quality dreamt of?

"Hullo, mama. We are playing a matching game." Robert gestured to the cards. "I am very good at it."

Stella grinned. "You are a very clever boy. He knows all his numbers and has a keen memory. He would make an excellent sharp."

"Don't tease her, Stella." Matthew's deep voice came from across the room.

Elizabeth turned as he strolled into the room. He looked so handsome in his burgundy vest over a crisp white shirt. His black jacket lay folded over one arm. His curly dark hair fell over his brow, and she wished she could push her fingers through it. A small smile turned up his full lips. How often had she seen him grin? A real smile that would crack his expression wide open? Perhaps just once, when they'd both been naked. A blush warmed her cheeks. Did he ever laugh? Did she for that matter? There was not much time for frivolity in her busy days. Matthew worked as hard as she to run his successful business and she admired that. What a pair they made. No, not a pair. That couldn't be. *Could it?*

She turned her attention back to the game on the floor. "What's a sharp?" she asked.

Stella's laugh rang out. Matthew's sister certainly had no trouble finding joy in the small things. "I was just teasing. A sharp is a cheater. Someone who is clever enough to see the patterns and take advantage of the house."

"Oh." She crouched down next to Robert. "Show me how your game works."

"You flip over two cards and see if the numbers match. If not, then it's the other person's turn. But you have to remember what numbers are where so that you can find pairs when it's your turn again. I have found threes, sixes, and queens so far. The Q is for queen, Stella said."

Stella nodded. "We have played several rounds, and he is very good at finding pairs."

"Thank you for entertaining him this afternoon."

"Oh, it's been fun." Stella's expression sobered. She tilted her head toward Robert. "I heard all about the break-in at your place."

"Did you?" She ran a hand over Robert's hair. "Are you still feeling scared about last night, darling?"

He looked up from the cards. "A little. Was anything stolen from my room?"

"No, nothing was taken from your room. Mr. Reeves had a new strong lock put on the back door. We should be very safe again."

"And I brought you some friends from your room." Matthew crossed to the table in the corner and scooped up the bag of toy soldiers he'd brought from her house. He handed it to Robert, and the joy that lit her son's face was priceless.

"My soldiers! And they were all there?"

"All accounted for, but I didn't bring the lot. Some stayed behind to keep watch."

"Good thinking." Robert rooted through the bag. "Thank you, Mr. Reeves."

Matthew's eyes crinkled with mirth. "My pleasure."

"Mama, will we go home already? I like it here. It's very busy with lots of people around. Not quiet, like our place."

"No." She met Matthew's gaze over her son's head. "I think we will stay for a few days at least."

His eyes warmed as he stared at her. She wished to see them melt. Her desire to be wrapped in his embrace, to feel his lips scorch her skin, flared low in her belly. She licked her lips and watched his gaze drop to her mouth. Her cheeks heated in response. She rose to her feet, breaking eye contact before she burst into flames.

"That's wonderful!" Stella exclaimed. "Will you come to see my show tonight? You never got a chance to see me sing last time you were here."

"Um, yes. I would be glad to. Did you have singing lessons growing up?" Elizabeth settled on the settee.

"No, Father didn't care for me to go about, singing. He was annoyed by it. I had a governess who taught me to paint and to embroider. Anything that was quiet. I did learn to ride. That was my favorite part of each day, getting to ride my horse across the countryside."

"I didn't realize. Do you miss it?" Matthew frowned. "We could get you a horse."

"The reason I loved it was because of the freedom it gave me. Before, I was constantly restricted. I was being molded to become the perfect wife to some ducal heir. But here I have so much to enjoy. I can sing to my heart's content and meet new people, and well, just be free to be myself. I don't need a horse to escape anymore."

Elizabeth sucked in a sharp breath. Stella's casual mention of how she had been groomed to be Robert's wife sent an unexpected wave of grief through her chest. Their broken betrothal was the reason that Robert was dead. Not for the first time, Elizabeth imagined that if Robert had never met her, he would be alive. He would be married to this sunny, darling girl sitting on the floor. Would they have been happy?

There was no use dwelling on the *might-have-beens*. She gazed over at her son, who sat across the room, setting up his regiments in neat rows. He was the product of her love affair with Robert, and she would forever be grateful for him. Glancing over at Matthew, she found him staring at her with a piercing look that said he understood the train of her thoughts. Elizabeth's hope that her grief hadn't shown on her face was further squashed when Stella scrambled to her feet and came to sit next to her.

"Matthew told me about what happened to your fiancé. You must hate me."

Elizabeth looked into Stella's wide, sad eyes. The girl was as much of a victim of her parentage as Matthew. "No. No, I do not hate either of you." She looked over at Matthew. "I can't blame you for what happened. In fact, I have often blamed myself. If Robert had never met me, he would still be alive."

Stella grasped her hand. "No, you must not think that. I don't yet understand much about how life unfolds. But it seems that you would be missing an important part of yours if you had never fallen in love." Stella gestured to where Robert played with his army across the room.

Elizabeth had difficulty swallowing around the lump in her throat.

"The only one to blame is our father. He was the one who shot the Duke of Hartwick that day." Matthew's voice was rough with anger.

"You are right. And whoever shot Robert to shut him up. One day, I will find out who, and I will get my retribution." Her chest expanded with anger at the unfairness of life. There had been no need for anyone to die that day. Men and their stupid pride. Equally to blame was the way these men protected each other. Even when they knew it was wrong. When someone was dangerous, like the current Viscount Griffen. Her nostrils flared as she pushed out a frustrated breath.

Across from her, Matthew grinned, wide and toothy. "Is it terrible that I find your fierce need for revenge very attractive?"

Elizabeth was so shocked by his grin that she didn't even try to stifle the chuckle that escaped her lips.

From next to her, Stella laughed out loud. "On that note, I will leave you two alone. I need to go to rehearsal."

Elizabeth tore her gaze from Matthew. "Can I come with you? Would it be all right to ask the other girls some questions about the night of Mary Beth's murder? Perhaps there are some clues to why she went outside. Of how she may have known him?"

Stella glanced at her brother. Matthew stood. "Yes, I think that is a good idea."

Elizabeth walked over to Robert. "Come darling, let's go downstairs to the kitchen for your supper."

"All right. Can I bring my horse?"

"Yes. Just one, though. Let's put the rest back into the bag." She turned to Matthew and Stella. "I will meet you in the theater shortly."

CHAPTER TWENTY-FIVE

MATTHEW STRODE INTO the theater with Stella at his side. Lizzie was right; he should have questioned the other girls already. He had spoken briefly to Mrs. Langley about Mary Beth and gathered that she had been young, but talented. She had lived with three other girls in a boarding house down the street. Mary Beth had been in her costume when they found her body. How had Jonas lured her outside to the alley? He had been at the Blue Angel that night, but Matthew had thrown him out before he even reached the gaming rooms. How would he have made contact with Mary Beth? Perhaps he knew the girl already? Is that what had led Jonas to the Blue Angel?

The dancers were all on stage, stretching and practicing dance steps. Matthew approached Mrs. Langley. "Anne, could I speak with the girls before you start rehearsal?"

"Sure, boss. What about?"

The door to the theater opened and he glanced back as Lizzie walked in. He gestured for her to come closer. "Ms. Harper and I have some questions about the night of Mary Beth's murder. We are trying to figure out why she was attacked."

"Such a shame that was. Been warning the girls to be extra careful and to stick together."

"Ms. Harper, this is Mrs. Langley, my theater manager. Miss Harper is the editor of the *Piccadilly Press* and a neighbor of Mary Beth's family."

"It's a pleasure to meet you, Mrs. Langley."

"Same to you." Mrs. Langley glanced over at him with a knowing gleam in her eye. "You are a right pretty lady. You ever been on the stage?"

Lizzie blushed. "Oh no. I think I would have terrible stage fright."

"Newspaper lady, huh? Must be smart then. You writing a story about Mary Beth's murder?"

"Yes, really, I am investigating a string of murders happening on the eastside. The magistrate doesn't seem to care about women who are attacked over here. And, well, Mary Beth's family are friends of mine. I want to make sure the person who killed her is punished."

Mrs. Langley waggled her eyebrows. "Working together, then, the two of you?"

Matthew took hold of Lizzie's elbow. "We'll just go talk to the girls now." He tugged Elizabeth away down the aisle before Mrs. Langley could pepper her with any more questions.

When they approached the stage, the dancers all paused and looked over at him. "Ladies, could I have a moment of your time?"

Stella came forward, and the rest of the girls followed her

lead. "This is Miss Harper. She is a friend of Mary Beth's family. We are trying to find out more about the events that led up to Mary Beth's death."

"Do any of you know who Mary Beth would have been meeting outside?" Lizzie asked.

Many of the girls shook their heads.

"Did she have a beau? It's all right to tell now. She can't get in trouble any longer."

Gertie stepped forward. "She was new, so we didn't know much about her, but I roomed with her. I never saw her with any blokes. I know she was kicked out of her father's house because her parents didn't want her to dance."

"Yeah," Jenny said. "She was real quiet. But nice."

"Why would she leave right before the show?" Stella said. "She was already in costume when she went out back, right?"

Matthew nodded. "That's what we want to know."

A loud sob came from the back of the group. Everyone turned. Fanny Cooper had her hand clapped over her mouth. Tears streamed down her face. A muffled sob escaped. Matthew narrowed his eyes at the girl. "Fanny, do you know something?"

Mrs. Langley stepped forward. "Come here, girl. Why are you crying? You wasn't friends with Mary Beth."

Stella went and wrapped an arm around the crying Fanny. "It's all right. Just tell us what you know."

"I didn't know she would get killed!" Fanny blurted out. "I never wanted her to be hurt."

Matthew stepped forward. "What did you do?"

She hiccupped loudly and huddled against Stella. "I just w-wanted her to be late for her mark. Get her in trouble with Mrs. Langley. I-I told her that her ma was out back and wanting to talk to her. She was always talking about how she missed her ma. I didn't know she would come to any harm. I swear!"

Stella stepped back from Fanny in horror. "Why would you want to get her in trouble?"

"She was so talented. Everyone loved her." Fanny wiped her hand under her nose with a loud sniffle. "She was going to get my spot in the front. I just knew it." Her eyes were wide as she looked around at the other girls. If she was looking for support, she would be very disappointed. Angry and aghast faces stared back at the girl.

Matthew clenched his jaw. This was the reason Mary Beth had died? Jealousy? "Fanny, you are fired. Get your things and leave immediately."

"What?! No, please, Mr. Reeves." She rushed forward and gripped his arm like she had that evening when Mary Beth died. He remembered the calculation in her eyes as she propositioned him. He should have known then that she would be trouble.

He looked her right in the eyes. "Get out of my club." Then he turned and walked down through the tables and out the door.

"Fuck!" He beat his fist down on the railing of the balcony. Leaning his arms on the smooth wood surface, he looked down at the front hall, empty but for Joe, who manned the door this evening. Voices echoed out from the gaming room. It was early still, but the club always had a few patrons from the moment the doors opened at five o'clock. Things would pick up around eight and be busy throughout the night. He didn't have an official closing time, but most days, by four in the morning, the place emptied out.

The door behind him banged open. "What a terrible person." Elizabeth's voice was sharp with anger.

He glanced over at her as she came to stand next to him. He agreed, but wasn't surprised. Most people were only looking out for themselves. "Poor Mary Beth. She went outside to see her mother and ended up in Jonas's clutches. Looks like he is just choosing women based on happenstance."

Lizzie hung her head. "Why was he in my home? Do you think it's true that he likes when I write about his misdeeds? Did I attract the attention of a killer?"

He moved closer to wrap his arm around her shoulders. "I honestly don't know if it was him, but my gut says it was. I just don't know how he would know who you are."

"I purposely keep my moniker the same as when my father ran the paper, just E. Harper, to preserve my anonymity."

He turned her gently by the shoulders to face him. The worry in her eyes gutted him. "Don't worry. He can't reach you here. You will be safe." He would make sure of it.

The front door below opened, and Seaton stepped through the threshold. He handed his hat to Joe and glanced up at them. Matthew let go of Lizzie as Rhys climbed the stairs. He didn't mince words. "What did you find out?"

"According to my man, Sunday afternoon, Griffen received a visit from the Duke of Lavensham. And then, Monday afternoon, two carriages, one piled with luggage, left the residence. Seth confirmed with a maid in the house that Griffen was leaving for his country estate in Derbyshire. According to this timeline, he couldn't have been the one to break into your home on Thursday evening."

"Bollocks!" Matthew pinched the bridge of his nose. "It's him. I can feel it. No ordinary thief would lay out her clothes like that. He's still in town."

"I checked the house myself and it's empty, but for the housekeeper and a maid," Seaton said. "Of course, that doesn't mean he doesn't have a place somewhere else in the city he keeps. The carriages might have just been for show."

"Yes," Lizzie said. "Last week at the party, I overheard two men discussing their concerns about him. One assured the other he would have a firm talk with him about his behavior. It was dark, and I couldn't identify the men. But it makes sense that Lavensham would be one of them. He was one of Griffen's club."

Seaton nodded. "Lavensham is one of only three left of their boyhood club. Blackpool and Fleming being the others, if you don't count Rawlings, who is in jail."

"I don't give a fuck about their boyhood club. What concerns me is that Jonas is skulking around the city, looking for my girls," Matthew said. Lizzie had gone quiet, and he studied her expression. Was she frightened? She looked more contemplative than anything else. "Lizzie?"

"I was thinking about him earlier today. And I think if we could plant something in the paper to flush him out, then maybe we could catch him before he hurts anyone else."

"We could use me."

Matthew swiveled around to find Stella walking through the door of the theater.

"If you printed something in the gossip page about spotting me in the city, it would drive him crazy. He would have to surface again to try and find me."

"Absolutely not," Matthew said. "We are not using you for bait."

Elizabeth laid a hand on his arm and squeezed. "I agree. Griffen has every right to come and take you, as he is your legal guardian. There is no reason to expose yourself."

Matthew swung back to frown at Elizabeth. "And there is also no need to expose yourself further. You should not be traipsing about the city until we can find him."

Her hand slipped from his arm. She raised her eyebrows high. "Traipsing about? What the hell does that mean? If you are referring to me doing my job, then you are stepping way out of bounds."

"I simply mean that you should lay low here for a while. The paper can wait."

Her eyes flashed fire at that, and he winced. She shoved past him to storm off down the hall. Staring at her retreating back, he fumed. Stubborn chit! He strode after her through the double doors to his wing. He caught her by the arm right before she went into her room.

"Lizzie, stop! I don't mean the paper is not important, but that, temporarily, perhaps it's your safety that should be more important."

She tore her arm from his grasp and stomped into her room. "I don't need you to tell me what's important. And I don't need you telling me what to do. I can take care of myself and my son. I have been doing it for three years now. I have *traipsed* through every neighborhood in this city, talking to people, investigating stories, and I am still here." She swung around to face him, practically vibrating with anger, cheeks flushed, and her hands clenched. All he could think about was how fucking magnificent she was.

He kicked the door shut and stalked over to her. She stepped backward, and he followed her until her back hit the wall. Grabbing her wrists, he pinned them to the wall next to her head. He blew out a frustrated breath. "Why won't you let me take care of you?"

"Because I can't."

"But why?" He pressed harder when she struggled against his grip.

"Because I can't." She turned her head, but not before he caught the flash of anguish in her eyes. "Because if I begin to rely on you, then it will just hurt all the more when things fall apart."

"Why would things fall apart?"

Her head snapped back to meet his searching gaze. "Because they do. Bad things happen. People die." The last words came out in a whisper.

His frustration drained. He released her arms and instead cupped her face with both hands. "I cannot promise that nothing bad will ever happen to me. That would be foolish when the world can be a dangerous place. But what I do know is that with all the uncertainties of life, all we can do is take care of each other. Love…each other." He stared into her wide green eyes, and in their depths, the vulnerability she normally hid so well shimmered. In that moment, he knew he would do anything for this woman and her child. They belonged with him now. He took a risk and dipped down to kiss her softly. "Let me love you."

She gripped his wrists. They stood staring at each other for what seemed like an eternity. Then she nodded almost imperceptibly. She still looked apprehensive, and he couldn't blame her. He knew what it was to have your whole life yanked away. To have to start over as something new.

Matthew captured her mouth in another kiss. Her lips tasted like heaven. He didn't know how she had become so important to him in such a short time, but his desire for her had grown far past the physical. He desired for her to be his, to have her love him in return. To belong to her.

"Take a risk with me. Perhaps the rewards could be great."

"You are in the business of risk. I don't know if I am built to gamble."

"Stick with me. Don't you know? The house always

wins." He grinned against her lips. The time for talking was over. He swept her up and sat her on the edge of the bed. Then he crossed to the door and turned the lock. He stripped off his coat as he walked back across the room, then made quick work of the buttons of his vest, letting it fall to the floor.

A small smile played across her lips as she watched him approach. "Don't you have to be downstairs?"

"That's the benefit of being the boss. I don't have to do anything." He tugged his cravat free as he stopped in front of her. "Especially when my beautiful lady needs me."

"Oh, I need you, do I?" Her hands spread across his chest, grazing across his nipples. He hummed low. God, he loved her hands on him.

"Yes. I think I need to prove just how well I can take care of you." Grasping her arms, he tugged her to her feet and kissed her. Her lips parted for him, and he licked into her mouth. Her kiss felt desperate, searching. He was more than happy to pour how he felt into their connection. He would kiss her all night long if that was what she needed to believe that he loved her. He slid his hands into her hair, dislodging hairpins. Working his fingers through the thick, luscious locks, he unwound the chignon she always wore.

Lizzie hummed against his lips and gripped his shirt. She shook her hair out. "That feels good."

He scratched her scalp. Her eyes fluttered closed and he buried his nose in the hair by her temple. "You smell sweet, like flowers."

"It's my hair oil, lily of the valley."

"Hmm." He kissed across her cheek and captured her lips once again. The tiny buttons down the front of her dress proved impossible without looking, and he huffed and pushed her onto her back before attacking the row. But he could not figure out how to slide the little round buttons free.

Lizzie chuckled. "They are hooks, not buttons." She unhooked the first two.

He brushed her hands away impatiently and finished the job, only to find a practical cotton chemise and stays underneath. He shook his head. "I'm still disappointed that I didn't get to fully unwrap you the other night when you wore nothing under that orange dress."

Bending over, he caged her with his arms and used his teeth to pull at the laces of her stays. He kept his eyes on hers. She watched him with such hunger that his cock went rock hard. He kissed up the smooth column of her throat, nibbling until he could pull her earlobe into his mouth for a slow suck. Her moan had all his plans for slow seduction fleeing. Matthew flipped her over and tore her clothes down and off. When he had her bare but for her stockings, he took a moment to admire her generous curves.

She looked back over her shoulder at him, her long mahogany waves spilling over her shoulder. "Matthew, please. I need you." She rolled her hips, rubbing that gorgeous ass along the front of his trousers.

Desperate, he tugged his shirt over his head and threw it

to the floor. His trousers were next. He smoothed a hand over her luscious ass. Giving it a small smack, he groaned as the spot turned a rosy pink. Lizzie whimpered and bit down on her bottom lip. Her eyes were fiery with lust. He brushed her hair to one side and leaned over to take her mouth in a sloppy kiss that set fire to his blood. He slid his aching cock up and down the seam of her backside. Another whimper of pure want came from Lizzie.

She tore her lips from his. "Stop teasing me, naughty boy."

Matthew straightened, and grabbing her hip, he notched his cock at her entrance. Sliding into the wet heat of her pussy had him rolling his eyes back in the pure pleasure that engulfed him. He pulled back and then impaled himself deep in her tight heat.

"Yes, that's it. Right there." She threw her head back and pushed her hips back against his thrusts.

He gave her ass another sharp tap. She made him feel like an animal, pulled only by his base instincts. That's not what he wanted, so he bent and slid an arm under her to bring her up flush against him. "You make me wild, Lizzie. I have never felt this need for anyone like I do for you."

His hips smacked against hers as he fucked into her. He dropped one hand to sift his fingers through the curls of her mons. Finding that swollen clit, he strummed it with his thumb and felt the rumble of her moan against the hand he had between her breasts. "That's my girl, come all over my cock. I won't stop until you are undone." He slid his hand up to her throat. Her gasps vibrated against his hold. His cock throbbed as he thrust into her, his orgasm barely leashed. "Trust me. Let go. I have you." He gave her clit a pinch.

With a low moan, she came, her pussy convulsing around his cock. He let her go and pulled out to paint her ass as his cock pulsed and pulsed through an orgasm that left him absolutely undone. He collapsed on top of Lizzie. Their breaths heaved in tandem for a minute before he rolled them so that they were facing each other side by side. *Fuck. This woman.* He pushed her hair away from her face and cupped her flushed cheeks. "I am so tangled up in love with you."

Her eyes went from sated to wary. Her mouth opened and then closed.

"It's okay. I know it's a risk to love such a bruised heart. But I'll take the gamble." He leaned in and placed a soft kiss against her mouth. "The house always wins."

CHAPTER TWENTY-SIX

IT WAS SO hard to be sensible when she was wrapped in Matthew's embrace. His declarations of love should scare her, but instead, her foolish heart only felt hopeful. She tried to tell herself that he was absolutely the wrong kind of man for her to love; she truly did. There were dozens of sensible reasons. He was too ruthless and rough, far too domineering and foul-mouthed. But as his lips sipped on hers, soft and sensual, she found it hard to keep those thoughts in the forefront.

He smelled so good, like tobacco and sex. His body was a hot furnace pressed up against her. She ran her hand through his inky curls and rubbed her nose in his soft beard. Never had she felt so sated and cared for as she did in his arms. Matthew seemed to know exactly how to unlock all her desires, ones she hadn't even known she had, like when he'd spanked her backside. Her cheeks flamed hot at how wet it had made her. She gazed into his eyes and kissed him again and again. Could she take the risk and let him unlock her heart as well?

"Perhaps I should call down for water for the bath. I would very much like to bathe you." His big hand smoothed slowly down her side to grasp her backside in a playful squeeze.

"Won't that be a lot of trouble for the staff when there are customers downstairs?" she asked.

The mention of customers had him sighing, but it did not stop his hand from roaming up to cup her breast. His clever fingers teased her nipple, and she gasped at the tingle of pleasure that raced through her. "And my son is surely done with his supper by now." She reminded both of them, because she was fast falling under his spell again. A warm bath and his hands soaping her body sounded like absolute heaven.

Matthew sat and then pulled her up with him. "Will you come to my room tonight? After Robert is asleep?" He pressed a kiss to her lips. "I want to come up at the night's end and wrap myself around you and sleep with my nose buried in your hair." He pressed another kiss behind her ear. "And wake you in the morning with my tongue buried in your pussy."

"You wicked man," she sighed. "Yes, I will come to your room and wait in your bed. And maybe in the morning, I will take you up on your offer of a bath."

He slid off the bed. "For now, let me clean you off so you can be presentable again." He crossed to the washstand to dip a cloth into the basin of water.

They cleaned up and helped each other get dressed. He watched her with hooded eyes as she pinned her hair back up. "Don't look at me like that, or we will never make it out of this room," she said to his reflection in the mirror. She shoved one more pin into her hair, then swiveled on her seat to face him. Lord, he was so handsome. Dark sultry eyes and broad shoulders. He stepped forward to reach for her just as a knock sounded at the door. The doorknob jiggled.

"Mama, are you in there?"

She stood and crossed to the door to turn the lock. When she opened it, Robert barreled inside. "Mrs. Todd says I should get ready for bed. Did you know there were mashed potatoes for supper tonight?" He stopped short when he spotted Matthew. "Oh, hullo, Mr. Reeves. Mashed potatoes are my favorite. What are you doing here?"

"I've just come to ask your mum if she wanted to come see the show tonight."

Robert glanced over at her. "Do you?"

"Um, yes. Stella wanted me to hear her sing," she replied. She glanced out to the corridor where Mrs. Todd stood with her eyebrows raised. "I will put you to bed, and Mrs. Todd will be right next door if you need anything."

"I wish I could go see Stella sing. She is so very nice and so is her kitten. I wish I could have a kitten. Do you think Stella likes mashed potatoes?"

Matthew laughed and ruffled his hand on Robert's head. "Yes, I believe she does. In fact, I shall go see if she has remembered to get her supper before I go downstairs. I'll see you tomorrow, Robert."

The causal gesture was so fatherly that it made her heart squeeze tight. Then Matthew sauntered out, but not before pausing to place a kiss on her cheek and give her a wink. Elizabeth caught the widening of Mrs. Todd's eyes. There was no censure there, just curiosity. *Good Lord, don't overthink it.* Elizabeth turned to her son. "Come, Robert, do you want to read the book about the mice family again tonight?"

"Yes!"

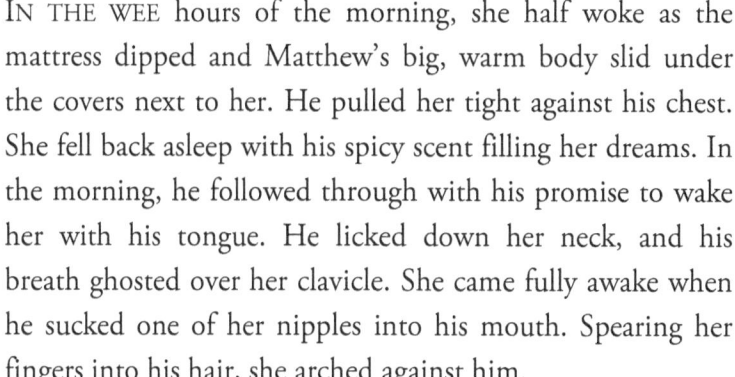

IN THE WEE hours of the morning, she half woke as the mattress dipped and Matthew's big, warm body slid under the covers next to her. He pulled her tight against his chest. She fell back asleep with his spicy scent filling her dreams. In the morning, he followed through with his promise to wake her with his tongue. He licked down her neck, and his breath ghosted over her clavicle. She came fully awake when he sucked one of her nipples into his mouth. Spearing her fingers into his hair, she arched against him.

He looked up at her with a wicked gleam in his eyes. Then, he slid further down the bed, settling himself between her thighs. His beard brushed along her sensitive skin, and she sighed in pleasure as he licked a slow stripe up her sex. "Matthew," she murmured.

"Hmm?" His voice vibrated against her clit. She rolled her hips, chasing the sensation.

It didn't seem to matter what she had meant to say; Matthew knew exactly what she needed. He feasted on her, licking and sucking her pearl until she was writhing and moaning uncontrollably. It felt so good, so decadent to have him moaning in tandem. "Fuck, my girl, you taste so good. I can't get enough of your delicious pussy."

His sweet, filthy words sent her over the edge. Her orgasm burst through her in a breathless wave of pleasure. And still, he kept lapping at her until she pushed his head away. "Too much…can't take any more," she managed to get out.

He chuckled. "Oh, I have so many ideas. It will take a lifetime to explore all the ways to make you moan in pleasure." He bit down on the flesh of her inner thigh, making her yelp. "But for now, I'll stop."

She propped herself on her elbows so she could admire Matthew as he sat back on his haunches between her spread legs. His hair was sticking up in all directions because of how she had gripped it; his beard was covered in her wetness, and his grin wide. She lowered her gaze to take in the glory that was his taut body, lean but strong, the muscles in his arms and chest well-defined. Those muscles tapered down his abdomen to the thick length of his erection, jutting out hard between his thighs and beaded with fluid at the tip. She licked her lips.

Scooting up to sit against the headboard, she crooked a finger. "Come here, naughty boy. You are not the only one that has ideas."

But before he could do as she instructed, a heavy knock sounded at the door. She startled, but Matthew laughed. "That would be the hot water I ordered for this morning. It must be eleven."

Elizabeth scrambled off the bed. "Eleven? The whole morning is gone." Robert would have been up for hours already. She pushed her hair off her face. She was a mess, lying around like a hedonist when there were things that needed to be done.

Matthew rolled off the bed and crossed to a wardrobe where he donned a pair of silky pajama pants and a matching banyan. "Don't fret about Robert; Mrs. Todd will watch him." He came over and cupped her face. "There is nothing you must do today except take a nice, long bath."

Another knock at the door reminded her that she was still entirely naked. Matthew turned her and gave her backside a tap. "Go behind the screen."

She hurried to do what he said as Matthew strode across the room to answer the door.

"Water's ready, boss." She heard Ben's voice. Then there was a clanging of metal buckets and footsteps.

Another robe hung on a hook on the wall behind her, and she quickly donned it. The blue satin hung down all the way to her feet. She tied the belt tight around her waist. There was the sound of another door opening and then a scraping and a loud bang. Curious, she peeked her head around the screen.

Ben was straightening an enormous copper tub. He glanced up and spotted her. "Mornin', Miz Harper. We'll have your bath ready in a jiff."

She knew her cheeks must be pink. There was no propriety in this place. But hell and damnation, she didn't know if she even cared. She stepped out from behind the screen. "I told you to call me Elizabeth."

"Yes, ma'am, you did." Ben grinned at Matthew's low growl. "But I value my job, so I think I'll stick with 'Miz Harper.' Fill it up, boys." He instructed the line of boys that each carried two buckets. When they had all filed back out, Matthew closed the door and turned the lock. He walked back to her and tugged loose the belt of her robe.

She stayed his hand. "Only if you take yours off as well."

He nodded and shrugged out of his robe. She followed suit. Then gasped as he swung her up into his arms and carried her over to the tub. As he lowered her into the steaming water, he kissed her languidly. The tub was enormous. She sank down until the water covered her breasts. Matthew straightened and walked over to grab a cloth and a bar of soap from the washstand.

He knelt down by the tub. "Let me take care of you?"

His words from last night seeped into her chest like warm honey. Instead of fear, this time she only felt longing. For this man, for what he offered. Trusting that they could have a future together was harder. She wasn't ready to risk her heart again. But trusting that he would take care of her for now? She could surrender to that. She nodded.

Matthew washed her, running the cloth slowly over every inch of her. Teasing and tormenting her as he kept his touches light, running the cloth over her most sensitive bits without the friction that she craved. Then he moved around so that he could wash her hair. His fingers worked the soapy lather into her hair, scratching gently at her scalp. Making her writhe with how good it felt.

She dipped her hand down to her clit and rubbed small circles to relieve the pressure that had built higher and higher with all his tantalizing touches. Matthew sucked in a sharp breath. "Feeling needy, my girl?"

She tipped her head back to stare up at him. "You know I am; you wanted to drive me mad."

He cupped his hands and scooped water carefully over her head, washing away the soap. His fingers ran through the entire length, untangling the ends. Then he bent over and gave her an open-mouthed kiss. Tangling her tongue with his, she let him plunder her mouth.

When he stood, she quickly rose to her knees. Water sloshed over the edge of the bathtub, splashing the floor, but she managed to grab hold of the waistband of his pajama bottoms. He wasn't going to get away this time. She shoved down the pants. His cock hard, the end red and weeping, sprang forth.

"I'm not the only one that's needy." She leaned forward and licked the salty tip. The groan that rumbled from Matthew was gratifying, and she gave in to her curiosity, taking him into her mouth.

Running her tongue along the underside, she found a vein that ran the length and made his cock twitch. She raised her gaze to assess his reaction to her efforts. His pupils were blown wide as he stared down at her. His jaw clenched tight.

She smiled and then sucked him into her mouth again. He was too long to swallow all of him, so she brought her hand up and grasped the base of his cock. When she gave it a rough squeeze, she was rewarded with another low groan. *Mmm.* This time, she was going to drive him mad with lust. She would ravish him until he lost control.

She sucked enthusiastically and used her hand in tandem. His moans got louder, his head fell back, and his hips thrust, pushing himself deeper into her mouth. It made her eyes water, but she wanted badly to make him come apart, so she breathed through her nose and swallowed around his tip.

"Fuck," he moaned. "Lizzie, you are a fucking goddess."

Then he jerked his hips again, and with a roar, he came. His seed spurted warm into her mouth. She swallowed as much as she could, but it still spilled down her chin as he pumped gently against her tongue. The bliss on his face was worth the mess. She grinned up at him, as he pulled in deep breaths, his chest heaving. Then he reached down to swipe his thumb across her chin. He hauled her to standing and kissed her, his tongue sweeping in to suck on her tongue.

"You are such a filthy beast," she murmured against his lips.

"I know." He grinned. "But you love it."

She did love it. Matthew had no inhibitions. He said whatever he was thinking. He didn't hold back any expressions of pleasure, and he demanded the same from her. The words he murmured against her lips or in her ear always ratcheted her desires to heights she had never experienced before. Her worries that she was too loud or too needy fell away one by one.

They spent the afternoon together, curled up in his drawing room with Stella and Robert as rain poured down outside. Matthew patiently explained the rules and tricks for playing loo as Robert played with Pitter-Patter and a ball of yarn Mrs. Todd had provided the pair.

Later, after she had put her son to bed, she again walked across the hall to Matthew's room to wait for him to return from downstairs. She closed the door behind her and wandered around his room, lighting a few tapers so she could explore. The large copper tub had been put away in its closet. And the other door along that same wall led to a shadowy sitting room. It held a small round breakfast table and a settee positioned in front of the fireplace. In one corner was an empty glass curio cabinet. Overall, the room had an air of disuse. She couldn't picture Matthew's tall frame lounging comfortably on that formal settee.

Back in his bedroom, the ambiance was entirely different. Cozy was the only word to describe it. Several large plush rugs covered the entire floor. Velvet curtains framed the windows. A large chaise covered in matching burgundy velvet sat in front of the fireplace. Along the far wall, a row of low bookcases stood sentry.

She wandered over to see what sorts of books Matthew owned. The books were shelved in no particular order. Lots of volumes containing plays—Shakespeare, Sophocles, and Molière. She ran her fingers down the row, holding the candle to see the titles, and stopped as she came to a small section of gothic novels by her favorite author, Ann Radcliffe. Her lips twitched in amusement. Why did it not surprise her at all that Matthew enjoyed novels with supernatural elements? She pulled *The Italian* off the shelf and climbed into Matthew's massive bed to read.

CHAPTER TWENTY-SEVEN

ROB NODDED TOWARD the gentleman at the dice table. Matthew sighed. The man in the middle of a small group was Lord Halifax, and he had been on a hot streak. Matthew walked past the bar and held out a hand. Val handed him a freshly opened bottle of champagne. Then he walked over to greet the three gentlemen who had been playing for the better part of an hour.

"Good evening, gentleman. How's the play tonight?" he asked.

"Bloody fantastic!" Halifax grinned wide, his crooked teeth on display.

"That's what I like to hear." He held up the bottle of wine. "Allow me to pour you a celebratory drink. Ruinart is simply the best."

All three men eagerly lifted empty glasses for a pour. After filling everyone's glasses, Matthew turned to Harry, who was running the table. "Time for a dice exchange." He withdrew a fresh set of dice from his right jacket pocket and handed it to Harry.

All the men around the table groaned. Matthew held up a hand. "Now, it's just standard practice. We exchange the dice on a strict schedule." He scooped up the dice on the table and pocketed them, but then he set the bottle of champagne next to Halifax. "Please enjoy the bottle. On the house." And with his task complete, he walked away before having to entertain any grumbling.

He ambled through the room, watching play and making eye contact with his employees to see if he needed to intervene anywhere else. Back at the bar, he leaned his elbows on the top and stared out at the room. His mind wandered to thoughts of the woman upstairs in his bed. He frowned; she damn well better be in his bed. He blew out a slow breath.

She drove him mad with wanting her. And not just her lush body, although being balls deep inside her was absolute heaven. Bloody hell, he wanted her to be his. To make a family with her and Robert. To spend his afternoons curled up next to her on the sofa, listening to her fume about all the ills in the city; to watch her work at her desk as she crafted the perfect article; to sit and play soldiers with Robert while the boy chattered about all the things he'd discovered about the world that day. To love them how they deserved to be loved. Matthew rubbed the heel of his hand against his chest where the longing to make a family of his own squeezed tight around his heart. How could he convince her to let him take care of them forever?

"Reeves." Seaton's voice came sharp in his ear.

Matthew blinked, surprised to find his friend standing right next to him. "Sorry, what?"

Seaton shook his head. "I said your name three times.

Val said he might as well have been talking about inventory to the wall for the past ten minutes."

Matthew swiveled around to where Val stood behind him wiping down the bar. "Sorry. My mind was wandering, I guess."

"S'aright, boss. If I had a lady as pretty as yours, I guess my mind would be wandering too." He chuckled and walked down a bit to serve a customer.

Matthew frowned. He didn't want the staff thinking about how pretty Lizzie was. Seaton took a puff of his cigarillo. He passed it over to Matthew. "So, she still here?"

"Yes." He took a drag and grinned as he exhaled the smoke. He passed it back to Rhys. "I plan to convince her to stay permanently."

"She's a risk. She is not going to just quit her newspaper and be the little wife."

Matthew turned his head and sent Rhys a sharp look. "What makes you think I want that shit? Naw, she's brilliant and passionate. I love that about her. And that kid of hers, just like his mother, full of questions all the time."

"Just checking." Rhys slapped him on the back. "If you marry her, we'd be family in a way, with Robert being my nephew."

Matthew shook his head. "You've been my family for a long time, brother."

Rhys's eyes flared with emotion. He nodded. Then he took a long drag of his smoke and stared out at the room. "You should go upstairs to your lady. I can handle things tonight."

"You sure?"

"I've got nothing going on. Go. She will need lots of convincing. She's got a bruised heart."

As Matthew strode away, heading for the front stairs, he thought about Rhys's comments about becoming family. It was absolutely true that Rhys was like a brother to him. Just like Ben and Val and so many others who worked at the Angel had become his family. He paused at the top of stairs and turned to survey the home that he had made for himself. His family might be a motley crew of misfits, but they were his. And maybe the ache in his chest wasn't so much a longing to make a family but rather a longing for her and Robert to become part of this family. Lord knew Lizzie and Robert had been on their own for long enough. Rhys was right; he would have to be persistent. He would have to show her how good it could be if she would stay, if she would be his.

He entered his room and found Lizzie asleep on the bed, a book open on her chest. A single taper on the nightstand flickered soft shadows across her beautiful features, so much softer in sleep. It was so warm. He crossed to push open the window and a gentle breeze raced into the room. He undressed and then blew out the candle before climbing into bed beside her. Setting aside the book, he pulled her into his arms with her backside nestled against him and her hair in his face.

He sucked in a deep breath of her scent, rubbing his nose in her hair. "Lizzie, you are mine now," he whispered. "I love you. Will you marry me? Be part of my family? Belong to me?" he practiced what he would say. "I want to take care of you and your son. Do you think you can take a risk on me?"

Yes, that was the real question. Would she take the gamble? He would get a ring, the biggest, gaudiest emerald he could get his hands on, to sweeten the pot. He gently squeezed her against him and then closed his eyes to go to sleep. This woman was meant to be his.

CHAPTER TWENTY-EIGHT

S UNDAY MORNING DAWNED bright and sunny. Elizabeth slipped out of bed to cross to the window and stare up at the clear blue sky. She took a deep breath. Life was strange. If anyone had told her a month ago, she would be living in a gaming hell and sharing the bed of its owner, she would have gasped in horror. Likewise, if anyone had said she would have anything to do with the Perrin family, let alone falling in love with one of them. She wrapped her arms around herself as a breeze skimmed over her bare arms and ruffled the hem of her thin cotton chemise.

But she did not regret where she was standing. Far from it.

Strong arms enveloped her from behind. Matthew's lips skimmed her ear. "Good morning, luv."

"Good morning. I didn't want to sleep in so late like yesterday. But you could have slept longer. I know you don't get to bed until the wee hours." She leaned back into his warmth.

"Told you before. I can sleep when I'm dead." His voice sounded scratchy first thing in the morning.

She smiled and turned her head to rub her nose against

his beard. "Robert will be up and ready for food. I swear he is growing. He has been eating so much lately. What do you have planned for today?"

"You mean besides fucking your sweet pussy? Nothing. The club is closed on Sundays."

She slapped his arm. "You have such a filthy mouth."

But he just turned her in his embrace so that they stood face-to-face. His eyebrows waggled up and down. "I think you secretly love it. I know you like how I use it." Then he dipped his head and kissed her.

She sighed and opened for him to plunder with his talented tongue. She kissed him back with equal eagerness. Would she ever be able to live without his kisses? She doubted it. Pressed against his hard body, she wished she could stay within his embrace forever. She reluctantly pulled back. "I have to get ready for the day." She extracted herself and crossed to grab her robe from the chaise. "I didn't know the club closed at all."

"Everyone deserves one day a week off. And because of church services, most people don't come to gamble on Sundays." He raised his arms in a languid stretch that had her breath quickening. "Suppose they think God is judging them."

She crossed back to him to run her hands down his chest and stomach all the way down to grip his hard cock. No one should be allowed to be this gorgeous. "I think perhaps I like your plan for the day after all." She bent to lick one of his nipples. "But we must be quick; I do have things to do today."

"That I can't promise." He threw her over his shoulder and smacked her backside as he strode over to the bed. She cackled with glee, the laughter cracking open her chest and releasing the last of her doubts. There was no other place she would rather be.

THEY WERE LATE for breakfast. Matthew explained that because the club was closed, even the chef had the day off. Ben and he shared the task of making food for the group that lived at the Angel full-time. Ben had breakfast duty this week. When they arrived in the kitchen, the big man was bustling around the kitchen, handing plates heaped with potatoes, sliced hard-boiled eggs, and toast to those who trickled in.

Mrs. Todd sat at the table with Robert, supervising his use of his fork and knife. She frowned at Ben as he moved around the kitchen.

Ben's head turned and he smiled at them. "Coffee, boss? And you, Miss Harper, tea?"

"Thank you, that would be lovely." Elizabeth slid onto a chair next to Robert and gave the top of his head a kiss. "Good morning, darling."

"Good morning, mama," he replied with his mouth full of potatoes.

"Don't talk with your mouth full." She turned to Mrs. Todd. "What's the matter?" she murmured softly.

"Ben won't let anyone help him. Even though he was up just as late as all the others." She didn't moderate her voice at all.

Ben looked over at her, his hands full of two more plates of food. "Oh, it's all right. I like taking care of people." He set the plates in front of two of the dancing girls.

They fluttered their lashes at him and flashed him big smiles. "Thanks, Big Ben."

The teakettle whistled shrill and loud. Mrs. Todd stood with a huff. "And who takes care of you, Ben?" She grabbed up a towel and pulled the kettle off the stove. She pushed Ben out of the way with her hip and poured hot water into the teapot on the counter.

Ben stared down at her with his mouth agape. Then he shook his head and reached for the canister of tea from a high shelf. He held it out. Mrs. Todd efficiently portioned tea into the sieve while Ben prepared Matthew's coffee. They stood side by side, and Mrs. Todd dished food onto plates as Ben tended to the pan of potatoes frying in the cast-iron skillet. He kept sneaking looks over at Mrs. Todd, and Elizabeth's heart melted a little.

Matthew slid into the spot next to her, vacated by Mrs. Todd, and Elizabeth bumped his shoulder with hers. She tipped her head at Ben. Matthew smiled at the goofy look in Ben's eyes. He leaned over and whispered in her ear, "Mrs. Todd has just won his undying devotion. He turns into a puddle at the smallest kindness."

Elizabeth accepted a plate of food from Mrs. Todd and

then watched the two of them interact while she ate. They were adorable. Ben flushing red anytime Mrs. Todd took charge and helped him with some small task. Mrs. Todd bustled over to the counter with the sink and called over the two girls who had finished eating. "If you two are done, you can come help me clean up these dishes." The girls glanced at each other in surprise but rose and cleared plates from the table. "Come, I'll wash, and you dry and put them away."

Ben picked up an apron and stepped up behind Mrs. Todd. He reached around her to tie the apron in place. "You don't want to get your pretty dress dirty."

Mrs. Todd tipped her head back to look up at him with a smile. "Thank you." They stood like that for a long minute before Ben stepped back.

Elizabeth exchanged a look with Matthew, who waggled his eyebrows, making her laugh. "I need to go to the market to buy food for supper. Would you and Robert like to come and help? Sunday at Covent Garden Market is always fun."

"Yes! Can we, mama?" Robert asked.

"Yes. If you don't mind, I need to stop by my house to see what's in the tip box, and I need to do a little bit of work. Then we could go shopping?"

"No problem. Robert, are there any other toys you'd like to bring from home?"

Robert screwed up his little face. "Maybe my blocks and another book. I'm tired of the one about the kittens."

"How could you possibly be tired of kittens?" Stella swept into the room with Pitter-Patter cradled in her arms.

Robert ran over to her and hugged her legs. "Oh, I would never get tired of Pitty-Pat. Can I hold him, please?"

"Of course. That would be a great help while I put some food together for his breakfast." She handed over the little cat, and Robert went over to sit with him on the rug in front of the hearth.

Elizabeth sighed. They were never going to get going now that he had that kitten to play with. She pulled out her pocket watch. It was already almost ten o'clock.

Matthew brushed his fingers across her cheek. "Why don't you go ahead and Robert and I will come in a bit and pick you up to go to the market."

"That would be lovely. I just need to get things ready for tomorrow when my staff arrives. I have one article to write, and then I need to look through the tips left in the box. Could you come fetch me in maybe two hours?"

He nodded. "But you must let Jim or Harry walk you to work. No arguing."

"All right." She bit back a smile at his shocked expression. "You said to let you take care of me."

"Yes, but I didn't think you would actually do it." He stood, grabbed a potato off his plate, and stuffed it in his mouth. "Go get your things, and I will find one of the lads."

CHAPTER TWENTY-NINE

T HE MARKET AT the Garden was always a crush on
Sundays. But she was strangely relaxed as she mean-
dered next to Matthew. He walked confidently through the
crowd with her son's hand firmly grasped in his. She had
grabbed her shopping basket from the house, but it was still
empty. Every place Matthew had purchased goods from, he
had simply had them delivered. He knew everyone by name,
and the vendors always replied, "Of course, Mr. Reeves. It'll
be delivered today."

Robert pointed to a stall that had a myriad of birds in
cages. These were not the kind one ate for dinner; no, these
had colorful plumage and curved beaks of bright yellow.
There was also a pair of lovebirds, dove gray, sitting next to
one another on the little swing in their cage. Matthew picked
Robert up in his arms so he could see better.

"Any juicy tips in your box this morning?" Matthew
asked her.

"Yes, but you'll have to read Tuesday's edition to find
out what they were," she teased.

"Look at the green one! Its hair is so tall." Robert pointed.

VICES, VILLAINS AND THE VISCOUNT

"Those are his feathers, darling. That's how they grow so long." She looked up at Matthew. "There was one unusual note in the box. A request to dine at the Marchioness of Rollinsford's home on Wednesday evening."

Matthew glanced over at her. "Your grandmother invited you to dine? Why is that strange?"

"Well, for one thing, I haven't spoken to her in six years."

"Oh. Will you go?"

"I don't know. I admit I am curious as to why she has summoned me." They moved past the birds and down the aisle to a large vegetable stand. She picked up a shiny green apple and handed it to Robert. Matthew tossed a coin to the vendor. "Perhaps you would accompany me? It didn't say I couldn't bring a guest." She bit her bottom lip and waited for him to laugh. These were the type of people he actively avoided.

Matthew set Robert down on his feet but kept his hand in a firm grasp. He stepped close and cupped her cheek. "Of course, if that's what you wish."

"Thank you." She turned her head and kissed his palm. Then they walked on. "I truly can't fathom why she is reaching out. Or why I am even considering going. She summarily cut me out of her life. Just as she had cut out my mother." Elizabeth frowned.

"Why are you accepting her invitation?" Matthew asked.

"Curiosity, I suppose. I can't help myself. Even if it is terrible, the dinner party could provide some good fodder for the gossip column. Nigel is going to faint when he hears."

Matthew reached out and grabbed the collar of a boy of about eleven who'd slipped between her and the candle stand. "Oy, just what do you think you're doing, lad?"

The boy struggled against his strong grip until Matthew brought them face-to-face. Then the boy froze. "S-sorry. Mr. Reeves. I didna know it was you. I swear." His dirty hair was covered by a threadbare cap, and his brown eyes were wide as saucers.

"Give the lady back her watch," Matthew ordered.

"Surely. Of course." He pulled her watch from the inner pocket of his jacket and, hand trembling, held it out.

"Oh, my goodness." She snatched it from the boy's grubby hand. "That was my father's watch."

"I'm sorry. Mr. Reeves, I didna know she was with you. Please don't tell Seaton." The boy's eyes shined with fear.

"It's all right. Just be more careful. Remember to watch for the fine ladies. They can afford to replace. Stick to the ones who have servants following them around. Those types make the best targets." He let go of the boy's collar, and the lad disappeared, weaving through the crowd.

Elizabeth pinned her watch back at her waist. "He didn't even break the clasp," she muttered.

"Sorry about that. These boys work the market. It's how they earn money to eat," Matthew said.

"How did you even know he had snatched my watch?"

He shrugged. "I'm familiar with the technique and the watch is the only thing on you of value."

"What about my coin purse?"

Matthew pulled her embroidered purse from the inside of his jacket. "I took it for safekeeping while we are in the market. I was going to give back."

She huffed. "But why did you take it without me knowing?"

"I didn't want to argue about it." His smile was sheepish.

Robert tugged on his hand. "Let's go see the bakery. Can I have a biscuit?"

As they headed down the aisle, Elizabeth glanced around more carefully at the people passing her by. She never thought too much about pickpockets, but then, she didn't do shopping here often. The shops in Bloomsbury had all the things they needed for the household. Glancing up at Matthew, she tried to picture him as an adolescent, weaving his way through the crowds, snatching purses and watches. She'd bet he had made an excellent thief, flashing his charming smile and distracting people from what his fingers were doing.

"So, I'm not a fine lady, am I?" she teased him.

"Nonsense. You are the finest lady I know. Isn't that right, Robert?" he winked at him.

"Yes, sir." Robert smiled up at her. "Can I have a biscuit, mama?"

She chuckled. "Yes, let's get enough to share with the others."

When they returned to the club, Elizabeth excused herself and left Robert downstairs in the kitchen with Mrs.

Todd and Ben. She had articles to write, and while the afternoon tooling around with her boys had been lovely, she was behind with her work. *Her boys?* Had she really just thought that? She plopped down in the chair. Staring out the window in the bedroom she and Robert were sharing, she tried to breathe through the sudden panic in her chest. What was she doing here? Getting comfortable at the club, spending nights in Matthew's bed? She was setting herself up for heartbreak.

Matthew's sweet whispered words last night felt like a hazy dream. One that she wanted to believe could be true, but she had believed in impossible dreams before, and they had been shattered. She had to be practical. They were here because Matthew thought she might be in danger. But they couldn't stay at the hell forever. This was no place to raise her son. She had to be practical.

Turning back to the desk, she straightened papers and sucked in a calming breath. Time to get work done. Time to focus on her real life.

<hr>

LATER, ELIZABETH MADE her way downstairs. The empty club felt strange, too quiet. She followed the smell of roasting meat as her stomach growled. She hadn't heard a peep from her son all afternoon, but she had gotten her articles drafted. Eager for some noise and distraction, she headed down the stairs to the kitchen, which she'd quickly learned was the heart of this place. She pushed open the door and entered its fragrant warmth.

"Evening, Elizabeth." Rhys Seaton leaned against the wall to her right.

"Evening, Mr. Seaton." She offered him a small smile. He really wasn't so bad. Enigmatic, for certain, but she respected his loyalty to his friend, and she had only ever observed him being kind to everyone who worked in the club. Perhaps she had been hasty in judging him. She thought about the boy in the market today. "Mr. Seaton, do the pickpockets in the market work for you?"

"The pickpockets? No. But I do occasionally pay them to run errands for me. Sometimes, I ask them to keep an ear out for a piece of information, which I will also pay them for. They know they can earn extra coin by staying on my good side."

"One tried to steal my watch today. Well, he did, but Matthew caught him in the act. The boy seemed scared we would tell you about it."

Seaton's lips twitched in amusement. "Matthew and I both did a fair share of pick-pocketing in our youth, so I'm not surprised he caught the thief in the act. Once you know the tactics, it's easy to spot. As for not telling me, well, a lot of the older lads do work for me, and your pickpocket probably didn't want to lose out on an opportunity to do the same in the future."

"Oh." She still didn't really understand what Seaton did for a living, but perhaps it was best she didn't. He was important to Matthew, and she was learning that not everything was as it appeared. She turned to observe the room.

Everyone had come down to supper, the long table full. Stella and the three other dancing girls who lived in the club sat together at one end of the table. Allan and Val sat in the middle, with a deck of cards between them. Ben and Mrs. Todd sat next to each other at the other end of the table, deep in conversation. A fire roared in the hearth, and a large piece of meat turned on a spit. In front of the stove, her son stood on a chair and stirred something in a large pot. At the counter next to the stove, Matthew sliced a crusty loaf of brown bread.

She went over to Mrs. Todd. "Is he all right by the stove?"

"Oh yes, I'm keeping an eye on him. Mr. Reeves has put him to work helping, and he is bursting with pride to be stirring the soup. Come and sit."

Elizabeth sat and tipped her head toward Matthew's back. "Does he need help?"

"Naw. He'll let us know when he wants it," Ben said. "He makes Sunday supper every week when Mr. Gregory is off."

"Every week?" To say she was surprised was an understatement. She watched Matthew move about the kitchen with practiced ease. He checked on Robert, ruffling her son's hair and giving him encouragement. Then he checked on the meat with a long fork. Turning to everyone, he clapped his hands together dramatically. "Supper is ready." He gave her a wink when he spotted her. "Val, Allan, will you get plates down? Ben, come help get this roast off the fire."

"Sure thing, boss." Ben and Matthew donned thick gloves and pulled the meat off the spit and over to the counter for carving.

Robert scrambled down from his perch and came over to give her a hug.

"I see you have been helping," she said.

"I am a good helper!" Robert grinned from ear to ear. Her heart overflowed with love as she looked down at him.

Then she glanced across at Matthew. He had donned an apron to protect his clothes as he carved the roast. He pushed the hair off his brow with the back of one hand. As though he sensed her gaze, he looked up, and her heart continued to spill over with emotion. Why had she ever thought that this man wasn't a family man? His family surrounded them, talking over each other and passing around bowls of soup. Matthew had orchestrated this atmosphere of home. She had tried hard not to label her feelings for him, too scared to love again. But it was no use denying that she had fallen in love with him.

She rose to her feet.

MATTHEW WATCHED ELIZABETH cross toward him. Her expression was one of determination. He wondered what was running through her head. He set down his knife. "What can I help you with, luv?"

She stopped right in front of him and placed a hand on his chest. Her chest rose and fell as she sucked in a deep breath. "Yes."

Confused, he covered her hand with his. "Yes?" he asked.

"Yes, to everything you whispered while you held me last night."

His breath caught. "You heard that?"

"Yes, I want to be yours. To be part of this family you have built." Her eyes shone with emotion. "Yes, I will marry you."

He cupped her face with both hands. Had she just agreed to be his wife? "Yes?"

She gripped his wrists. "I love you, Matthew Reeves. And for the first time in a long time, I feel hopeful. I want to take a risk on a future with you."

Overcome, he leaned down and kissed her. "I love you," he murmured against her lips. Then he slid to his knees. The room went silent, but he didn't care. All he could see was Lizzie, so fierce and independent, agreeing to be his.

He grasped her hands. "I was going to buy you a big ring to sweeten the deal. But for now, you'll have to just take my sincere declaration. Everything I have is yours, my heart most of all. I promise to take care of you and your son with every breath I take. I don't know what the future might bring, but I can promise to stand by your side and fight for the good things and help to fix the bad things."

A tear slipped down her cheek. She nodded over and over again, a smile stretching across her beautiful face. "Yes."

Clapping erupted around them. He rose to his feet and grabbed her around the waist. With his heart overflowing with joy, he kissed her long and slow, dipping her back until she giggled against his lips.

"Don't let 'im forget about the ring," one of the girls called out.

He laughed and kept on kissing his girl.

CHAPTER THIRTY

MATTHEW HANDED LIZZIE down from the coach in front of the large mansion in Berkeley Square. He whistled low as they stared up at the manse. "That's your grandmother's house? Why is it you are not speaking to her?"

Lizzie slid him a wry, sideways look. "Because she unceremoniously cut me out of her life for getting pregnant out of wedlock."

"Even though Robert's father was a ducal heir?"

"Our engagement hadn't been announced, and after Robert and his father were murdered, I was too afraid to say who the father was to people like her. Not that she ever gave me a chance to explain. All she could see was that I had ruined my season by mooning over a man who died. There were plenty of rumors that circulated about the circumstances of their deaths." She sighed. "My father always supported me, and that was a blessing."

He squeezed her hand. "Are you sure you want to go inside? I say, fuck her."

"Yes, my curiosity is piqued. I am glad you're here."

They climbed the steps to the front door. A starchy butler took Elizabeth's wrap and showed them into a large, opulent drawing room. He spotted her grandmother immediately. The Marchioness of Rollinsford stood in the center of a group of elegantly dressed guests, holding court. Her silver hair was piled high, and set within it was a golden tiara dotted with sapphires. When she saw them, she immediately headed toward them, the guests in the crowded room parting to give her way.

The marchioness held out both hands as she stopped in front of Lizzie. "My dear, I'm so glad you could come to my little dinner party."

"Thank you for inviting me," Lizzie replied. "I must admit, I was quite surprised to hear from you at all."

He placed a hand at her waist and squeezed. Good for her. Don't give the old biddy any quarter.

"I hope you don't mind that I brought a dinner partner. May I introduce my fiancé, Matthew Reeves?"

"It's a pleasure to meet you, Lady Rollinsford," he replied politely.

"Your fiancé?" Her grandmother looked between them with clear surprise. "Oh, I hadn't heard."

"I can't imagine how you would have, since you have not been a part of my life for the past six years." Lizzie's normally expressive features were set into a blandly polite facsimile, but he could see the tightness in the lines around her eyes. Damn it, they shouldn't have come.

Lady Rollinsford's expression briefly showed a flash of pain. She smoothed a hand down her gown. "Actually, I rather like your paper. I am a subscriber."

He felt a tiny jolt of surprise run through Lizzie, and he gave her waist another small squeeze.

"I invited you tonight because I received a request from a gentleman of my acquaintance for an introduction. It seems he became quite enamored of you at Lady Cheltenham's ball." She waved her hand at Matthew. "But that is moot, if you are already engaged to be married."

Matthew's stomach dropped at the mention of the Cheltenham party; the night he had followed his brother. He glanced around the crowded room, but didn't see him anywhere. No, it couldn't be him.

"Please excuse me. I see new guests have just arrived. Mr. Reeves, please have a drink. The refreshment table is over on the far wall." Lady Rollinsford walked away with a bright smile aimed at a couple who had just entered the room.

Lizzie's posture deflated as her grandmother walked away. He studied her face. "I think we could both use a drink. I hope she has brandy."

"I will wait for you here. I haven't the slightest inclination to make small talk with anyone. I prefer to be an observer."

"I'll be right back." He weaved his way through the room. Some curious looks were sent his way, but he paid them no mind. His girl needed a drink to settle her nerves. At the refreshment table, he ordered two snifters of brandy. As he turned, a glass in each hand, he saw his brother across the room. Jonas stood with two other men by the windows. He was impeccably dressed in all black, except for a blood-red cravat and waistcoat. His black hair was slicked back with pomade. Matthew's reaction was, as usual, a terrible, gut-tightening unease.

But tonight, he paused to study his brother. As children, Jonas had always seemed larger than life. As the older brother, he had been bigger physically, but more so, it had been his cruel personality that had been so intimidating. Now, as Matthew really looked at him, he saw that Jonas had not aged well. He was soft around the middle. His face was puffy and bloated, probably from excessive drink. This was a man who had spent his life in the lap of luxury, never having to fight to survive, and it showed. Matthew might be the younger brother, but he was certainly no longer the weaker one. And he was done hiding. Jonas could go to fucking hell.

Jonas sipped from his drink. Matthew saw the moment he noticed Lizzie. His brother's expression turned absolutely predatory. Jonas turned to the man next to him and excused himself. Then he started for where Lizzie stood by herself. *Oh, hell no.* Matthew pushed through groups of people to take the most direct route to his girl. When he arrived next to her, Jonas was mid-sentence.

"—I hoped you would wear the green dress."

"Pardon?" Lizzie recoiled. "Are we acquainted?"

Matthew handed her the brandy glass and then snaked his arm around her waist to pull her snug against his side. "No, you are not acquainted. Allow me to introduce the Viscount Griffen."

Lizzie stiffened next to him. Then she took a long swallow from her glass.

Jonas's gaze narrowed on the hand he had at her waist and then snapped up to his face. A flare of recognition widened his brother's eyes. "Matthew?" He glanced between the two of them.

Matthew nodded. "Let me introduce my fiancée, Miss Elizabeth Harper."

His brother's expression darkened. His eyes narrowed; his jaw clenched. "It is a pleasure to finally make your acquaintance, Miss Harper." He reached for her free hand.

But Matthew was quicker and pulled her behind him. "I won't ever let you touch her, you bastard," he snarled.

Jonas flinched and took a step back.

Lady Rollinsford appeared at his elbow. "Lord Griffen, I see you are finally getting an introduction to my granddaughter."

Smoothing his lapels, Jonas's smile was saccharine. "Yes. Unfortunately, it has also turned into an unexpected reunion with my younger brother."

Lady Rollinsford's head swept up to stare at him. "The missing spare, Lord Perrin?"

Matthew shook his head. "No, I ain't no toff. I am Matthew Reeves, nephew to businessman and theater owner, Harry Reeves. I run the Blue Angel, a gaming establishment and theater. And I am the soon-to-be husband to Elizabeth Harper and father to Robert Harper. This is who I am."

Lizzie squeezed his hand. He stared down into the emerald depths of her eyes as they shone with soft emotion, and something inside his chest shifted. A sense of rightness slid into place.

"Grandmother, please excuse us," Lizzie said. Her gaze stayed fastened on him. "I don't think we will stay for dinner."

He nodded, and with her hand still grasped in his, he turned and led her from the room. In the front hall, he asked the footman at the door to send around for his carriage. He was helping her into her wrap when his brother appeared across the foyer.

"Has Stella been hiding with you?" he called out.

Matthew strode across the black-and-white marble floor. He leaned into Jonas's space. "We are not hiding anymore. We know what you have done. And mark my words, you'll pay for your sins."

CHAPTER THIRTY-ONE

E LIZABETH PACED BACK and forth across the carpet in
Matthew's study. "I don't think this is a good idea."
She watched Seaton and Matthew strap weapons to themselves. Seaton slid two wickedly sharp knives into slots in a
leather holster he wore fastened across his chest. Matthew
tucked a pistol into the inner pocket of his jacket.

He crossed to stand in front of her. "We have to confront him. Now that he knows where you and Stella are, I
can't risk him coming for either of you. We will attempt to
intimidate him into staying away. Seaton can be very persuasive." He glanced over at Seaton. The look they exchanged
said they found it very unlikely that intimidation would
work.

"What are you doing?" Stella's voice came from the open
doorway. Her eyes were glued to Seaton's knives. He
shrugged into his jacket and turned to pick up a short club
from the desk.

"They are going out to be vigilantes," Elizabeth said.
"We ran into your older brother this evening at my grandmother's house."

"What? Why was he there?" Stella came into the room.

Elizabeth rubbed her arms, still chilled from her encounter with a murderer. "He wanted an introduction to me. According to my grandmother, he has become enamored of me."

Matthew growled low. "He recognized me, and we had words. He knows you're here, Stella. The time has come to deal with him."

Stella's eyes were round with fear. Elizabeth crossed and put an arm around her. She looked over at the men. "Can't we still go to the magistrate? Tell him what we know. Perhaps you could search Griffen's house. Maybe there is evidence of his wrongdoings there?"

Stella shook her head. "No, if Jonas has fixed on you, he won't stop. I have seen it time and again." She locked eyes with her brother. "Go deal with him."

"We are going back to Lady Rollinsford's house to wait for him. The dinner should last at least three hours, right?"

She bit down on her bottom lip and nodded.

Matthew came over and kissed Stella on the cheek. Then he kissed her, hard but brief. "Stay inside." He strode out of the room with Seaton at his back.

SHE PLACED DOWN her trick with a loud sigh. Across the table from her, Stella sat in her sparkly blue costume. After Elizabeth had put Robert to bed, Stella had come to find her, fretting about what could be happening with the men. They had decided to play cards to pass the time while they waited for them to return.

"It's no use," Elizabeth said. "I can't concentrate."

"Let's go downstairs. Matthew said to stay inside; he didn't say anything about staying trapped up here. We can go bother Val behind the bar. He always has funny stories to tell. I still have an hour before the show."

"All right," she found herself agreeing. She would go crazy, sitting here waiting all night, and she still wore the apricot satin dress from earlier in the evening, so at least she was dressed appropriately. "But we must stick together. I don't want to lose sight of you for any reason."

"You are worse than Big Ben with your mother-hen routine." Stella stood and gripped her hand. "Come on. What could happen inside the club?"

Val good-naturedly lifted the end cap on the bar and let them come behind. "This one is always hanging out behind here." He jerked his thumb at Stella.

"It's the best place to watch people from. Busy tonight, Val?"

"For mid-week, a fair amount of customers." He poured a glass of wine and handed it to Elizabeth.

"Thank you." She took a long drink.

"Where's the boss tonight?"

"He and Seaton went out hunting," Stella said cryptically.

Val seemed to understand perfectly. He nodded, then grabbed the wine bottle and topped off her half-empty glass.

"He'll be fine. No tougher kids than those two."

She snorted at Val calling them kids. Suppose that's how he saw all of them. The graying and grizzled former sailor must be at least sixty-five. "How long have you been working for Mr. Reeves?"

"Since he opened the place. But I knew him from when he and Seaton worked as hooks down at the docks."

A roar of voices rose from around the hazard table. Stella grinned. "Play is hot tonight."

But then a scream rent the air. A man lay on the floor, a brick next to his head. All hell broke loose as more of the front windows were broken by bricks sailing through them. A bottle with a rag set on fire sailed through one of the broken windows and landed in the middle of a table, setting the felt covering on fire. Another came through the far window. It rolled across the floor and set the curtains aflame.

"We're under attack!" Val lifted the end cap. "Come girls, get out of here."

People were streaming out of the room, pushing and shoving each other through the double doors. Ben yanked the flaming curtains off the wall and tried to stomp out the flames. But two more fire bombs hurtled through the windows. Men came running from the back of the house to help stomp out flames. She and Stella huddled by the bar as they tried to stay out of the stampede of men streaming out of the club. Ben caught her eye, muscled his way over to them, grabbed her and Stella each by an arm, and guided them out of the room, which was filling with smoke at an alarming rate. In the main foyer, he pulled them over by the stairs.

"Are you harmed?"

Elizabeth shook her head. Stella dashed up the stairs. "I have to tell the dancers in the theater to get outside," she called over her shoulder.

Elizabeth looked up at Ben. "I have to go get Robert." Panic filled her as she imagined the smoke and fire reaching the second floor. She and Ben raced up the stairs after Stella. They burst through the doors to the suite. "Mrs. Todd!" she shouted.

A door opened and the lady appeared, wrapping her robe around her. "What's happening?"

"Fire. Downstairs in the main gaming room. We need to get everyone outside," Ben said.

Elizabeth wrenched open the door to Robert's room. He sat up in bed, rubbing his eyes. She hurried to the bed and scooped into her arms. "We must get outside, darling."

"What's the matter, mama?"

"There's a fire downstairs." She turned and met up with Ben and Mrs. Todd. They raced down the corridor. As they came out of the wing, Elizabeth saw a man disappear through the doors into the theater. His oiled black hair and scarlet cravat were unmistakable. *Jonas!* Of course, he would be the orchestrator of the chaos. She turned to Ben. "I have to go find Stella. I will never forgive myself if she is hurt. Please take Robert."

"No, Miz Harper. You should come with us." Ben argued.

"I have to make sure Stella is safe. Please, take care of my son."

Ben nodded and took Robert from her arms. "At the back of the stage, there are two doors that lead to a wooden staircase that will take everyone safely to the alley out back. Mrs. Langley knows the way. Make sure she knows what's happening."

"I will." Elizabeth flew across the landing and flung open the doors to the theater room. It was empty and eerily quiet. She ran through the tables and climbed onto the stage. Pushing past the curtains, she finally saw people across the backstage area. The back door was open, and Mrs. Langley stood at the opening with a candelabra in her hand. She ushered the girls outside. "Anne, where is Gertie?" Mrs. Langley called out.

"I'm here!" A girl called out as she raced down the hall-way.

Elizabeth hurried over. "Mrs. Langley, have you seen Stella?"

"Yes, she came back here to tell us about the fire. How bad is it?"

"I don't know. Flaming bottles were thrown through the windows in the main gaming room. The men were trying to stomp out the flames, but there was a lot of smoke. Ben and I ran upstairs to get my son and Mrs. Todd. Ben has them." She looked around. "Where is Stella?"

"Perhaps she already went down the stairs?" Mrs. Langley said.

"Go down and see, please. Call up if she is there."

"But Miss Harper, you should come down too."

"No, we are far from the smoke. I'll be all right. I can't leave without knowing if she is safe."

Mrs. Langley followed the last of the girls down the stairs. Elizabeth stood in the doorway, waiting. She had a horrible feeling in her gut. Where was Griffen? He definitely came in here. Then she heard a crash from down the hallway that led to the dressing rooms. She raced toward the sound.

"You thought you could get away from me?"

Elizabeth careened to a halt outside Stella's dressing room. The girl was on the floor, clutching her cheek. Griffen loomed over her, his face a mask of fury.

"Get away from her!" she yelled. She rushed at him with all her body weight, pushing him against the dressing table with a crash. His surprise had him stumbling and falling over a stool to sprawl on the floor.

Elizabeth grasped Stella's hand and hauled her to her feet. But they weren't quick enough. With a roar, Griffen grabbed his sister by the hair to pull her against him. He wrapped an arm around her throat. "You have fire, I will give you that, Miss Harper. Good thing I like it when they fight." His features morphed into an eerily calm expression. All but his eyes. The candlelight flickered and reflected an unholy gleam in them.

Stella scraped with her fingernails against the arm around her neck.

"Don't hurt her. Please!" Elizabeth cried out.

His arm relaxed slightly. Stella sucked in a breath, her chest rising and falling.

"You both are coming with me. Don't try to run, or I'll snap her neck." He jerked his head to the door. "Slowly."

Elizabeth headed through the door with Griffen pushing Stella behind her. Out in the hallway, the pitiful mew of Stella's kitten echoed. Its yellow eyes glowed in the dark hallway. She reached down and scooped Pitter-Patter up. Then she turned left toward the stage. "There are back stairs, where we can go out to the alley."

When they got to the back doors. Griffen muscled past her and out onto the small landing. He looked down and spotted Mrs. Langley and the other women. Then he looked up. "We will climb to the roof and go over to the next building. You first." He jerked his head to the shadowy stairs that led up to the roof.

Elizabeth glanced down and contemplated screaming to call attention.

"Don't even think of screaming if you value her neck." Stella let out a gasp as he tightened his hold on her. Elizabeth held up her hands to stay him. She grasped her skirts and began to climb the wooden stairs.

At the top of the stairs, they stepped over a low ledge and onto the rooftop. Smoke rose from the front of the house. She moved slowly to the middle of the roof and spotted a plank of wood lying nearby. Stella began to struggle against her brother's grip, kicking her legs back against his shins.

Taking advantage of his distraction, Elizabeth dropped

the kitten and stumbled to grab up the plank. Turning, she swung it with all her might at the back of his legs. With a yelp of pain, he dropped Stella and fell to his knees. His hand snaked out and grasped Elizabeth's skirt, pulling her off-balance, and she fell onto her backside. She twisted to Stella. "Run!" she screamed.

CHAPTER THIRTY-TWO

MATTHEW KICKED HIS horse into a gallop as they turned the corner. *Jesus Christ.* Smoke and fire poured out of the front of his club. He leapt from the saddle after coming to a stop in front. Ben stood in the street with little Robert in one arm and the other wrapped around Mrs. Todd.

He raced over to them. Seaton was hot on his heels. "What the hell happened?"

"We was ambushed, boss." Ben's face was twisted in anguish. "They threw firebombs through the front windows. The men are inside with the buckets. Someone's run to get the fire brigade. Elizabeth went into the theater to find Stella, but they haven't come out yet."

"No, no." He twisted to look up at the house.

Seaton's heavy hand clapped onto his shoulder. "They probably went out the back stairs. That's why we had it installed. I'm sure they are safe in the alley."

A shrill scream from above their heads rent the air. He tipped his head back and saw shadows struggling on the roof. A low male shout was followed by Lizzie's voice screaming, "Run!"

Matthew's heart dropped to his stomach. They were on the roof. Trapped. He ran to the corner of the building. Ignoring the smoke billowing out, he began to scramble up the wooden drainpipe. One hand over the other, he climbed. Fear clogged his throat, mingling with smoke and making his lungs burn. Still, he climbed. He had to get to his girls. At the roofline, he flung himself over the ledge. It was so much worse than he imagined. Jonas had Lizzie pulled flush against him with his arm around her throat, his back to Matthew.

Stella, her eyes streaming with tears, was on her knees in front of them screaming, "Stop!"

Matthew slid his knife from his boot and took aim. Throwing it with accuracy born from pure fury, it sank into Jonas's shoulder. With a howl of pain, his brother let go of Lizzie and swung around, trying to reach the knife with wide, desperate grabs. Lizzie scrabbled on her knees over to Stella, throwing her arms around his sister.

Matthew strode over, pulled his knife out, and tossed it to the ground. Then he grabbed Jonas around the throat in the same hold he had just had on Lizzie. He pressed his forearm into Jonas's windpipe, cutting off his air. "How does it feel, you bastard?"

Jonas scratched at his arm, his movements jerky and un-coordinated as he ran out of breath. Matthew spoke low, right in his ear. "This is how your victims felt. Desperate for air. How does it feel to know your life is draining away? Just like you drained so many others."

"Matthew," Lizzie's voice cut through the haze of his fury. He looked over at her. Eyes wide and frightened, she held his sister in her arms, cradling Stella's head as she sobbed against her shoulder.

What was he doing? He wasn't like his brother. He didn't kill. Matthew shook his head to clear the madness that had filled him with such rage and loosened the pressure on Jonas's throat.

Seaton's lithe form emerged from the smoke. He pulled a knife from its holster. Without pausing, he strode up and shoved it right between Jonas's ribs. His brother gasped and let out a wet gurgle. Blood began to trickle out of his mouth. Matthew released him, letting Jonas's body slither to the ground.

He met Seaton's flinty gaze. "Thank you."

Seaton nodded. "Go take care of your family." He looked down at Jonas's lifeless body at their feet. "I will handle this."

Matthew walked over to his girls. Falling to his knees in front of them, he gently grasped each of their chins. "It's over. He's dead." He swept his thumb across Lizzie's cheek as she nodded. Then he switched his gaze to Stella.

His sister's dark eyes were filled with tears, but her jaw clenched. "I'm glad. He was going to kill us."

"You're both safe now. Except we need to get off this roof." He stood and reached down for each of their hands, pulling them to their feet.

Stella glanced around. "Where is Pitter-Patter? Come here, girl."

Elizabeth stood there, shaking, her eyes focused on where Jonas lay behind him. Matthew enfolded her in his arms. Kissing her hair, he held her tight, letting the solid feel of her seep into his bones. She was alive and unharmed.

She tipped her head back to look up at him. "I'm glad he's dead too. Now he can't hurt anyone else."

"Come, luv. Let's get you safely downstairs." He led the way down the wooden staircase. Lizzie behind him, Stella cradling her cat, and Seaton bringing up the rear. At the bottom, Mrs. Langley was waiting anxiously. She enveloped Stella in her embrace. "Girl, you'll be the death of me. Why did you run off?"

"I needed to go get Pitter-Patter. He was in my dressing room."

"That damn kitten," Mrs. Langley muttered. She led the way down the alley and around the building.

The smoke was thick as they rounded the building, but Matthew could not see any more flames. The fire brigade with their water tank on wheels was in front, men pumping the handles and the hose snaking through the window into the house. He led the ladies over to where Ben still stood across the street.

Lizzie stumbled toward him, her arms outstretched for her son. "Mama!" Robert cried out as Ben passed him over to her. She hugged him tight, her eyes squeezed shut.

Matthew turned on his heel and headed for the club's front doors. He coughed as the smoke hit his lungs. He covered his nose and mouth with his neckcloth as he entered the foyer. Val and Rob came out of the big gaming room, covered in soot and coughing. He strode over to them. "What's the status?"

"Boss!" Rob wiped the back of his hand across his forehead. "The flames are out. There is plenty of smoke damage, but thanks to the fire brigade arriving on the scene, we were able to drown the last of the flames."

"The fire was contained to the big room. Thank fuck for the stone walls these old manses are built from. The bar and most of the furniture are a charred mess. The tables in the back end of the room are salvageable, but the wall coverings all caught fire and burned away," Val inventoried the damage before bending over in a coughing fit.

"Come on, let's get you both out of here," Matthew said. "Who's left inside?"

"Harry and Frank and Paul, I think," Rob replied.

"I'll get them. I need to see the damage for myself. Get outside where you can breathe." He walked into the gaming room, still holding the cloth over his nose and mouth. The only light was the moonlight streaming through the broken windows. It painted large stripes across the floor. "Come on, boys," he called out to the remaining men, who were sifting through the charred tables for any signs of fire that might be still smoldering.

Matthew surveyed the damage as best he could, with the room swathed in so much shadow. He walked over to the bar that he and Seaton had built with so much hope and ambition. Its surface was charred, the bottles lined on the shelves behind just shards of broken glass now. His chest ached. Not with anger, but with relief. This room had been destroyed, but the building still stood. Nobody he loved had died tonight. His family was safe, and that's what he needed to focus on now.

On his way out, he kicked at a piece of wood, maybe a table leg, and underneath, gleaming in a shaft of moonlight, was a pair of dice. Matthew scooped them up and closed his hand around them. He would rebuild. Not just the club, but his life. No more hiding from the past. He could start fresh with Elizabeth and Robert, free to be his authentic self.

CHAPTER THIRTY-THREE

A RAGTAG GROUP of ten staff that lived at the Blue Angel walked into the Fairmont Hotel at one in the morning. Seaton organized and paid for rooms for everyone. Elizabeth carried her sleeping son, who felt like he weighed one hundred pounds by the time they arrived. Matthew and Ben had both offered to carry him, but she needed to hold on to his sweet warmth. She let it seep into her bones as the events of the night swirled and then settled in her mind.

"We have plenty of rooms ready, Mr. Seaton." The man at the front desk rang a bell and several other employees arrived from a back room. Stella was guided by Mrs. Langley to go with three of the other dancers to share a room. Elizabeth glanced over at Matthew. He had been worriedly quiet ever since coming out of the Angel earlier. He moved woodenly, putting one foot in front of the other, but his mind seemed to be far away.

Mrs. Todd came over to Elizabeth. "Here now, hand him over. He can sleep with me tonight." She glanced at Matthew. "You take care of your fella. He looks dead on his feet."

Elizabeth nodded and, with relief, passed the sleeping

Robert to Mrs. Todd. "Thank you. As usual, you are my savior."

Mrs. Todd cupped her cheek with one hand. "I'm just so grateful you are unharmed."

Elizabeth nodded again, only able to muster a wobbly smile. Then she turned to Matthew. Slipping her hand in his, she gave a gentle tug. "Come, love. Let's go to our room."

He looked down at her. His eyes blinked as though he was trying to focus. "Yes, of course."

They followed a maid to the second-floor room. The woman stoked a fire for them and left with a polite curtsy. Elizabeth locked the door and then slipped her shoes off her aching feet. She dug her toes into the plush carpet with a long sigh. She glanced over her shoulder at Matthew. "Would you get me out of this dress, please?"

He nodded and crossed to unbutton the back of the apricot dress. She looked down at the dirty, torn skirt and grimaced. "I will need to pay my friend for ruining her beautiful creation."

"It's no problem. I will pay her for it."

Her dress hit the floor in a whoosh of fabric. She turned to face Matthew as she unlaced her short stays. No teasing kisses along her neck, no roaming hands; something was definitely wrong. Perhaps Mrs. Todd was right. He was just exhausted. She took his arm and led him over to a chair on the other side of the room by the fireplace. She stripped his jacket off and then unbuckled the holster that housed his pistol. Giving him a gentle shove, she pushed him to sit.

He ran a hand through his hair. With a tired smile, he looked up at her.

"Your face is covered with soot." She went over to the washbasin and poured water into it from a nearby pitcher. "What is the status of the building?" She dipped a cloth from the stack next to the basin into the cool water before gently wringing it out. "Matthew?"

When she returned to him, she gently wiped his face off. She gripped his chin. What was really at the crux of his feelings? She tried again with a different question. "How do you feel now that he is gone?"

With a shake of his head, his gaze focused on her. He leaned forward and rested his forehead on her stomach. His hands rested on her hips. A full minute passed before he began to speak. "Jonas has always been a specter, floating in the back of my existence, something to be feared. And then, tonight, at your grandmother's house, I looked at him and realized I wasn't afraid of him any longer. That there was no reason to hide."

He raised his head. "I shouldn't have provoked him like that. But when he tried to touch you... You've seen just how rotten my family tree is. I wouldn't blame you if you wish to run away, screaming." He gripped her tight. "But I won't let you go." His gaze filled with yearning. "Obsession must run in my family because I need you like I need to breathe air. I cannot fathom life without you."

Elizabeth climbed onto his lap to straddle his thighs. She

cupped his face, sinking her fingers into his beard. "Matthew, I am not going anywhere. Don't you see how much I want all that you promised me? I fell in love with you so easily. That was part of why I was so scared to admit it, to risk my heart again. The first time I fell in love, it was a whirlwind, a fairy tale without the happy ending. But I have become a different person than I would have been if Robert hadn't been killed. I am stronger. I am passionate about helping people. I am proud of my paper, and that I can support myself and my son."

"I love all those things about you."

She smiled. "You see, I don't wish for the fairy tale anymore. I want a partner who will walk beside me, love me, and help me tackle the ups and downs of real life." She kissed him deeply. "And even though this was not a fairy-tale day, you were my hero, scaling the side of the building to rescue me."

He grinned. It transformed his face and lit his eyes from within. She ran a hand through his hair, pushing his curls back off his brow. There was the Matthew she knew and loved. "How did you get up to the roof, anyway?"

"I climbed up the downspout. It's how we always got into people's houses. An old skill that came in handy tonight." He wrapped his arms around her, and his lips captured hers. His tongue, hot and frantic, plundered her mouth. His hands raced up her back and into her hair. Pins scattered to the floor. She gripped his hair as she licked into his mouth. This is what she needed—the passion between them to burn away the events of the day.

He kissed across her cheek and down her neck. She flinched at the brush of his beard against abraded skin. Matthew growled low as he saw the red marks his brother had left on her. "Where else are you hurt?" He grabbed handfuls of her shift and pulled it over her head. Then he stood with her in his arms and stalked over to set her down on the bed. He brought a candelabra over to the bedside table so he could examine her skin. Frowning over each of the bruises that had begun to bloom. Kissing each spot that he found.

Elizabeth stretched her arms above her head and writhed under his ministrations. "Are you done frowning yet? They are just bruises. Soon to fade." His head popped up. His eyes met hers. She gave him a pleading look. "Matthew, I need you to strip off your clothes, come here, and make love to me. Please."

"Well, since you asked so nicely." He grabbed the collar of his shirt and pulled it up and over his head.

She bit her bottom lip as the expanse of muscles was revealed. Then she watched him slowly unbutton his falls. He pushed his trousers off and stepped out of them. His eyes never left hers as he climbed over her. Then he dipped down to take one of her nipples into his mouth, giving it a long suck. She arched her back, chasing the delicious sensations his lips left behind as he licked across her breasts. She reached for his hair, but his head popped up.

"Keep those hands above your head, naughty girl. Your

body is mine to worship. Lay back and take what I give you."

She whimpered, but her body came alive for him. Each touch of his fingers across her skin, each caress of his lips, had her on the razor's edge between pleasure and frustration. She wanted to touch him. To feel his body press against hers.

As though he could read her thoughts, he lowered himself on top of her. His cock nudged her entrance, and she spread her legs wide to let him in. He kissed her deeply. She finally sank her hands into his hair as he began to move inside her, filling her up so good. She moaned against his mouth.

"Lizzie, may I spill inside you? I promise to always take care of you and to be a father to any children we have. I will never leave your side."

She nodded and wrapped her legs around him. "Yes, yes, fill me up with your seed. I am yours."

He closed his eyes with a low moan. Then his hips ravished her. She met each of his thrusts with her own sighs of pleasure. His lips raced across her neck. "I love you, Lizzie. Come for me, love."

"Oh God, Matthew, I love you." Her orgasm exploded in a burst of light behind her eyelids. She felt his cock pulse inside her over and over, spilling inside her, marking her as his. She held him close, reveling in the heavy weight of him between her legs. This was the happy ending she craved. This man loving her and making love to her every night. Building their family. Building a life together.

CHAPTER THIRTY-FOUR

M ATTHEW TUCKED STELLA'S hand into the crook of his arm. "Are you ready?"

"Yes." She looked up at him. "Are you?"

"Not really." He shrugged. "But no more hiding." He turned the knob to the heavy wooden door that marked the front office of Harrington and Sibley. The firm had been handling the business of the viscountcy since his grandfather's time. He and Stella walked inside and approached the man at the front desk, a nervous-looking gentleman who jumped up and gave a sharp bow.

"Viscount Griffen, I presume?"

Matthew gave a terse nod. *Damn title. Rotten family tree. Bad luck, for sure.* He should turn around now while he still had the chance. Go home to his girl and what…admit that he was a coward? He sighed. *Fuck this.* He was not a scared ten-year-old boy. He was a grown man who ran his own bloody business. He could take care of this piece of business. All he had to do was sign the paperwork and then sell everything off. Be done with it.

Stella squeezed his arm. Her wide dark eyes questioning. He gave her a nod, then turned back to the clerk. "Yes, and this is my sister, Miss Estella Perrin. We are here for our three o'clock appointment."

"Yes, my lord. Right this way." The man gestured for them to follow him as he led them down a corridor to the left of the desk. The thick carpeting and dark wood paneling on the walls all lent to a quiet, rarefied atmosphere. They were ushered into a room with tall windows along one wall. In the center of the room sat a large mahogany table, and around it, a half dozen chairs.

"Please have a seat. May I bring you any refreshments? Tea? Coffee?" the clerk asked them.

"No, thank you," Stella answered. When the man left, she turned to him. "This place makes me feel as though I am walking back into the cage. Did you see all those portraits hanging in the hallway? It was as though the eyes were following us as we walked past."

Matthew couldn't hold back a laugh at her expression of mock horror. He kissed the top of her head. "Thank you for coming with me today. Don't worry. We are about to be handed the keys to the cage. We can dismantle it. We can do whatever we wish. I promise, no rules."

"Even if I want to go sing for Mr. Spencer at the Hill wood Theater?"

Matthew studied her upturned face, eyes full of hope. "Is that really what you want?"

Stella nodded. "Yes!"

"You could have a proper season in society. Go to balls and such things."

"No, thank you." She scrunched her nose and shook her head.

He sighed. "All right. We will talk again with Spencer. But you must live at home, where I can keep an eye on you."

"Absolutely." She clapped her hands together in glee. The smile on her face erased any reservations he had. He had promised no rules, and he meant it. Stella deserved her freedom.

The door opened and three men walked into the room. "Good afternoon, Lord Griffen. Miss Perin." One man gave a short bow. "I am Mr. Harrington and this is Mr. Sibley."

"Mr. Travers," Stella exclaimed.

The third man to enter the room stilled, and a huge smile broke across his weatherworn face. "Miss Stella!" He crossed the carpet to grasp her hands. "I'm so glad to see you safe and sound."

Stella stepped forward to buss his cheek. "I am just fine. I have been safe with Matthew this whole time."

Mr. Travers's gaze snapped to him. "The missing spare. By golly, never thought I would see the day."

Mr. Harrington coughed. "Why don't we all take a seat? This is Mr. Travers, the land steward for Foxglove Glen, the entailed estate in Norfolk. We are here today to confirm your identity and to explain the extent of your holdings and accounts."

"That's Matthew Perrin. I'd recognize the boy anywhere. Even with a grown man's beard. Spitting image of his father," Mr. Travers said.

Matthew frowned at that. Was he? He supposed so. All three siblings shared the dark hair and eyes from his father's side. But he had never wanted to emulate his father. Cold, pious, and unloving, his father had never been the man he wanted to be. He shook his head. "Let's get this over with. Please continue, Mr. Harrington."

It took much of the afternoon. But in the end, Matthew had gained new holdings in Norfolk, a house in Bath, and the large townhome in London he thought his brother let, actually belonged to the estate. There was a sizable dowry for Stella. She and Matthew decided to close up the manor house for now. Neither of them was interested in returning to their childhood home haunted with bad memories.

Matthew leaned back in his chair after signing his name to the last of the papers. It was all a bit unbelievable, this large windfall, as though he had won a lucrative hand at the tables. He ran a hand over his beard. The whole afternoon had been strange. It wasn't that the business of it all didn't make sense. Instead, it was the way they all kept referring to him as Lord Griffen, which was the hard part to swallow. As Stella had said earlier, it felt like a cage, and all of a sudden, his chest tightened painfully.

Stella's hand gripped his under the table. "Remember, you have the key," she whispered. "You can make this whatever you wish. No rules."

He squeezed her hand back. No rules. He leaned forward to address the solicitors. "The first thing I want you to do is sell the house in Berkley Square. We won't be needing it."

INSTEAD OF WORKING, Elizabeth stared out her window at the cloudless blue sky. A bird trilled from a nearby tree and a small breeze raced through the open casement to cool her brow. The last two weeks had been blissfully slow and peaceful. Oh, there were articles to write and curious boys to rescue from trees, but after the day was done, she would curl up with Matthew in his big bed, and they would talk about the work of the day, and he would distract her with passionate kisses and roaming hands. The club had been closed while they worked on repairs, but he hoped to have a grand reopening this weekend.

"Hello, pretty lady," a deep voice called out.

Pulled from her thoughts, she leaned out the window, glancing over at the front walk to find Matthew grinning at her, looking so handsome with his wild tangle of curls falling across his brow and his hands in his pockets. She smiled back. "Well, hello to you, fine gentleman. What brings you to Bloomsbury this afternoon?"

"I have something to show you. Will you come for a walk with me?"

"Love to." Elizabeth pulled the window closed and hurried through the front room to grab her bonnet and keys. She pulled the front door closed and locked it. When she turned, Matthew was right behind her. His hands came to her waist and his lips slid against hers in a warm welcome.

Lord, she was such a fool for his kisses. She smiled against his mouth, and he pulled back to bump his nose gently against hers.

"How's my girl today? Get your article written?"

She nodded. They walked down to the pavement, and he led her to the left. "I should have been organizing the page proofs, but I got distracted by the fine weather and found myself woolgathering instead."

"Nothing wrong with a little woolgathering," he said.

"Says the man who has worked every moment of the past two weeks."

"Not every moment." He took her hand and placed a kiss in the center of her palm.

She blushed. No, not every moment. "You need to sleep sometimes."

"I told you; I'll sleep when I am dead. There is too much to do to get the Angel up and running again. Seaton and I finished the last coat of varnish on the new bar today and it looks fucking fantastic, if I do say so myself."

Elizabeth looked around. They had entered Bloomsbury Square. The large green lawn in the middle of the square was dotted with children playing under the watchful eyes of their nannies. The houses in the square were far bigger than the narrow townhomes along the adjoining streets, like hers. But still, the warm brick facades lent a homey feel to the square. "Where are we going?" she asked.

Matthew stopped in front of a house at the far corner. Its white stone exterior gleamed in the sunlight and the front door was painted a cheerful, azure blue. "Here."

She raised an eyebrow. "Here?"

"Well, I know that I said I would buy you an engagement ring, but then I got to thinking that ostentatious jewelry is not your style. So instead, I bought you this house."

Elizabeth's mouth fell open. "You bought me a house?"

He took both her hands in his. "I bought us a house."

"But I have a house."

"And you can keep it as your place of business. I chose this house because it is only three blocks for you to walk to work. As you expand the paper's readership, you will be able to hire more employees and have plenty of space to expand into the other rooms. Maybe even offer the bedrooms upstairs for let to employees."

She nodded. The possibilities buzzing in her head. "What about the hell?"

Matthew chuckled. "The hell was fine for a bachelor, but it is no place to raise a family." He turned her by the shoulders to face the house and wrapped his arms around her waist.

She leaned her head back against his shoulder. "You bought me a house." A house. A place to make a home together. Tears gathered in her eyes, and she swallowed hard.

"Do you like it?" he spoke low next to her ear.

She nodded. Turning, she grasped his face between her hands and kissed him. "I love it. But most of all, I love you."

"Good. Because they are all excited about the house."

The front door opened, and in the threshold, Stella and Robert waved at them. Ben and Mrs. Todd stood behind them, his arm around her shoulders, and smiles wreathing their faces.

"Do you love it? Isn't it the finest house you have ever seen?" Stella called out.

Robert rushed out and hugged her legs. "Matthew said we might live here if you said yes. Did you see the big garden? It has a very tall tree right in the middle. I bet I could climb to the very top."

Elizabeth ruffled his hair. "Yes." She looked back up into Matthew's warm, chestnut eyes. Happiness flowed through her. "Yes."

He cupped her face and brushed away a tear that had slipped down her cheek. "I love you, Lizzie. Don't be scared."

How did he always see her so clearly? "I don't want to be. All of this is worth the risk. I want my happy ending."

"We will build our happy ending side by side." Matthew's grin was cocky as ever. "Remember, the house always wins."

EPILOGUE

Christmastide

E LIZABETH GRIPPED LUCY'S hands and kissed her cheek. "Thank you for inviting us. The house looks beautiful dressed for Christmas."

The main ballroom of Hartwick House was draped in festive greenery woven with bright-red ribbon. The refreshment table was laden with sweet treats and tureens of wassail. The tall windows were painted with delicate snowflakes, and more snowflakes dangled by ribbons from the chandeliers.

"Thank you for coming, Lord and Lady Griffen," Lucy replied.

Standing next to her, Matthew grunted. "I prefer Mr. and Mrs. Reeves still. I have not yet come to terms with the title."

Elizabeth lowered her voice. "He still thinks it's cursed, or bad luck anyway."

"The title is whatever you make of it." Hartwick, stoic as ever, gripped Matthew's shoulder and gave it a friendly squeeze. The two men had become fast friends. Perhaps it was all the time that Hart had spent in the last month playing cards at the newly refurbished Angel. He said he much preferred the atmosphere and clientele at the Angel as opposed to the pretty, citified dandies that overran his club in St. James Square. And when word spread that the Blue Angel was the Duke of Hartwick's new favorite place, it had brought in a set of new, monied clients. "You and Elizabeth are starting a fresh branch of your family tree. I am sure it will grow strong and healthy."

She exchanged a look with Matthew. "Yes, well, about that." She slipped her hand in his. "Robert is going to be an older brother by next summer."

Lucy bounced on her toes. "Ah! That's wonderful news!" She flung her arms around Elizabeth. Lucy's large protruding belly pressed against her. "Our babies will not be that far apart. They can become the best of friends."

People around them were staring at Lucy's overt show of affection, but that didn't dampen her enthusiasm. With her duke scowling at anyone who looked sideways at them, no one would ever twitter unkindly about their hostess.

Lucy pulled her aside. "Have you been feeling all right? Sick?"

"No, thankfully, but I have had to"—she lowered her voice again—"um, have had to relieve myself ten times a day. I feel like I am spending all my time in the privy." She slid her husband a look and watched his lips twitch. She knew he'd heard her and was suppressing a smile. Matthew thought it hilarious how often she had to pee. The beast.

Lucy nodded sagely. "It was the same for me at the beginning, and now this baby seems to be squishing my insides. I hope it comes soon, or there won't be any more room for it."

Elizabeth felt the familiar twinge low in her belly. *For goodness' sake.* "Speaking of said issue, I need to head to the ladies retiring room. Watch out for my husband for a few minutes? I told him no cursing at a toff party, but I can't promise you anything."

Matthew grunted again. "I can behave for now." He waggled his eyebrows at her, his gaze salacious.

Lucy put her hand over her mouth to stifle a giggle. "Upstairs, first door on the left has been set up as the retiring room."

"Thank you." Elizabeth hurried out of the ballroom. Following the directions, she climbed the stairs. The retiring room was blissfully empty except for a maid sitting in the far corner. Elizabeth went behind the screen and relieved herself. Once she had straightened her skirts, she came back around the screen and found that a young woman had entered the room. The lady sat at the dressing table, fussing with a lace fichu tucked into her neckline. Elizabeth tilted her head and studied the lady's reflection in the mirror.

"Violet?" she asked. She had only had the opportunity to meet Lucy's friend on a couple of occasions last year. But had not seen her since the lady's marriage. Although Lucy had spoken at length about her concerns, that her friend had been squirreled away by her husband at his estate and that she never got to see Violet anymore.

"Elizabeth Harper?" Violet met her gaze in the mirror.

"It's Elizabeth Reeves now. I was married three months ago."

"Oh, how lovely to hear." Violet's smile looked forced. Again, she attempted to straighten the fichu. "Do you think you might help me? I think maybe the ties for the sleeves have come loose. They keep slipping off my shoulders."

"Certainly." Elizabeth approached her, and sure enough, the ribbon that attached the long velvet sleeves to the bodice had come partially loose. She untangled ribbons for the right sleeve, then tugged the strings tighter in order to bring the dress back to where it should rest on the shoulder. "Lucy must be happy to have you back in town. She has often said lately how much she misses you."

Violet's smile brightened. "Yes. I can't believe how big her belly has grown. She is positively glowing these days."

Elizabeth frowned down at a large blackish-blue bruise on Violet's shoulder blade. She pulled the edge of the neckline over it and tied the ribbons tight. Then she turned her attention to the left sleeve. It had almost come entirely undone and had separated from the bodice. There, in the gap, she spotted more small bruises on Violet's upper arm. Spaced in a neat row, they could have been made by fingers gripping roughly into her pale skin. Appalled, she studied Violet more closely in the mirror.

By all appearances, Violet looked elegant and beautiful. Her honey-blonde hair was piled in an intricate style with a small, tasteful tiara tucked into the ringlets. Large diamond earrings swung from her ears. But dark smudges marred the delicate skin underneath her eyes, making her look weary, if one paid close enough attention. And was she thinner than last year? Her cheekbones were a stark relief in her previously rounder face. Elizabeth efficiently retied the ribbons for the sleeve and tucked them away.

Violet rose from the padded stool. "Thank you for your help."

But when Violet went to move past her, Elizabeth simply could not let her walk away. She grabbed hold of Violet's hands. "I couldn't help but notice the bruises that mar your skin," she said in a low voice. "Is someone hurting you?"

Violet's gaze slid to where the maid sat across the room, picking at her nails and paying them absolutely no attention. "No, of course not. Everything is fine."

Violet would not meet her gaze, her eyes downcast. Elizabeth squeezed her hands. "I do not believe you."

At that, Violet did look up with wide, wary eyes.

Elizabeth pushed up the flowing sleeves of the gown and quietly gasped as more bruises were revealed right above Violet's wrists and further up around the soft flesh of her upper arm. Violet stepped back and shook the sleeves back into place. Her cheeks stained pink.

"Violet, you must know that if you need help, Lucy and Hartwick would slay dragons to protect their friends," she said quietly.

Violet shook her head. "No, you must not tell them. It's not as bad as it looks." Her voice desperate. "I have family counting on me. My younger sister is out this season and my marriage to the ducal heir assures her a good match just as did for my other sister. There cannot be any scandal or rumors."

Elizabeth bit down on her bottom lip to keep from arguing further. Violet looked so lost and wary that every motherly instinct she had called out for her to wrap this woman in her arms and abscond with her. She did again reach out and take one of Violet's hands. "If you ever need anything, anything at all, please come and see me. I have a house in Bloomsbury Square, or you can come to the *Piccadilly Press* offices, also in Bloomsbury."

Violet's eyes shuttered. A polished, polite smile turned up the corners of her lips as she pulled her hand from Elizabeth's. Violet smoothed down her skirts. "Thank you for your kind help and for your kind words. But there is nothing to be done. Good evening." Then she swept past Elizabeth and out of the room.

The End

If you enjoyed *Scandal, Secrets, and the Marquess,* you'll love the other books in…

The Lost Lords series

Book 1: *Rumors, Ruin and the Duke*

Book 2: *Scandal, Secrets, and the Marquess*

Book 3: *Vices, Villains and the Viscount*

Available now at your favorite online retailer!

More Books by Karla Kratovil

The Maidens of Marbury series

Book 1: *A Perfect Engagement*
Book 2: *Saving a Scoundrel*
Book 3: *Christmas at Belhaven Hall*
Book 4: *Making the Marquess Mine*

Available now at your favorite online retailer!

About the Author

From the time she read fairytales as a child, Karla Kratovil
was hooked on stories that ended in Happily Ever After.
Now as an author of sexy historical romance she gets to craft
her own happy endings. Karla lives right on the edge of
Northern Virginia's wine country with her college
sweetheart, two terrific teenagers, and two blond terriers. She
is a Taurus. Like any good earth sign she loves good food,
good wine, and getting her hands dirty growing things in
her garden.

Thank you for reading

Vices, Villains and the Viscount

If you enjoyed this book, you can find more from all our great authors at TulePublishing.com, or from your favorite online retailer.

TULE
PUBLISHING